Joel Barlow

The Vision of Columbus

A Poem in Nine Books, Ed. 5

Joel Barlow

The Vision of Columbus
A Poem in Nine Books, Ed. 5

ISBN/EAN: 9783741126826

Manufactured in Europe, USA, Canada, Australia, Japa

Cover: Foto ©Andreas Hilbeck / pixelio.de

Manufactured and distributed by brebook publishing software
(www.brebook.com)

Joel Barlow

The Vision of Columbus

THE
VISION
OF
COLUMBUS.
A POEM,
IN NINE BOOKS.
BY JOEL BARLOW.

THE FIFTH EDITION, CORRECTED.

Tu spiegherai, Colombo, a un novo polo
Lontane sì le fortunate antenne,
Ch'a pena seguirà con gli occhi il volo
La Fama, c'hà mille occhi e mille penne.
Canti ella Alcide, e Bacco, e di te solo
Basti a'posteri tuoi, ch' alquanto accenne
Che quel poco darà lunga memoria
Di Poema degnissima, e d'istoria.

Gierusalemme Liberata. Canto XV. Sta. 32.

TO WHICH IS ADDED,

THE CONSPIRACY OF KINGS:
A POEM,
BY THE SAME AUTHOR.

PARIS:

PRINTED AT THE ENGLISH PRESS, RUE DE VAUGIRARD, N.° 1214; AND SOLD BY BARROIS, SENIOR, QUAI DES AUGUSTINS; AND B. THOMSON, RUE DE L'ANCIENNE COMEDIE FRANÇAISE, N.° 42.   1793.

ADVERTISEMENT.

THIS Poem was firſt publiſhed in America, in the year 1787. During that year it went through two editions in that country, and one in England. The Author is informed, that it has been once reprinted in America ſince that period. He now offers this edition to the Engliſh Preſs in Paris, merely for the ſake of preſerving the numerous corrections and ſome few additional notes which he has found leiſure to make in it ; as a traveller, eſpecially in countries at war, is expoſed to loſe his papers. Theſe were of a nature not to be replaced ; and they may ſerve, in a conſiderable degree, to diminiſh the imperfections of the work.

Paris, 12 *July* 1793.

INTRODUCTION.

EVERY circumstance relating to the discovery and settlement of America, is an interesting object of enquiry. Yet, it is presumed, from the present state of literature in the United States, that many persons, who might be entertained with an American production of this kind, are but slightly acquainted with the life and character of that great man, whose extraordinary genius led him to the discovery of the continent, and whose singular sufferings ought to excite the indignation of the world.

CHRISTOPHER COLUMBUS was born in the republic of Genoa, about the year 1447, at a time when the navigation of Europe was scarcely extended beyond the limits of the Mediterranean. The mariner's compass had been invented and in common use for more than a century; yet with the help of this sure guide, prompted by the most ardent spirit of discovery, and encouraged by the patronage of princes, the mariners of those days rarely ventured from the sight of land. They acquired great applause by sailing along the coast of Africa, and discovering some of the neighbouring islands; and after pushing their researches with the

A

greatest

greatest industry and perseverance for more than half a century, the Portuguese, who were the most fortunate and enterprising, extended their discoveries southward no farther than the equator.

The rich commodities of the East had, for several ages, been brought into Europe by the way of the Red-Sea and the Mediterranean; and it had now become the object of the Portuguese to find a passage to India, by sailing round the southern extremity of Africa, and then taking an eastern course. This great object engaged the general attention of mankind, and drew into the Portuguese service adventurers from every maritime nation in Europe. Every year added to their experience in navigation, and seemed to promise a reward to their industry. The prospect, however, of arriving at India was extremely distant; fifty years perseverance in the same track, had brought them only to the equator; and it was probable that as many more would elapse before they could accomplish their purpose. But Columbus, by an uncommon exertion of genius, formed a design no less astonishing to the age in which he lived, than beneficial to posterity. This design was to fail to India by taking a western direction. By the accounts of travellers who had visited India, that country seemed almost without limits on the east; and, by

attending

attending to the spherical figure of the earth, Columbus drew this conclusion—that the Atlantic ocean muſt be bounded on the weſt either by India itſelf, or by ſome great continent not far diſtant from it.

THIS extraordinary man, who was now about twenty-ſeven years of age, appears to have poſ-ſeſſed every talent, requiſite to form and execute the greateſt enterpriſes. He was early educated in all the uſeful ſciences that were taught in that day. He had made great proficiency in geography, aſtronomy and drawing, as they were neceſſary to his favourite purſuit of navigation. He had now been a number of years in the ſervice of the Portugueſe, and had acquired all the expe-rience that their voyages and diſcoveries could afford. His courage and perſeverance had been put to the ſevereſt teſt, and the exerciſe of every amiable and heroic virtue rendered him univerſally known and reſpected. He had married a Portu-gueſe lady, by whom he had two ſons, Diego and Ferdinand ; the younger of whom is the hiſtorian of his life.

SUCH was the ſituation of Columbus, when he formed and thoroughly digeſted a plan, which, in its operation and conſequences, unfolded to the view of mankind one half of the globe, diffuſed wealth and dignity over the other, and extended commerce and civilization through the whole. To corroborate the theory which he had formed of the exiftence of a weftern continent, his difcerning mind, which always knew the application of every circumftance that fell in his way, had obferved feveral facts, which by others would have paffed unnoticed. In his voyages to the African iflands, he had found, floating afhore after a long weftern ftorm, pieces of wood carved in a curious manner, canes of a fize unknown in that quarter of the world, and human bodies with very fingular features. Fully confirmed in the opinion that a confiderable portion of the earth was ftill undifcovered, his genius was too vigorous and perfevering to fuffer an idea of this importance to reft merely in fpeculation, as it had done in the minds of Plato and Seneca, who appear to have had conjectures of a fimilar nature. He determined therefore to bring his favourite theory to the teft of experiment. But an object of that magnitude required the patronage of a prince; and a defign fo extraordinary, met with all the obftructions, delays and difappointments, which an age of fuperftition could invent, and which perfonal jealoufy and malice could magnify and encourage. Happily for mankind, in this inftance, a genius, capable of devifing the greateft

under-

undertakings, aſſociated in itſelf a degree of patience and enterpriſe, modeſty and confidence, which rendered him ſuperior, not only to theſe misfortunes, but to all the future calamities of his life. Excited by the moſt ardent enthuſiaſm to be the diſcoverer of new continents, and fully ſenſible of the advantages that would reſult to mankind from ſuch diſcoveries, he had the mortification to waſte away eighteen years of his life, after his ſyſtem was well eſtabliſhed in his own mind, before he could obtain the means of executing his deſigns. The greateſt part of this period was ſpent in ſucceſſive and fruitleſs ſolicitations, in Genoa, Portugal, and Spain. As a duty to his native country, he made his firſt propoſal to the Senate of Genoa; where it was ſoon rejected. Conſcious of the truth of his theory, and of his own abilities to execute his deſign, he retired without dejection from a body of men who were incapable of forming any juſt ideas upon the ſubject; and applied with freſh confidence to John the Second, king of Portugal, who had diſtinguiſhed himſelf as the great patron of navigation, and in whoſe ſervice Columbus had acquired a reputation which entitled him and his project to general confidence and approbation. But here he ſuffered an inſult much greater than a direct refuſal. After referring the examination of his

A 3

ſcheme

scheme to the council who had the direction of naval affairs, and drawing from him his general ideas of the length of the voyage and the course he meant to take, that great monarch had the meanness to conspire with this council to rob Columbus of the glory and advantage he expected to derive from his undertaking. While Columbus was amused with this negotiation, in hopes of having his scheme adopted and patronised, a vessel was secretly dispatched, by order of the king, to make the intended discovery. Want of skill and perseverance in the pilot rendered the plot unsuccessful; and Columbus, on discovering the treachery, retired with an ingenuous indignation from a court capable of such duplicity.

HAVING now performed what was due to the country that gave him birth, and to the one that had adopted him as a subject, he was at liberty to court the patronage of any prince who should have the wisdom and justice to accept his proposals. He had communicated his ideas to his brother Bartholomew, whom he sent to England to negotiate with Henry the Seventh; at the same time that he went himself into Spain to apply in person to Ferdinand and Isabella, who governed the united kingdoms of Arragon and Castile. The circumstances of his brother's application in England,
which

which appears to have been unfuccefsful, is not to my purpofe to relate ; and the limits prefcribed to this Introduction will prevent the detail of all the particulars relating to his own negotiation in Spain. In this negotiation Columbus fpent eight years in the various agitations of fufpence, expectation and difappointment ; till at length his fcheme was adopted by Ifabella, who undertook, as queen of Caftile, to defray the expences of the expedition ; and declared herfelf, ever after, the friend and patron of the hero who projected it.

Columbus, who, during all his ill fuccefs in the negotiation, never abated any thing of the honours and emoluments which he expected to acquire in the expedition, obtained from Ferdinand and Ifabella a full ftipulation of every article contained in his firft proposals. He was conftituted high admiral and viceroy of all the feas, iflands, and continents which he fhould difcover ; with power to receive one tenth of the profits arifing from their productions and commerce. Thefe offices and emoluments were to be hereditary in his family.

These articles being adjufted, the preparations for the voyage were brought forward with rapidity ; but they were by no means adequate to the importance of the expedition. Three fmall veffels,

A 4

scarcely

scarcely sufficient in size to be employed in the coasting business, were appointed to traverse the vast Atlantic; and to encounter the storms and currents that might be expected in so long a voyage, through distant and unknown seas. These vessels, as might be expected in the infancy of navigation, were ill constructed, in a poor condition, and manned by seamen unaccustomed to distant voyages. But the tedious length of time which Columbus had spent in solicitation and suspence, and the prospect of being able soon to obtain the object of his wishes, induced him to overlook what he could not easily remedy, and led him to disregard those circumstances which would have intimidated any other mind. He accordingly equipped his small squadron with as much expedition as possible, manned with ninety men, and victualled for one year. With these, on the 3d of August 1492, amidst a vast crowd of anxious spectators, he set sail on an enterprise, which, if we consider the ill condition of his ships, the inexperience of his sailors, the length and uncertainty of his voyage, and the consequences that flowed from it, was the most daring and important that ever was undertaken. He touched at some of the Portuguese settlements in the Canary Isles; where, although he had been but a few days out, he found his vessels

needed

needed refitting. He soon made the neceſſary re-
pairs, and took his departure from the weſtermoſt
iſlands that had hitherto been diſcovered. Here he
left the former track of navigation, and ſteered his
courſe due weſt.

Not many days after he had been at ſea, he
began to experience a new ſcene of difficulty.
The ſailors now began to contemplate the dangers
and uncertain iſſue of a voyage, the nature and
length of which was left entirely open to conjecture.
Beſides the fickleneſs and timidity natural to men
unaccuſtomed to the diſcipline of a ſea-faring life,
ſeveral circumſtances contributed to inſpire an ob-
ſtinate and mutinous diſpoſition, which required
the moſt conſummate art, as well as fortitude, in
the admiral to controul. Having been three weeks
at ſea, and experienced the uniform courſe of the
trade winds, which always blow in a weſtern direction, they contended that, ſhould they continue the
ſame courſe for a longer period, the ſame winds
would never permit them to return to Spain. The
magnetic needle began to vary its direction. This
being the firſt time that phenomenon was ever
diſcovered, it was viewed by the ſailors with aſtoniſhment, and conſidered as an indication that nature itſelf had changed her courſe, and that Providence was determined to puniſh their audacity, in
venturing

venturing so far beyond the ordinary bounds of man. They declared that the commands of their sovereign had been fully obeyed, in their proceeding so many days in the same direction, and so far surpassing the attempts of all former navigators, in quest of new discoveries. Every talent, requisite for governing, soothing and tempering the passions of men, is conspicuous in the conduct of Columbus on this occasion. The dignity and affability of his manners, his surprising knowledge and experience in naval affairs, his unwearied and minute attention to the duties of his command, gave him a complete ascendency over the minds of his men, and inspired that degree of confidence which would have maintained his authority in almost any possible circumstances. But here, from the nature of the undertaking, every man had leisure to feed his imagination with all the gloominess and uncertainty of the prospect. They found, every day, that the same steady gales carried them with great rapidity from their native country, and indeed from all countries of which they had any knowledge. Notwithstanding all the variety of management with which Columbus addressed himself to their passions—sometimes by soothing them with the prognostics of discovering land, sometimes by flattering their ambition and feasting their avarice with the glory

and

and wealth they would acquire from diſcovering thoſe rich countries beyond the Atlantic, and ſometimes by threatening them with the diſpleaſure of their ſovereign, ſhould their timidity and diſobedience defeat ſo great an object —their uneaſineſs ſtill increaſed. From ſecret whiſperings, it aroſe to open mutiny and dangerous conſpiracy. At length they determined to rid themſelves of the remonſtrances of Columbus, by throwing him into the ſea. The infection ſpread from ſhip to ſhip, and involved officers as well as common ſailors. They finally loſt all ſenſe of ſubordination, and addreſſed their commander in an inſolent manner, demanding to be conducted immediately back to Spain, or, they aſſured him, they would ſeek their own ſafety by taking away his life. Columbus, whoſe ſagacity and penetration had diſcovered every ſymptom of the diſorder, was prepared for this laſt ſtage of it, and was ſufficiently appriſed of the danger that awaited him. He found it vain to contend with paſſions he could no longer controul. He therefore propoſed that they ſhould obey his orders for three days longer; and, ſhould they not diſcover land in that time, he would then direct his courſe for Spain. They complied with his propoſal; and, happily for mankind, in three days they diſcovered land. This was a ſmall iſland, to

which

which Columbus gave the name of San Salvador. Their firſt interview with the natives was a ſcene of amuſement and compaſſion on the one part, and of aſtoniſhment and adoration on the other. The natives were entirely naked, ſimple and timorous; and they viewed the Spaniards as a ſuperior order of beings, deſcended from the Sun, which, in that iſland, and in moſt parts of America, was worſhipped as a Deity. By this it was eaſy for Columbus to perceive the line of conduct proper to be obſerved toward that ſimple and inoffenſive people. Had his companions and ſucceſſors, of the Spaniſh nation, poſſeſſed the wiſdom and humanity of that great diſcoverer, the benevolent mind would have had to experience no ſenſations of regret, in contemplating the extenſive advantages ariſing to mankind from the diſcovery of America.

In this voyage, Columbus diſcovered the iſlands of Cuba and Hiſpaniola; on the latter of which he erected a ſmall fort, and having left a garriſon of thirty-eight men under the command of an officer of the name of Arada, he ſet ſail for Spain. Returning acroſs the Atlantic, he was overtaken by a violent ſtorm, which laſted ſeveral days, and increaſed to ſuch a degree, as baffled all his naval ſkill and threatened immediate deſtruction. In this

ſituation,

situation, when all were in a state of despair, and it was expected that every sea would swallow up the crazy vessel, he manifested a serenity and presence of mind, perhaps never equalled in cases of like extremity. He wrote a short account of his voyage and of the discoveries he had made, wrapped it in an oiled cloth, enclosed it in a cake of wax, put it into an empty cask, and threw it overboard, in hopes that some accident might preserve a deposit of so much importance to the world.

THE storm however abated, and he at length arrived in Spain, after having been driven by stress of weather into the port of Lisbon, where he had opportunity, in an interview with the king of Portugal, to prove the truth of his system by arguments more convincing than those he had before advanced, in the character of an humble and unsuccessful suitor. He was received every where in Spain with royal honours, his family was ennobled, and his former stipulation respecting his offices and emoluments was ratified in the most solemn manner, by Ferdinand and Isabella; while all Europe resounded his praises, and reciprocated their joy and congratulations on the discovery of a new world.

THE immediate consequence of this was a second voyage; in which Columbus took charge of a squadron

dron of feventeen fhips of confiderable burthen. Volunteers of all ranks and conditions folicited to be employed in this expedition. He carried over fifteen hundred perfons, together with all the ne-ceffaries for eftablifhing a colony and extending his difcoveries. In this voyage he explored moft of the Weft-India Iflands; but, on his arrival at Hifpaniola, he found that the garrifon he had left there had been totally deftroyed by the natives, and the fort demolifhed. He however proceeded in the planting of his colony; and, by his prudent and humane conduct towards the natives, he effec-tually eftablifhed the Spanifh authority in that ifland. But while he was thus laying the founda-tion of their future grandeur in South America, fome difcontented perfons, who had returned to Spain, together with his former enemies in that kingdom, confpired to accomplifh his ruin.

They reprefented his conduct in fuch a light at court, as to create uneafinefs and diftruft in the jealous mind of Ferdinand, and made it neceffary for Columbus again to return to Spain, in order to counteract their machinations, and to obtain fuch farther fupplies as were neceffary to his great po-litical and benevolent purpofes. On his arriving at court, and ftating with his ufual dignity and confi-dence the whole hiftory of his tranfactions abroad,

every

every thing wore a favourable appearance. He was received with ufual honours, and folicited to take charge of another fquadron, to carry out farther fupplies, to purfue his difcoveries, and in every refpect to ufe his difcretion in extending the Spanifh empire in the new world. In this third voyage he difcovered the continent of America at the mouth of the river Oronoque. He rectified many diforders in his government of Hifpaniola, which had happened in his abfence; and every thing was going on in a profperous train, when an event was announced to him, which completed his own ruin, and gave a fatal turn to the Spanifh policy and conduct in America. This was the arrival of Francis de Bovadilla, with a commiffion to fupercede Columbus in his government; and with power to arraign him as a criminal, and to judge of his former adminiftration.

It feems that by this time the enemies of Columbus, defpairing to complete his overthrow by groundlefs infinuations of mal-conduct, had taken the more effectual method of exciting the jealoufy of their fovereigns. From the promifing famples of gold and other valuable commodities brought from America, they took occafion to reprefent to the king and queen, that the prodigious wealth and extent of the countries he had difcovered would

foon

foon throw fuch power into the hands of the viceroy, that he would trample on the royal authority, and bid defiance to the Spanifh power. Thefe arguments were well calculated for the cold and fufpicious temper of Ferdinand, and they muft have had fome effect upon the mind of Ifabella. The confequence was the appointment of Bovadilla, who had been the inveterate enemy of Columbus, to take the government from his hands. This firft tyrant of the Spanifh nation in America began his adminiftration by ordering Columbus to be put in chains on board of a fhip, and fending him prifoner to Spain. By relaxing all difcipline, he introduced diforder and licentioufnefs throughout the colony. He fubjected the unhappy natives to a moft miferable fervitude, and apportioned them out in large numbers among his adherents. Under this fevere treatment perifhed, in a fhort time, many thoufands of thofe innocent people.

COLUMBUS was carried in his fetters to the Spanifh court, where the king and queen either feigned or felt a fufficient regret at the conduct of Bovadilla towards this illuftrious prifoner. He was not only releafed from confinement, but treated with all imaginable refpect. But, although the king endeavoured to expiate the offence by cenfuring and recalling Bovadilla, yet we may judge of

his

his sincerity, from his appointing Nicholas de Ovando, another bitter enemy of Columbus, to succeed in the government, and from his ever after refusing to reinstate Columbus, or to fulfil any of the conditions on which the discoveries were undertaken. After two years of solicitation for this or some other employment, he at length obtained a squadron of four small vessels to attempt new discoveries. He now set out, with the ardour and enthusiasm of a young adventurer, in quest of what was always his favourite object, a passage into the South Sea, by which he might sail to India. He touched at Hispaniola, where Ovando, the governor, refused him admittance on shore, even to take shelter during a hurricane, the prognostics of which his experience had taught him to discern. By putting into a small creek, he rode out the storm, and then bore away for the continent. He spent several months, in the most boisterous season of the year, in exploring the coast round the gulph of Mexico, in hopes of finding the intended navigation to India. At length he was shipwrecked, and driven ashore on the island of Jamaica.

His cup of calamities seemed now completely full. He was cast upon an island of savages, without provisions, without any vessel, and thirty leagues from any Spanish settlement. But the greatest physical misfortunes are capable of being imbit-

B tered

tered by the infults of our fellow-creatures. A few
of his hardy companions generoufly offered, in two
Indian canoes, to attempt a voyage to Hifpaniola,
in hopes of obtaining a veffel for the relief of the
unhappy crew. After fuffering every extremity of
danger and hardfhip, they arrived at the Spanifh
colony in ten days. Ovando, through perfonal
malice and jealoufy of Columbus, after having de-
tained thefe meffengers eight months, difpatched a
veffel to Jamaica, in order to fpy out the condition
of Columbus and his crew, with pofitive inftructions
to the captain not to afford them any relief. This
order was punctually executed. The captain ap-
proached the fhore, delivered a letter of empty com-
pliment from Ovando to the admiral, received his
anfwer, and returned. About four months afterwards a veffel came to their relief; and Columbus,
worn out with fatigues and broken with misfortunes, returned for the laft time to Spain. Here a
new diftrefs awaited him, which he confidered as
one of the greateft he had fuffered in his whole life:
this was the death of queen Ifabella, his laft and
greateft friend.

He did not fuddenly abandon himfelf to defpair.
He called upon the gratitude and juftice of the king;
and, in terms of dignity, demanded the fulfilment
of his former contract. Notwithftanding his age
and infirmities, he even folicited to be farther employed

ployed in extending the career of difcovery, without
a profpect of any other reward but the confcioufnefs
of doing good to mankind. But Ferdinand, cold,
ungrateful, and timid, dared not to comply with a
fingle propofal of this kind, left he fhould increafe
his own obligations to a man, whofe fervices he
thought it dangerous to reward. He therefore de-
layed and avoided any decifion on thefe fubjects, in
hopes that the declining health of Columbus would
foon rid the court of the remonftrances of a man,
whofe extraordinary merit was, in their opinion, a
fufficient reafon for deftroying him. In this they
were not difappointed. Columbus languifhed a
fhort time, and gladly refigned a life, which had
been worn out in the moft effential fervices, perhaps, that were ever rendered, by any one man, to
an ungrateful world.

SOME time in this gloomy interval, before his
death, this Vifion is fuppofed to have been prefented
to him; in order to fatisfy his benevolent mind, by
unfolding to him the importance of his difcoveries,
in their extenfive influence upon the intereft and
happinefs of mankind, in the progrefs of fociety.

THE author has indulged a fmall anachronifm in
the opening of the poem, for the fake of grouping
the misfortunes of the hero; as the time of his real

im-

imprifonment was previous to his laft voyage and to the death of Ifabella.

THE author, at firft, formed an idea of attempting a regular epic poem, on the difcovery of America. But on examining the nature of that event, he found that the moft brilliant fubjects incident to fuch a plan would arife from the *confequences* of the difcovery, and muft be reprefented in vifion. Indeed to have made it a patriotic poem, by extending the fubject to the fettlement and revolutions of North America, and their probable effect upon the future progrefs of fociety at large, would have protracted the vifion to fuch a degree as to render it difproportionate to the reft of the work. To avoid an abfurdity of this kind, which he fuppofed the critics would not pardon, he rejected the idea of a regular epic form, and has confined his plan to the train of events which might be reprefented. to the hero in vifion. This form he confiders as the beft that the nature of the fubject would admit ; and the regularity of the parts will appear by obferving, that there is a fingle poetical defign conflantly kept in view, which is, to gratify and footh the defponding mind of the hero : it being the greateft poffible reward of his fervices, and the only one that his fituation would permit him to enjoy, to convince him that his labours had not been beftowed in vain, and that he was the author of fuch extenfive happinefs to the human race.

THE

VISION of COLUMBUS.

BOOK I.

B 3

ARGUMENT.

Condition and soliloquy of Columbus. Appearance and speech of the Angel. They ascend the Mount of Vision, supposed to be on the western coast of Spain. Continent of America draws into view, and is described by the mountains, rivers, lakes, soil, temperature, and some of the natural productions.

THE

VISION of COLUMBUS

BOOK I.

LONG had the Sage, the first who dar'd to brave
The unknown dangers of the western wave,
Who taught mankind where future empires lay
In these fair confines of descending day,
With cares o'erwhelm'd, in life's distressing gloom,   5
Wish'd from a thankless world a peaceful tomb ;
While kings and nations, envious of his name,
Enjoy'd his labours and usurp'd his fame,
And gave the chief, from promis'd empire hurl'd,
Chains for a crown, a prison for a world.   10
    Now night and silence held their lonely reign,
The half-orb'd moon declining to the main ;
Descending clouds, o'er varying ether driven,
Obscur'd the stars and shut the eye from heaven ;
Cold mists through op'ning grates the cell invade,   15
And deathlike terrors haunt the midnight shade ;
When from a visionary, short repose,
That rais'd new cares and temper'd keener woes,

B 4   Co-

Columbus woke, and to the walls addrefs'd
The deep-felt forrows of his manly breaft.   20
    Here lies the purchafe, here the wretched fpoil,
Of painful years and perfevering toil.
For thefe dread walks, this hideous haunt of pain,
I trac'd new regions o'er the pathlefs main,
Dar'd all the dangers of the dreary wave,   25
Hung o'er its clefts and topp'd the furging grave,
Saw billowy feas in fwelling mountains roll,
And burfting thunders rock the reddening pole,
Death rear his front in every dreadful form,
Gape from beneath and blacken in the ftorm ;   30
Till, toft far onward to the fkirts of day,
Where milder funs difpens'd a fmiling ray,
Through brighter fkies my happier fails defcry'd
The golden banks that bound the weftern tide,
And gave th'admiring world that bounteous fhore   35
Their wealth to nations and to kings their power.
    Oh land of wonders ! dear, delufive coaft,
To thefe fond aged eyes for ever loft !
No more thy flowery vales I travel o'er,
For me thy mountains rear the head no more,   40
For me thy rocks no fparkling gems unfold,
Or ftreams luxuriant wear their paths in gold ;

From

From realms of promis'd peace for ever borne,
I hail dread anguish, and in secret mourn.

But dangers paſt, a world explor'd in vain,   45
And foes triumphant, ſhew but half my pain.
Diſſembling friends, each earlier joy who gave,
And fir'd my youth the ſtorms of fate to brave,
Swarm'd in the funſhine of my happier days,
Purſu'd the fortune and partook the praiſe,   50
Bore in my doubtful cauſe a two-fold part,
The garb of friendſhip and the viper's heart,
Now paſs my cell with ſmiles of four diſdain,
Infult my woes and triumph in my pain.

One gentle guardian Heav'n indulgent gave,   55
And now that guardian ſlumbers in the grave.
Hear from above, thou dear departed Shade,＊
As once my joys, my prefent forrows aid,
Burſt my full heart, afford that laſt relief,
Breathe back my fighs and reinſpire my grief;   60
Still in my fight thy royal form appears,
Reproves my filence and demands my tears.
On that bleſt hour my foul delights to dwell,
When thy protection bade the canvaſs ſwell ;

＊ The death of queen Iſabella, which happened previous to
the laſt return of Columbus from America, was his moſt bitter
ſubjeċt of regret; as in her he loſt his only friend.

When

When kings and courtiers found their factions vain,   65
Blind Superstition shrunk beneath her chain,
The sun's glad beam led on the circling way,
And isles rose beauteous in the western day.
But o'er those silv'ry shores, that new domain,
What crouds of tyrants fix their horrid reign!   70
Again bold Freedom seeks her kindred skies,
Truth leaves the world, and Isabella dies.

Oh, lend thy friendly shroud to veil my sight,
That these pain'd eyes may dread no more the light,
These welcome shades shall close my instant doom,   75
And this drear mansion moulder to a tomb.

Thus mourn'd the hapless man, a thundering sound
Roll'd round the shuddering walls and shook the ground;
O'er all the dome, where solemn arches bend,
The roofs unfold and streams of light descend;   80
The growing splendor fill'd th'astonish'd room,
And gales etherial breath'd a glad perfume;
Mild in the midst a radiant seraph shone,
Rob'd in the vestments of the rising sun;
Tall rose his stature, youth's primeval grace   85
Adorn'd his limbs and brighten'd in his face,
His closing wings, in golden plumage dress,
With gentle sweep came folding o'er his breast,

His

His locks in rolling ringlets glittering hung,
And founds melodious mov'd his heav'nly tongue :   90
   Rife, trembling Chief, to fcenes of rapture, rife,
This voice awaits thee from th'approving fkies ;
Thy juft complaints, in God's own prefence known,
Have call'd compaffion from his bounteous throne ;
Affume no more the deep defponding ftrain,   95
Nor count thy toils, nor deem thy virtues vain.
Tho' faithlefs men thy injur'd worth defpife,
'Tis thus they treat the bleffings of the fkies ;
For look thro' nature, Heav'n's own conduct trace,
What power divine fuftains th'unthankful race !   100
From that great fource, that life-infpiring foul,
Suns drew their light and fyftems learn'd to roll,
Time walk'd the filent round, and life began,
And God's fair image ftamp'd the mind of man ;
His cares, his bounties fill the realms of fpace,   105
And fhine fuperior in thy favour'd race ;
Men fpeak their wants, th' all-bounteous hand fupplies,
And gives the good that mortals dare defpife.
In thefe dark vales where blinded faction fways,
Wealth, pride and conqueft claim the palm of praife,   110
Aw'd into flaves, while grov'ling millions groan,
And blood-ftain'd fteps lead upwards to a throne.

                                          Far

Far other wreaths thy virtuous temples claim,
Far nobler honours build thy sacred name;
Be thine the joys immortal minds that grace,   115
And thine the toils that bless a kindred race.
Now raise thy ravish'd soul to scenes more bright,
The vision'd ages rising on thy sight;
For, wing'd with speed, from worlds of light I came,
To sooth thy grief and show thy distant fame.   120
    As that great Seer, whose animating rod
Taught Israel's sons the wonder-working God,
Who led, thro' dreary wastes, the murm'ring band
To the rich confines of the promis'd land,
Oppress'd with years, from Pisgah's beauteous height, 125
O'er boundless regions cast the raptor'd sight;
The bliss of unborn nations warm'd his breast,
Repaid his toils and sooth'd his soul to rest;
Thus, o'er thy subject wave, shalt thou behold
Far happier realms their future charms unfold,   130
In nobler pomp another Pisgah rise,
Beneath whose foot thy new-found Canaan lies;
There, rapt in vision, hail the distant clime,
And taste the blessings of remotest time.
    The Seraph spoke; and now before them lay   135
(The doors unbarr'd) a steep ascending way,

That,

That, through difparting fhades, arofe on high,
Reach'd o'er the hills, and lengthen'd up the fky,
Show'd a clear fummit, rich with rifing flowers,
That breathe their odours through celeftial bowers;   140
O'er proud Hifpanian fpires, it looks fublime,
Subjects the Alps and levels all the clime.
Led by the Power, Columbus gain'd the height,
A touch from heav'n fublim'd his mortal fight,
And, calm beneath them, flow'd the weftern main,   145
Far ftretch'd, immenfe, a fky-encircled plain;
No fail, no ifle, no cloud invefts the bound,
Nor billowy furge difturbs th'unvaried round;
Till, deep in diftant heav'ns, the fun's dim ray
Topp'd unknown cliffs and call'd them up to day;   150
Slow glimmering into fight wide regions drew,
And rofe and brighten'd on th'expanding view;
Fair fweep the waves, the leffening ocean fmiles,
And breathes the fragrance of a thoufand ifles;
Near and more near the long-drawn coafts arife,   155
Bays ftretch their arms and mountains lift the fkies,
The lakes, unfolding, point the ftreams their way,
The plains, the hills, their fpreading fkirts difplay,
The vales draw forth, high walk th'approaching groves,
And all the majefty of nature moves.   160

O'er

O'er the wild climes his eyes delighted rove,
Where lands extend and glittering waters move;
He saw, through central realms, the winding shore
Spread the deep Gulph, his sail had trac'd before,
The Darien isthmus meet the raging tide,   165
Join distant lands and neighb'ring seas divide,
On either side the shores unbounded bend,
Push wide their waves, and to the poles ascend;
While two great continents united rise,
Broad as the main and lengthen'd with the skies.   170
     Silent the Hero gaz'd; when thus the Guide:
Here spreads the world, thy daring sail descry'd,
Ages unborn shall bless the happy day,
That saw thy streamers shape the trackless way,
While through the growing realms thy sons shall tread, 175
And following millions trace the path you led.
Behold yon isles, where first thy flag unfurl'd,
Wav'd peaceful triumph o'er the western world,
Where, aw'd to silence, savage bands gave place,
And hail'd with joy the sun-descended race!*   180

* The original inhabitants of Hispaniola were worshippers
of the sun. On the first landing of the Europeans, they were
suppofed to be gods, and consequently descended from the sun.

See

See there the banks that pureſt waters lave,
Swift Oronoque rolls back the ocean's wave,
The well-known current cleaves the lofty coaſt,
Where Paria's walks thy former footſteps boaſt!
Theſe ſcanty ſhores no more thy joys ſhall bound,   185
See nobler proſpects lead their ſwelling round,
Nature's ſublimeſt ſcenes before thee roll,
And years and empires open on thy ſoul!

High to yon ſeats exalt thy roving view,
Where Quito's lofty plains o'erlook Peru,   190
On whoſe broad baſe, like clouds together driven,
A world exalted props the ſkirts of heaven.
From ſouth to north, what long blue fronts ariſe!
Ridge over ridge, and loſt in ambient ſkies!
Approaching near, they heave expanding bounds,   195
The yielding concave bends ſublimer rounds,
Earth's loftieſt towers there lift the daring height,
And all the Andes fill the bounded ſight.

Round the low baſe what ſloping breaches bend!
Hills form on hills, and trees o'er trees extend,   200
Aſcending, whitening, how the crags are loſt!
O'erwhelm'd with ſummits of eternal froſt;
Broad fields of ice give back the morning ray,
Like walls of ſuns, or heav'n's perennial day.

                                        There

There folding ftorms on eaftern pinions ride,   205
Veil the black heav'n, and wrap the mountain's fide,
The thunders rake the crags, the rains defcend,
And the long light'nings o'er the vallies bend,
While blafts unburden'd fweep the cliffs of fnow,
The whirlwinds wheel above, the floods convolve below. 210
There molten rocks, explofive rend their tomb,
And dread volcanoes ope the nations' doom,
Wild o'er the regions pour the floods of fire,
The fhores heave backward and the feas retire.
There flumbering vengeance waits th'Almighty's call, 215
Long ages hence to fhake fome guilty wall;
Thy pride, O Lima, fwells the fulph'rous wave,
And fanes, and priefts, and idols crowd thy grave.

But ceafe, my fon, thefe dread events to trace,
Nor learn the woes that wait thy kindred race.   220
Beyond thofe glimmering hills, in lands unknown,
O'er the wide gulph, beyond the flaming zone,
Thro' milder climes, fee gentler mountains rife,
Where yon dim regions bound the northern fkies.
Back from the fhore afcending champaigns run,   225
And lift their heights to hail the eaftern fun,
Through all the midland realm, to yon blue pole,
The green hills lengthen and the rivers roll.

So

So spoke the blest Immortal; when, more near,
The northern climes in various pomp appear;   230
Lands yet unknown, and streams without a name
Rise into vision and demand their fame.
As when some saint, in heav'n's sublime abode,
Extends his views o'er all the works of God;
While earth, his kindred orb, before him rolls,   235
Here glows the centre, and there point the poles;
O'er land and sea his eyes exalted rove,
And joys of mortals kindle heav'n with love;
With equal glance the raptur'd Hero's sight
Rang'd the low vale, or climb'd the cloudy height,   240
As, led by heav'n's own hand, his ardent mind,
Explor'd the realms that here await mankind.

  From sultry Mobile's rich Floridian shore,
To where Ontario bids hoarse Laurence roar,
Stretch'd o'er the plains and hills, in long array,   245
The beauteous Alleganies met the day.
Round the clear mountain-tops and o'er the streams,
The forest azure streak'd the morning beams;
Fair spread the scene, the Hero gaz'd sublime,
And thus in prospect hail'd the happy clime: 250
Blest be the race, in future ages led,
Where these wide realms their various bounties spread!

What treasur'd stores the lofty hills combine!
Sleep there ye diamonds, and ye ores refine,
Exalt your heads, ye oaks, ye pines, afcend,   255
Till future navies bid your branches bend,
Then fpread the canvafs o'er the watery way,
Explore new worlds and teach the old your fway.

He faid, and northward caft his wondering eyes,
Where other cliffs, in other climes, arife,   260
Where bleak Acadia fpreads the dangerous coaft,
And ifles and fhoals their latent horrors boaft,
High in the diftant heav'n, the hoary height
Heaves the glad failor an eternal light.*
Nor could thofe hills, unnotic'd, raife their head,   265
That look fublime o'er Hudfon's winding bed;
Tho' no bold fiction rear them to the fkies,
Tho' neighb'ring fummits far fuperior rife;
Yet the blue Kaatfkill, where the ftorms divide,
Would lift the heav'ns from Atlas' lab'ring pride.   270
Awhile the ridgy heights his notice claim,
And hills unnumber'd rofe without a name,
Which plac'd, in pomp, on any eaftern fhore,
Taurus would fhrink, the Alps be fung no more;

* The White Hills of Nova Scotia, though fifty miles from
the fea, are the firft land to be difcovered in approaching that
part of North America, and ferve as a land mark for a confiderable length of coaft, of very difficult navigation.

For

For here great Nature, more exalted show'd   275
The last ascending footsteps of her God.

He saw those mountains ope their watery store,
Floods leave their caves, thro' hills disparting pour,
Cleave the wide plains and seek the distant strand,
And lave their beauteous banks, where future towns
    must stand.   280

   First, from the dreadful Andes' opening side,
He saw Maranon * lead his sovereign tide.
A thousand hills for him dissolve their snow,
A thousand streams obedient bend below,

* This river, from different circumstances, has obtained several different names. It has been called *Amazon*, from an idea that some part of the neighbouring country was inhabited by a race of warlike women, resembling what Herodotus relates of the Amazons of Scythia. It has been called *Orellana*, from its having been discovered by a Spanish officer of that name, who, on a certain expedition, deserted from the younger Pizarro, on one of the sources of this river, and navigated it from thence to the ocean. *Maranon* is the original name given it by the natives of the country; which name I choose to follow.

If we estimate its magnitude by the length of its course, and the quantity of its water, it is much the greatest river that has hitherto come to our knowledge. Its navigation is said to be uninterrupted for four thousand miles from the sea, its breadth, within the banks, is sixty geographical miles; it receives in its course a variety of great rivers, besides those described in the succeeding paragraphs of the text. Many of these descend from elevated countries and mountains covered with snow, the melting of which annually swells the Maranon above its banks; when it overflows and fertilizes a vast extent of territory.

From different climes their devious courses wind,   285
Sweep beds of ore and leave their gold behind,
In headlong ~~characters~~ *cataracts* indignant heave,
Rush to his opening banks and swell the sweeping wave.
    Ucayla, chief of all his mighty sons,
From Cusco's heights a boundless journey runs ;   290
Yutay moves gently in a shorter course,
And rapid Yatva pours a gathering force ;
Far in a wild, by nameless tributes fed,
The silent Chavar wears a lonely bed ;
Aloft, where northern Quito sits on high,   295
The roaring Napo quits his misty sky ;
Down the long steeps, in whitening torrents driven,
Like Nile descending from his fabled heaven.
While other waves and lakes unknown to fame,
Discharge their urns and fill the swelling stream,   300
That, far, from clime to clime, majestic goes,
Enlarging, widening, deepening as it flows ;
Approaching ocean hears the distant roar,
Moves up its bed, nor finds th' expected shore ;
His freshening waves, with high and hoary tide,   305
Whelm back the flood, and isles and champaigns hide,
Till mingling waters lead the downward sweep,
And waves, and trees, and banks roll whirling to the deep.
                                        Now,

Now, where the sun in milder glory beams,
Brazilia's hills pour down their spreading streams,   310
The smiling lakes their opening sides display,
And winding vales prolong the devious way;
He saw Xaraya's * diamond banks unfold,
And Paraguay's deep channel pav'd with gold,
Saw proud Potosi lift his glittering head,   315
Whence the clear Plata wears his tinctur'd bed;
Rich with the spoils of many a distant mine,
In one broad silver sea their floods combine;
Wide o'er the realms its annual bounties spread,
By nameless streams from various mountains fed;   320
The thirsty regions wait its glad return,
And drink their future harvests from its urn.

Round the cold climes, beneath the southern sky,
Thy path, Magellan, caught the Hero's eye;
The long cleft ridges wall'd the spreading way,   325
Fair gleaming westward to the placid sea.

* Some of the richest diamond mines are found on the banks
of the lake *Xaraya*. The river *Paraguay* is remarkable for the
quantities of gold dust found in it's channel. The *Rio de la
Plata*, properly so called, has its source in the mountains of
Potosi; and it is probably from this circumstance, that it received
its name, which signifies the *River of Silver*. This river, after
being joined by the Paraguay, which is larger than itself, retains
its own name till it joins the sea. Near the mouth, it is ninety
miles wide; but it is in other respects far inferior to the
Maranon.

Soon as the diftant wave was feen to roll,

His ancient wifhes * fill'd his rifing foul,

Warm from his heaving heart an anxious figh

Breath'd o'er his lips; he turn'd his moiften'd eye,   330

And thus befought the angel : Speak, my guide,

Where leads the pafs ? and whence yon purple tide ?

How the dim waves in blending ether ftray,

No lands behind them rife, no ftreamers in them play !

　　In thofe low fkies extends the boundlefs main,   335

I fought fo long, and fought, alas, in vain.

Reftore, celeftial Power, my youthful morn,

Call back my years, and bid my fame return ;

Grant me to trace, beyond that pathlefs fea,

Some happier fhore from luft of empire free ;   340

In that far world to fix a peaceful bower,

From envy fafe, and curft Ovando's power.

Earth's happieft realms, let not their diftance hide,

Nor feas for ever roll their ufelefs tide.

Bid unborn nations burft the womb of time,   345

And rife to birth in that indulgent clime ;

* The great object of Columbus in moft of his voyages was to difcover a weftern paffage to India. For this purpofe he navigated the gulph of Mexico, with great care, and was much difappointed in not finding a pafs into the South Sea. The view he is here fuppofed to have of that ocean would therefore naturally recall his former defire of failing round the world.

　　　　　　　　　　　　　　　　　　And

And grant me still, this final task to dare,
One vent'rous bark, and be my life thy care.

   The Hero spoke; the seraph mild replies,
While warm compassion soften'd in his eyes: 350
Though still to virtuous deeds thy mind aspires,
And heav'nly visions kindle new desires ;
Yet hear with reverence what attends thy state,
Nor wish to pass th' eternal bounds of fate.
Led by this sacred light thy soul shall see, 355
That half mankind shall owe their bliss to thee,
And joyous empires claim their future birth,
In these fair bounds of sea-encircled earth ;
While unborn times, by thine example prest,
Shall call forth heroes to explore the rest. 360

   Beyond those seas, the well-known climes arise,
Where morning splendors gild the Indian skies.
The circling course to Madagascar's shores,
Round Afric's cape, bold Gama now explores ;
Another pass these opening straits provide, 365
Nor long shall rest the daring search untry'd ;
This watery glade shall open soon to fame,
Here a lost hero fix his lasting name,*

  * The Straits of Magellan; so called from having been difcovered by that navigator, who first attempted to go round the
world, and lost his life in the attempt.

C 4

From

From that new main in furious waves be toft,
And fail neglected on the barb'rous coaft.   370
    But fee the chief from Albion's ftrand arife,
Speed in his pinions, fame before his eyes!
Hither, O Drake, difplay the haftening fails,
Widen ye paffes, and awake ye gales,
Move thou before him, heav'n-revolving fun,   375
Wind his long courfe, and teach him where to run,
Earth's diftant fhores, in circling bands unite,
Lands, learn your fame, and oceans, roll in light,
Round all the beauteous globe his flag be hurl'd,
A new Columbus to th'aftonifh'd world!   380
    He fpoke; and filent tow'rd the northern fky,
Wide o'er the realms the Hero caft his eye;
Saw the long floods thro' devious channels pour,
And wind their currents to the opening fhore;
While midland feas and lonely lakes difplay   385
Their glittering glories to the beams of day.
Thy capes, Virginia, towering from the tide,
Rais'd their blue banks, and ftretch'd their borders wide;
To future fails unfold a circling way,
And guard the bofom of thy beauteous Bay.   390
Where, from each diftant Alleganian height,
Thy fpreading ftreams lay glimmering to the light;

York

York led his wave, imbank'd in flowery pride,
And nobler James fell winding by his fide ;
Back tow'rd the hills, through many a filent vale,   375
Wild Rappahanock feem'd to lure the fail,
While, far o'er all, in fea-like azure fpread,
The great Potowmac fwept his lordly bed.

When thus he faw the mingling waters play,
And feas, in loft diforder, idly ftray,   400
The frowning forefts ftretch the dufky wing,
And deadly damps forbid the fruits to fpring,
No feafons clothe the field with beauteous grain,
No buoyant fhip attempt the ufelefs main,
With fond impatience, heav'nly feer, he cry'd,   405
When fhall my children crofs the lonely tide ?
Here, here, my fons, the hand of culture bring,
Here teach the lawns to fmile, the groves to fing ;
Ye facred floods, no longer vainly glide,
Ye harvefts, load them, and ye forefts, ride,   410
Bear the deep burden from the joyous fwain,
And tell the world where peace and plenty reign.

Now round the coaft, where other floods invite,
He fondly turn'd ; they fill'd his eager fight :
Here Del'ware's waves the yielding fhores divide,   415
And here majeftic Hudfon pours his tide ;

Thy

Thy parent ſtream, fair Hartford, met his eye,
Far leſſening upward to the northern ſky ;
No watery glades thro' richer valleys ſhine,
Nor drinks the ſea a lovelier wave than thine.   420
Myſtick and Charles adorn'd their bloomy iſles,
And gay Piſcat'way caught his paſſing ſmiles ;
Swift Kenebeck, deſcending from on high,
Swept the tall hills and lengthen'd down the ſky ;
When hoarſe reſounding through the gaping ſhore,   425
He heard cold Laurence' dreadful ſurges roar.
Tho' ſoftening May had wak'd the vernal blade,
And happier climes her fragrant garb diſplay'd,
Yet howling winter, in this bleak domain,
Shook the wide waſte, and held his gloomy reign ;   430
Still groans the flood, in frozen fetters bound,
And iſles of ice his angry front ſurround ;
Cloth'd in white majeſty, the foaming main
Leads up the tide and tempts the wintery chain,
Billows on billows lift the maddening brine,   435
And ſeas and clouds in battling conflict join,
The daſh'd wave ſtruggling heaves in ſwelling ſweep,
Wide craſh the portals of the frozen deep ;
Till, forc'd aloft, high-bounding in the air,
Moves the blear ice and ſheds a hideous glare,   440

The

The torn foundations on the furface ride,
And wrecks of winter load the downward tide.

Now where the lakes, thofe midland oceans lie,
Columbus turn'd his heav'n-illumin'd eye.
Ontario's banks, unfolding on the north,   445
With fweep majeftic, pour'd his Laurence forth;
Above, bold Erie's wave fublimely ftood,
Look'd o'er the cliff * and heav'd his headlong flood;
Far circling in the north, great Huron fpread,
And Michigan o'erwhelm'd a weftern bed;   450
While, ftretch'd in circling majefty away,
The deep Superior clos'd the fetting day.
Wide opening round them, lands delightful fpread,
Deep groves innumerous caft a folemn fhade;
Slow mov'd the fettling mift in lurid ftreams,   455
And dufky radiance brown'd the folar beams;
O'er all the fcene the great difcoverer ftood,
And thus addrefs'd the meffenger of good:
But why thefe feats, that feem referv'd to grace
The virtuous toils of fome illuftrious race,   460
Why fpread fo wide, and form'd fo fair in vain?
And why fo diftant rolls th'unconfcious main?
Thefe defert fountains muft for ever reft,
Of man unfeen, by native beafts poffeft.

* The falls of Niagara.

For, fee! no fhip can point the canvafs here,   465
No ftream conducts, nor ocean wanders near,
Eternal winter clothes the fhelvy fhores,
Where yon far northern * fon of Neptune roars;
Or fhould bold barks his frozen entrance brave,
And climes by culture warm his leffening wave,   470
Yon frightful Cataract exhalts the brow,
And frowns defiance to the world below.
    To whom the Seraph.   Here extended lies
The happieft realm that feels the foftering fkies;
Led by this arm thy fons fhall hither come,   475
And ftreams obedient yield the heroes room;
Nor think no pafs can find the diftant main,
Or heav'n's laft polifh touch'd thefe climes in vain.
See the bold Miffifippi bend his way
Thro' all the weftern boundlefs tracts of day;   480
From lonely lakes behold his current led,
And filent waves adorn his infant head;
Far fouth thro' happy regions fee him wind,
By gathering floods and nobler fountains join'd,
Yon opening gulph receive the beauteous wave,   485
And thy known ifles his frefh'ning current lave.
To his broad bed their tributary ftores,
Akanfa here, and there Miffouri pours,

                    * St. Laurence.

Rouge, from the weſtern wild, his channel fills,
Ohio, gather'd from a thouſand hills,   490
The Black, the Yazoes fed by Georgian ſprings,
And Illinois his northern tribute brings ;——
There lies the path thy future ſons ſhall trace,
And ſpread o'er theſe wide realms the glory of thy race.

    So taught the Saint. The regions nearer drew,   495
And other objects claim'd the Hero's view.
Retiring far round Hudſon's frozen bay,
Where leſſening circles ſhrink beyond the day,
The ſhivering ſhrubs ſcarce brave the diſmal clime,
Snows ever-riſing with the years of time ;   500
The beaſts all whitening roam the lifeleſs plain,
And caves unfrequent ſcoop the couch for man.

    Where ſpring's coy ſteps, in cold Canada, ſtray,
And joyleſs ſeaſons hold unequal ſway,
He ſaw the pine its daring mantle rear,   505
Break the rude blaſt and mock th'inclement year,
Secure the limits of the angry ſkies,
And bid all ſouthern vegetation riſe.
Wild o'er the vaſt impenetrable round,
The untrod bow'rs of ſhadowy nature frown'd ;   510
The neighb'ring cedar wav'd its honours wide,
The fir's tall boughs, the oak's reſiſtleſs pride,

The

The branching beech, the aspen's trembling shade,
Veil'd the dim heav'ns and brown'd the dusky glade.
Here in huge crouds those sturdy sons of earth,   515
In frosty regions, claim a nobler birth ;
Where heavy trunks the shelt'ring dome requires,
And copious fuel feeds the wint'ry fires.
While warmer suns that southern climes emblaze,
A cool deep umbrage o'er the woodland raise ;   520
Floridia's shores their blooms around him spread,
And Georgian hills erect their shady head.
Beneath tall trees, in livelier verdure gay,
Long level walks a humble garb display ;
The infant maize unconscious of its worth,   525
Points the green spire and bends the foliage forth ;
Sweeten'd on flowery banks, the passing air
Breathes all th'untasted fragrance of the year ;
Unbidden harvests o'er the regions rife,
And blooming life repays the genial skies.   530
Where circling shores around the gulph extend,
The bounteous groves with richer burdens bend ;
Spontaneous fruits th'uplifted palms unfold,
The beauteous orange waves a load of gold,
The untaught vine, the wildly-wanton cane   535
Bloom on the waste, and clothe th'enarbour'd plain ;

The

The rich pimento scents the neighbouring skies,
And woolly clusters o'er the cotton rise.
Here, in one view, the same glad branches bring
The fruits of autumn and the flowers of spring;   540
No wint'ry blasts th'unchanging year deform,
Nor beasts unshelter'd fear the pinching storm;
But vernal breezes o'er the blossoms rove,
And breathe the ripen'd juices thro' the grove.
Beneath the crystal wave's inconstant light,   545
Pearl's undistinguish'd sparkle on the sight;
From opening earth, in living lustre, shine
The various treasures of the blazing mine;
Hills, cleft before him, all their stores unfold,
The quick mercurius and the burning gold;   550
While gems of various hues, in bright array,
Illume the changing rocks and shed the beams of day.

THE

THE

VISION of COLUMBUS.

BOOK II.

D

ARGUMENT.

THE
VISION OF COLUMBUS.

BOOK II.

HIGH o'er the scene, as thus Columbus gaz'd,
Th' indulgent Power his arm sublimely rais'd ;
When round the realms superior lustre flew,
And call'd new wonders to the Hero's view.

He saw, at once, as far as eye could rove, 5
Like scattering herds, the swarthy people move,
In tribes innumerable ; all the waste,
Beneath their steps, a varying shadow cast.
As airy shapes, beneath the moon's pale eye,
When broken clouds sail o'er the curtain'd sky, 10
Spread thro' the grove and flit along the glade,
And cast their grisly phantoms through the shade ;
So move the hordes, in thickets half conceal'd,
Or vagrant stalking o'er the open field.
Here ever-restless tribes, despising home, 15
O'er shadowy streams and trackless deserts roam ;
While others there, thro' downs and hamlets stray,
And rising domes a happier state display.

D 2

The

The painted chiefs, in death's grim terrors dreft,
Rife fierce to war, and beat the favage breaft ;   20
Dark round their fteps collecting warriors pour,
And dire revenge begins the hideous roar ;
While to the realms around the fignal flies,
And tribes on tribes, in dread diforder, rife,
Track the mute foe and fcour the diftant wood,   25
Wide as a ftorm, and dreadful as a flood ;
Or deep in groves the filent ambufh lay,
Or wing the flight or fweep the prize away,
Unconfcious babes and reverend fires devour,
Drink the warm blood, and paint their cheeks with gore. 30

    Awhile he gaz'd, with dubious thoughts oppref's'd,
And thus his wavering voice the Power addref's'd :—
Say, to what clafs of nature's fons belong
The countlefs tribes of this untutor'd throng ?
Where human frames and brutal fouls combine,   35
No force can tame them, and no arts refine.
Can thefe be fafhion'd on the focial plan,
Or boaft a lineage with the race of man ?
In yon fair ifle, * when firft my wandering view
Rang'd the glad coaft and met the favage crew ;   40

* The ifland of Hifpaniola ; where Columbus planted a
colony in his firft voyage. See the Introduction.

A

A timorous herd, like harmless roes, they ran,
And call'd us gods, from whom their tribes began.
But when, their fears allay'd, in us they trace
The well-known image of a mortal race;——
When Spanish blood their wondering eyes beheld,   45
Returning rage their changing bosoms swell'd;
They rous'd their bands from numerous hills afar,
To feast their souls on ruin, waste and war.
Nor plighted vows, nor sure defeat, controul
The same indignant savageness of soul.   50
    Tell then, my Seer, from what dire sons of earth
The brutal people drew their ancient birth?
Whether in realms, the western heav'ns that close,
A tribe distinct from other nations rose,
Born to subjection; when, in happier time,   55
A nobler race should hail their fruitful clime.
Or, if a common source all nations claim,
Their lineage, form, and reas'ning powers the same,
What sovereign cause, in secret wisdom laid,
This wond'rous change in God's own work has made? 60
Why various powers of soul and tints of face
In different climes diversify the race?
    To whom the Guide: — Unnumber'd causes lie
In earth, and sea, and round the varying sky,

D 3

That

That fire the foul, or damp the genial flame, 65
And work their wonders on the human frame.
See beauty, form, and colour change with place—
Here charms of health the blooming vifage grace;
There pale difeafes float in every wind,
Deform the figure, and degrade the mind. 70
    From earth's own elements, thy race at firft
Rofe into life, the children of the duft;
Thefe kindred elements, by various ufe,
Nourifh the growth and every change produce;
In each afcending ftage the man fuftain, 75
His breath, his food, his phyfic, and his bane.
In due proportions, where thefe virtues lie,
A perfect form their equal aids fupply;
And, while unchang'd th'efficient caufes reign,
Age foll'wing age th'unvaried race maintain. 80
But where crude elements diftemper'd rife,
And caft their fick'ning vapours round the fkies,
Unlike that harmony of human frame,
Where God's firft works and Nature's were the fame,
Th' unconfcious tribes, attemp'ring to the clime, 85
Still vary downward with the years of time;
Till fix'd, at laft, their characters abide,
And local likenefs feeds their local pride.

The

The foul too, varying with the changing clime,
Feeble or fierce, or groveling or fublime,   90
Forms with the body to a kindred plan,
And lives the fame, a nation or a man.

    Yet think not clime alone the tint controuls,
On every fhore, by altitude of poles;
A different caft the glowing zone demands,   95
In Paria's blooms,* from Tombut's burning fands.
Internal caufes, thro' the earth and fkies,
Blow in the breeze or on the mountain rife,
'Thro' air and ocean, with their changes run,
Breathe from the ground, or circle with the fun.·   100

    Where thefe long fhores their boundlefs regions fpread,
See the fame form all different tribes pervade;
Thro' all alike the fertile forefts bloom,
And all, uncultur'd, fhed a folemn gloom;
Thro' all great nature's boldeft features rife,   105
Sink into vales and tower amid the fkies;
Streams, darkly winding, ftretch a broader fway,
The groves and mountains bolder walks difplay;
A dread fublimity informs the whole,
And wakes a dread fublimity of foul.   110

    * Paria is a country near the river Oronoque; the only part
of the continent of America that Columbus had feen. Tombut,
in the fame latitude, is the moft fteril part of Africa.

Yet time and art shall other changes find,
And open still and vary still the mind.
The countless swarms that tread these dark abodes,
Who glean spontaneous fruits and range the woods,
Fix'd here for ages, in their swarthy face   115
Display the wild complexion of the place.
Yet when their tribes to happy nations rise,
And earth by culture warms * the genial skies;

* Without entering into any discussion on the theory of heat and cold, the author, in vindication of the expression in the text, would just observe, that some solid mass of matter, such for instance as the surface of the earth, seems absolutely necessary to the production of heat. At least it must be a matter more compact than that of the sun's rays; and perhaps its power of producing heat is in proportion to its solidity. That the warmth communicated to the atmosphere is generated by the combined causes of the earth and the sun, he is not disposed to deny; but he thinks the agency of the former much more powerful in this operation than that of the latter, and its presence more indispensible; as masses of matter will produce heat by friction, without the aid of the sun; but no experiment has yet proved that the rays of the sun are capable of producing heat, without the aid of earthy matter. The air is temperate in those cavities of the earth where the sun is the most effectually excluded; whereas, the coldest regions of which we have any knowledge are the tops of the Andes; where the sun's rays have the most direct operation, being the most verticle and the least obstructed by vapours. Those regions are too far removed from the broad surface of the earth, which is requisite to warm the surrounding atmosphere by its co-operation with the action of the sun.

From these principles we may conclude that cultivation tends to warm the atmosphere and meliorate the climate of a cold country; as by removing the forests and the marshes, the solid earth is open to the sun, and acts upon the air.

According to the descriptions given of the middle parts of
Europe

A fairer tint and more majeſtic grace
Shall fluſh their features and exalt the race;   120
While milder arts, with ſocial joys refin'd,
Inſpire new beauties in the growing mind.

Thy foll'wers too, fair Europe's nobleſt pride,
When future gales ſhall wing them o'er the tide,
A ruddier hue * and deeper ſhade ſhall gain,   125
And ſtalk, in ſtatelier figures, o'er the plain.
While nature's grandeur lifts the eye abroad
O'er theſe dread footſteps of the forming God,
Wing'd on a wider glance the vent'rous ſoul
Bids greater powers and bolder thoughts unroll;   130
The ſage, the chief, the patriot, unconfin'd,
Shield the weak world and meliorate mankind.

But think not thou, in all the range of man,
That different pairs, in different climes, began;
Or tribes diſtinct, by ſignal marks confeſt,   135
Were born to ſerve or ſubjugate the reſt.

Europe by Cæſar and Tacitus, it appears that thoſe countries
were much colder in the days of thoſe writers, than at preſent;
cultivation has already ſoftened the climate to a great degree.
The ſame effect begins to be perceived in North America, and
will doubtleſs one day be as apparent as the preſent difference in
the temperature of the two continents.

* The complexion of the inhabitants of North America, who
are deſcended from the Engliſh and Dutch, is evidently darker,
and their ſtature taller, than thoſe of the Engliſh and Dutch in
Europe

The Hero heard, and thus refum'd the ftrain :—
Who led thefe wand'rers o'er the dreary main ?
Could their weak fires, unfkill'd in human lore,
Build the bold bark, to feek an unknown fhore ;   140
A fhore fo diftant from the world befide,
So dark the tempefts, and fo wild the tide,
That Greece and Tyre, and all who tempt the fea,
Have fhunn'd the tafk, and left the fame to me ?

When firft thy roving race, the Power reply'd,   145
Learn'd by the ftars the devious fail to guide,
From ftormy Hellefpont explor'd the way,
And fought the bound'ries of the Midland fea ;
Ere great Alcides form'd the impious plan
To check the fail, and bound the fteps of man,—   150
Driv'n from the Calpian ftraits, a haplefs train
Roll'd on the waves that fweep the weftern main ;
While eaftern ftorms the bill'wing fkies o'erfhade,
Nor fun nor ftars afford their wonted aid.
For many a darkfome day, o'erwhelm'd and toft,   155
Their fails, their oars in fwall'wing furges loft ;
At length, the clouds withdrawn, they fail defcry
Their courfe directing from their native fky ;
No hope remains ; while, o'er the flaming zone,
The wind ftill bears them with the circling fun ;   160

Till

Till the wild walks of this delightful coaſt
Receive to lonely ſeats the ſuffering hoſt.
The fruitful plains invite their ſteps to roam,
Renounce their ſorrows, and forget their home ;
Revolving years their ceaſeleſs wand'rings led, 165
And from their ſons deſcending nations ſpread.

Theſe round the ſouth and middle region ſtray,
Where cultur'd fields their growing arts diſplay ;
While northern tribes a later ſource demand,
A race deſcended from the Aſian ſtrand. 170
Now tow'rd the diſtant pole thy view extend ;
See iſles and ſhores and ſeas Pacific blend ;
That peopled coaſt, where Amur's current glides,
From thy own world a narrow frith divides ;
There Tartar hoſts, for numerous years, have ſail'd, 175
And changing tribes theſe fruitful regions hail'd:

He look'd : the north-weſt ſhores beneath him ſpread,
And moving nations on the margin tread.
As, when autumnal ſtorms awake their force,
The ſtorks foreboding tempt their ſouthern courſe ; 180
From all the fields collecting throngs ariſe,
Mount on the wing and crowd along the ſkies ;
Thus, to his eye, from far Siberia's ſhore,
Thro' iſles and ſeas, the gath'ring people pour ;

From

From those cold regions hail a happier strand,   185
Leap from the wave and tread the welcome land;
The growing tribes extend their southern sway,
And widely wander to a milder day.
    But why—the Chief replied—if ages past
Have led these vagrants o'er the wilder'd waste—   190
If human souls, for social compact given,
Inform their nature with the stamp of heaven,
Why the dread glooms for ever must they rove,
And no mild joys their temper'd passions move?
Ages remote and dark thou bring'st to light,   195
When the first leaders dar'd the western flight.
On other shores, in every eastern clime,
Since that unletter'd, distant tract of time,
What arts have shone! what empires found their place!
What golden sceptres sway'd the human race!   200
What guilt and grandeur from their seats been hurl'd,
And dire divulsions shook the changing world!
Ere Rome's bold Eagle clave th'affrighted air,
Ere Sparta form'd her death-like sons of war,
Ere proud Chaldea saw her towers arise,   205
Or Memphian columns heav'd against the skies;
These tribes have stray'd beneath the fruitful zone,
Their souls unpolish'd, and their name unknown.

The

The voice of heav'n reply'd :—A fcanty train,
In that far age, approach'd the wide domain ;   210
Where fertile groves, with game and fruitage crown'd,
Supply'd their wifhes from th'uncultur'd ground.
By nature form'd to rove, the reftlefs mind,
Of freedom fond, will ramble unconfin'd,
Till all the realm is fill'd, and rival right   215
Reftrains their fteps, and bids their force unite ;
When common fafety builds a common caufe,
Conforms their interefts and infpires their laws ;
By mutual checks their different manners blend,
Their fields bloom joyous, and their walls afcend.   220

  Here, to their growing hofts, no bounds arofe,
They claim'd no fafeguard, as they fear'd no foes ;
Round all the land their fcatt'ring fons muft ftray,
Ere civil arts could claim a fettled fway.
And what a world their mazy wand'rings led !   225
What ftreams and wilds in boundlefs order fpread !
See the fhores lengthen, fee the rivers roll,
To each far main and each extended pole !

  Yet circling years the deftin'd courfe have run,
The realms are peopled and their arts begun.   230
Behold, where that mild region ftrikes the eyes,
A few fair cities glitter to the fkies ;

There

There move, in eastern pomp, the toils of state,
And temples heave, magnificently great.

The Hero look'd; when from the varying height,   235
Three growing splendors, rising on the sight,
Flam'd like a constellation : high in view,
Ascending near, their opening glories drew ;
In equal pomp, beneath their roofs of gold,
Three spiry towns, in blazing pride, unfold.   240
So, led by visions of the guiding God,
The sacred Seer* in Patmos' waste who trod,
Saw the dim vault of heav'n its folds unbend,
And gates and spires and streets and domes descend ;
With golden skies, and suns and rainbows crown'd,   245
The new-form'd city lights the world around.

Fair on the north, bright Mexico arose,
A mimic morn her sparkling towers disclose,
An ample range the op'ning streets display.
Give back the sun, and shed internal day ;   250
The circling wall with sky-built turrets frown'd,
And look'd defiance to the realms around ;
A glimmering lake, without the walls retires,
Inverts the trembling towers, and seems a grove of spires.

Bright, o'er the midst, on columns lifted high,   255
A rising structure claims a loftier sky ;

* 'St. John's vision of the new Jerusalem.' *Rev.* ch. xxi.

O'er the tall gates fublimer arches bend,
Courts larger lengthen, bolder walks afcend,
Starr'd with fuperior gems the porches fhine,
And fpeak the royal refidence within.   260

There, rob'd in ftate, high on a golden throne,
Mid fuppliant kings, dread Montezuma fhone :
Mild in his eye a temper'd grandeur fate,
Great feem'd his foul, with confcious power elate ;
In afpect open, focial and ferene,   265
Enclos'd with fav'rites and of friends unfeen.

Round the rich throne, with various luftre bright,
Gems undiftinguifh'd caft a changing light ;
Sapphires and em'ralds deck the fplendent fcene,
Sky-tinctures mingling with the vernal green ;   270
The ruby's blufh, the amber's flames unfold,
And diamonds brighten from the burning gold ;
Through all the doom the living blazes blend,
And caft their rainbows where the arches bend.
Wide round the walls, with mimic action gay,   275
In order rang'd, hiftoric figures ftray,
And fhow, in Memphian ftyle,* with rival grace,
The boafted feats of all their regal race.

* The Mexicans had the art of recording their hiftory in hieroglyphics; and had carried this art to a degree of perfection nearly equal to that of the ancient Egyptians.

Thro'

Thro' the full gates, and round each ample ſtreet,
Unnumber'd throngs, in various concourſe meet,   280
Ply different toils, new walls and ſtructures rear,
Or till the fields, or train the ranks of war.
Thro' ſpreading realms the ſkirts of empire bend,
New temples riſe and other plains extend;
Thrice ten wide provinces, in culture gay,   285
Bleſs the ſame monarch and enlarge his ſway.

 A ſmile benignant kindling in his eyes,
Oh happy clime ! the glad Columbus cries,
Far in the midland, ſafe from foreign foes,
Thy joys ſhall ripen, as thy grandeur grows,   290
To endleſs years thy riſing fame extend,
And ſires of nations from thy ſons deſcend.
May no gold-thirſty race thy temples tread,
Nor ſtain thy ſtreams, nor heap thy plains with dead;
No Bovadilla ſeize the tempting ſpoil,   295
Ovando dark, or ſacrilegious Boyle,*

* Bovadilla and Ovando are mentioned in the Introduction
as the enemies and ſucceſſors of Columbus in the government
of Hiſpaniola. They began that ſyſtem of cruelty towards the
natives which, in a few years, almoſt depopulated that iſland,
and was afterwards purſued by Cortez, Pizarro and others, in
all the firſt ſettlements in Spaniſh America.
   Boyle was a fanatical prieſt who accompanied Ovando, and
under pretence of chriſtianizing the natives by the ſword, gave
a ſanction to the moſt ſhocking and extenſive ſcenes of ſlaughter.

In

In mimic prieſthood grave, or rob'd in ſtate,
O'erwhelm thy glories in oblivious fate!
   Vain are thy fondeſt hopes, the Power reply'd,
Theſe rich abodes from rav'ning hoſts to hide,   300
To teach hard guilt and cruelty to ſpare
The guardleſs prize, and check the waſte of war.
Think not the vulture, o'er the field of ſlain,
Where baſe and brave promiſcuous ſtrow the plain,
Where the young hero, in the pride of charms,   305
Pours deeper crimſon o'er his ſpotleſs arms,
Will paſs the tempting prey, and glut his rage
On harder fleſh, and carnage black with age;
O'er all alike he darts his eager eye,
Whets the dire beak and hovers down the ſky,   310
From countleſs corſes picks the dainty food,
And ſcreams and fattens in the pureſt blood.
So the vile boſts, that trace thy daring way,
On happieſt tribes with fierceſt fury prey.
Thine the dread taſk, O Cortez, here to ſhow   315
What unknown crimes can heighten human woe,
On theſe fair fields the blood of realms to pour,
Tread ſceptres down, and print thy ſteps in gore,
With gold and carnage ſwell thy ſateleſs mind,
And live and die the blackeſt of mankind.   320
E

He gains the ſhore.   Behold his fortreſs riſe,
The fleet in flames * aſcends the darken'd ſkies.
The march begins; the nations, from afar,
Quake in his ſight, and wage the fruitleſs war;
O'er the rich provinces he bends his way,   325
Kings in his chain, and kingdoms for his prey;
While, rob'd in peace, great Montezuma ſtands,
And crowns and treaſures ſparkle in his hands,
Proffers the empire, yields the ſceptred ſway,
Bids vaſſall'd millions tremble and obey;   330
And plies the victor, with inceſſant prayer,
Thro' ravag'd realms the harmleſs race to ſpare.
But prayers, and tears, and ſceptres plead in vain,
Nor threats can move him, nor a world reſtrain;
While bleſt religion's proſtituted name,   335
And monkiſh fury guides the ſacred flame:
O'er fanes and altars, fires unhallow'd bend,
Climb the wide walls, and up the towers aſcend,

* The conduct of Cortez, when he firſt landed on the coaſt
of Mexico, was as remarkable for that hardy ſpirit of adventure,
to which ſucceſs gives the name of policy, as his ſubſequent
operations were for cruelty and perfidy. As ſoon as his army
was on ſhore, he diſmantled his fleet of ſuch articles as would be
neceſſary in building a new one; he then ſet fire to all his ſhips,
and burnt them in preſence of his men; that they might fight
their battles with more deſperate courage, knowing that it would
be impoſſible to ſave themſelves from a victorious enemy by
flight. He conſtructed a ſmall fort on the ſhore, in which the
iron and the rigging were preſerved.

Pour, round the lowering ſkies, the ſmoky flood,
And whelm the fields, and quench their rage in blood. 340
    The Hero heard; and, with a heaving ſigh,
Dropp'd the full tear that ſtarted in his eye:
Oh hapleſs day! his trembling voice reply'd,
That ſaw my wand'ring ſtreamer mount the tide!
Oh! had the lamp of heav'n, to that bold ſail,   345
Ne'er mark'd the paſſage nor awak'd the gale;
Taught eaſtern worlds theſe beauteous climes to find,
Nor led thoſe tygers forth to curſe mankind.
Then had the tribes beneath theſe bounteous ſkies,
Seen their walls widen and their ſpires ariſe;   · 350
Down the long tracts of time their glory ſhone,
Broad as the day and laſting as the ſun:
The growing realms, beneath thy ſhield that reſt,
O hapleſs monarch, ſtill thy power had bleſt,
Enjoy'd the pleaſures that ſurround thy throne,   355
Survey'd thy virtues and ſublim'd their own.
Forgive me, prince; this impious arm hath led
The unſeen ſtorm that blackens o'er thy head;
Taught the dark ſons of ſlaughter where to roam,
To ſeize thy crown and ſeal thy nation's doom.   360
Arm, ſleeping empire, meet the daring band,
Drive back th'invaders, ſave the ſinking land——

E 2

Yet

Yet vain the ſtrife! behold the ſtreaming blood!
Forgive me, Nature, and forgive me, God.
Thus, from his heart, while ſpeaking ſorrows roll,   365
The Power, reproving, ſooth'd his tender ſoul :—
Father of this new world, thy tears give o'er,
Let virtue grieve and heav'n be blam'd no more.
Enough for man, with perſevering mind,
To act his part and ſtrive to bleſs his kind ;   370
Enough for thee, o'er thy dark age to ſoar,
And raiſe to light that long-ſecluded ſhore.
For this my guardian care thy youth inſpir'd,
To virtue rais'd thee, and with glory fir'd,
Bade in thy plan each diſtant world unite,   375
And wing'd thy veſſel for the vent'rous flight.

  Nor think no bleſſings ſhall thy toils attend,
Or theſe fell tyrants can defeat their end.
Such impious deeds, in heav'n's all-ruling plan,
Lead in diſguiſe the ſolid bliſs of man.   380
Long have thy race, to narrow ſhores confin'd,
Trod the ſame round that cramp'd the roving mind ;
Now, borne on bolder wings, with happier flight,
The world's broad bounds unfolding to the ſight,
The mind ſhall ſoar ; the nations catch the flame,   385
Enlarge their treaties and extend their fame ;

And

And buried gold, drawn bounteous from the mine,
Give wings to commerce and the world refine.
   Now to yon fouthern walls extend thy view,
And mark the rival feats of rich Peru.   390
There Quito's airy plains, exalted high,
With loftier temples rife along the fky;
And elder Cufco's richer roofs unfold,
Flame on the day, and fhed their funs of gold.
Another range, in thefe delightful climes,   395
Spreads a broad theatre for unborn crimes.
Another Cortez fhall the treafures view,
The rage rekindle and the guilt renew;
His treafon, fraud, and every dire decree,
O curft Pizarro, fhall revive in thee.   400
   There reigns a prince, whofe hand the fceptre claims,
Thro' a long lineage of imperial names:
Where the brave roll of following Incas trace
The diftant father of their realm and race,
Immortal Capac. He, in youthful pride,   405
With young Oella, his illuftrious bride,
In virtuous guile, proclaim'd their birth begun,
From the pure fplendors of their God, the fun;
By him commiffion'd o'er thefe realms around,
A polifh'd ftate on peaceful laws to found,   410

To crush the gods that human victims claim,
And point all worship to a nobler name,
With cheerful rites, the due devotions pay
To the bright beam, that gives the changing day.

On this great plan, the children of the skies   415
Bade, in the wild, a growing empire rise;
Beneath their hand, and sacred to their fame,
Arose yon walls, that meet the solar flame.
Succeeding sovereigns spread their bounds afar,
Enlarg'd their leagues, and sooth'd the rage of war;   420
Till these surrounding realms the sceptre own,
And pay their homage to the sacred sun.
Behold, o'er yon wide lake their temple rise,
Seat of the sun and pillar of the skies.
The roofs of burnish'd gold, the blazing spires   425
Light the glad heav'ns and lose their upward fires;
Fix'd in the flaming front, with living ray,
A diamond circlet gives the rival day;
In whose bright face for ever looks abroad
The radiant image of the beaming God.   430
Round the wide courts, and in the solemn dome,
A white-rob'd train of holy virgins bloom;
Whose pious hands the sacred rites require,
To grace the offerings, and preserve the fire.

On

On this bleſt iſle, with flowery garlands crown'd,   435

That ancient Pair, in charms of youth, were found,

Whoſe union'd ſouls the myſtic code deſign'd,

To bleſs the nations * and reform mankind.

* From the traditions of Capac and Oella, mentioned by the Spaniſh hiſtorians, they appear to have been very great and diſtinguiſhed characters. About three centuries previous to the diſcovery of that country by the Spaniards, the natives of Peru were as rude ſavages as any in America. They had no fixed habitations, no ideas of permanent property; they wandered naked like the beaſts, and, like them, depended on the events of each day for a precarious ſubſiſtence. At this period, Manco Capac, and his wife Mama Oella, appeared on a ſmall iſland in the lake Titiaca; near which the city of Cuſco was afterwards erected. Theſe perſons, in order to eſtabliſh a belief of their divinity in the minds of the people, were clothed in white garments of cotton; and declared themſelves deſcended from the ſun, who was their father and the god of that country. They affirmed, that he was offended at their cruel and perpetual wars, their barbarous modes of worſhip, and their neglecting to make the beſt uſe of the bleſſings he was conſtantly beſtowing, in fertilizing the earth and producing vegetation; that he pitied their wretched ſtate, and had ſent his own children to inſtruct them, and to eſtabliſh a number of wiſe regulations, by which they might be rendered happy.

By ſome extraordinary method of perſuaſion, theſe perſons drew together a number of the ſavage tribes, laid the foundations of the city of Cuſco, and eſtabliſhed what was called the kingdom of the Sun, or the Peruvian empire. In the reign of Manco Capac, the dominion was extended about eight leagues from the city; and at the end of three centuries, it was eſtabliſhed fifteen hundred miles on the coaſt of the Pacific ocean; and from that ocean to the mountains of the Andes. During this period, through a ſucceſſion of twelve monarchs, the original conſtitution, eſtabliſhed by the firſt Inca, remained unaltered; and was at laſt overturned by an accident, which no human wiſdom could foreſee or prevent.

For a more particular diſquiſition on the character and inſtitutions of this great legiſlator, the reader is referred to a diſſertation prefixed to the third book.

E 5

Mama

The Hero heard, and thus the Power befought :—

Declare what arts the wonderous bleffings wrought ;   440

What human fkill, in that benighted age,

In favage fouls, could quell the barb'rous rage ?

With leagues of peace combine a wide domain ?

And teach the Virtues in their laws to reign ?

    Long is their ftory, faid the Power divine,   445

Their labours great, and glorious the defign ;

Mama Oella is faid to have invented many of the domeftic arts, particularly that of making garments of cotton and other vegetable fubftances.

In the paffage preceding this reference, I have alluded to moft of the traditions, relating to the manner of their introducing themfelves, and eftablifhing their dominion. In the remainder of the fecond, and through the whole of the third book, I have given what may be fuppofed a probable narrative of their real origin and conduct. I have thrown the epifode into an epic form, and given it fo confiderable a place in the poem, for the purpofe of exhibiting *in action* the characters, manners, and fentiments of the different tribes of favages, that inhabit the mountains of South America.

In reviewing this part of my fubject, I have to lament, that fo extraordinary and meritorious a poem, as the Araucana of Don Alonfo de Ercilla, of the fixteenth century, has never yet appeared in our language. The account given of that work by Voltaire, excited my curiofity at an early day ; as I conceived the manners and characters of the mountain favages of Chili, as defcribed by that heroic Spaniard, muft have opened a new field of poetry, rich with uncommon ornaments.

That elegant and concife fketch of it, lately given to the public by Mr. Hayley, has come into my hands, fince I have been writing thefe notes, and preparing this poem for the prefs : yet it gives me reafon to hope, with every friend of literature, that the whole of that great work will ere long be prefented to the Englifh reader by the fame hand.

And

And tho', to earthly minds, their actions rest,
By years obscur'd, in flowery fiction drest,
Yet my glad voice shall wake their honour'd name,
And give their virtues to immortal fame. 450

Led by his father's wars, in early prime,
Young Capac wander'd from a northern clime;
Along these shores, with richer blooms array'd,
Thro' fertile vales the vent'rous armies stray'd.
He saw the tribes unnumber'd range the plain, 455
And rival chiefs, by rage and slaughter, reign;
He saw the fires their dreadful gods adore,
Their altars staining with their children's gore;
Yet mark'd their reverence for the sun, whose beam
Proclaims his bounties and his power supreme; 460
Who fails in happier skies, diffusing good,
Demands no victim, and receives no blood.

In peace return'd with his victorious sire,
Fair glory's charms his youthful soul inspire,
To conquer nations on a nobler plan, 465
And build his greatness on the bliss of man.

By nature form'd to daring deeds of fame,
Tall, bold and beauteous rose his stately frame.
Strong mov'd his limbs, a mild majestic grace
Beam'd from his eyes and open'd in his face; 470

O'er

O'er the dark world his mind superior shone,
And soaring, seem'd the semblance of the sun.
Now fame's prophetic visions lift his eyes,
And future empires from his labours rise;
Yet softer fires his daring views controul,
Sway the warm wish and fill his changing soul.
Shall the bright genius, kindled from above,
Bend to the milder, gentler voice of love,
That bounds his glories, and forbids to part,
From that calm bower, that held his plighted heart?
Or shall the toils, imperial heroes claim,
Fire his bold bosom with a patriot flame,
Bid sceptres wait him on Peruvia's shore,
And bleft Oella meet his eyes no more?
  Retiring pensive, near the wonted shade,
His unseen steps approach the beauteous maid.
Her raven-locks roll on her heaving breaft,
And wave luxuriant round her slender waift,
Gay wreaths of flowers her lovely brows adorn,
And her white raiment mocks the pride of morn.
Her busy hand suftains a bending bough,
Where cotton clufters spread their robes of snow,
From opening pods unbinds the fleecy store,
Ands culls her labours for the evening bower.

For she before, by deep invention led,   495
Had found the skill to turn the twisting thread,
To spread the woof; the shuttle to command,
Till various garments grac'd her forming hand.
Here, while her thoughts with her own Capac rove,
O'er former scenes of innocence and love,   500
Through many a field his fancied dangers share,
And wait him glorious from the distant war;
Blest with the ardent wish, her sprightly mind
A snowy vesture for the prince design'd;
She seeks the purest wool, to web the fleece,   505
The sacred emblem of returning peace.
Sudden his near approach her breast alarms;
He flew enraptur'd to her yielding arms,
And lost, dissolving in a softer flame,
The distant empire and the fire of fame.   510
At length, retiring o'er the homeward field,
Their mutual minds to happy converse yield,
O'er various scenes of blissful life they ran,
When thus the warrior to the maid began :—

Joy of my life, thou know'st my roving mind,   515
With these grim tribes, in dark abodes, confin'd,
With grief hath mark'd what vengeful passions sway
The bickering bands, and sweep the race away.

Where

Where late my diftant fteps the war purfu'd,
The fertile plains grew boundlefs as I view'd ;   520
Increafing nations trod the waving wild,
And joyous nature more delightful fmil'd.
No changing feafons there the flowers deform,
No dread volcano, and no mountain ftorm ;
Rains ne'er invade, nor livid lightnings play,   525
Nor clouds obfcure the radiant power of day.
But, while the God, in ceafelefs glory bright,
Rolls o'er the day, and fires his ftars by night,
Unbounded fulnefs flows beneath his reign,
Seas yield their treafures, fruits adorn the plain ;   530
Warm'd by his beam, their mountains pour the flood,
And the cool breezes wake beneath the God.
My anxious thoughts indulge the great defign,
To form thofe nations to a fway divine ;
Deftroy the rites of every dreadful power,   535
Whofe crimfon altars glow with human gore ;
To laws and mildnefs teach the realms to yield,
And richer fruits to grace the cultur'd field.
  But great, my charmer, is the tafk of fame,
The countlefs tribes to temper and to tame,   540
Full many a fpacious wild my foul muft fee,
Spread dreary bounds between my joys and me ;

                                        And

And yon bright Godhead circle many a year,
Each lonely evening number'd with a tear.
Long robes of white * my shoulders must embrace,   545
To speak my lineage of etherial race ;
That wondering tribes may honour and obey
The radiant offspring of the Power of day.

And when thro' cultur'd fields their bowers increase,
And streams and plains survey the works of peace,   550
When these glad hands the rod of nations claim,
And happy millions bless thy Capac's name,
Then shall he feign a journey to the sun,
To bring the partner of the peaceful throne ;
So shall descending kings the line sustain,   555
And unborn ages bloom beneath their reign.

Will then my Fair, in that delightful hour,
Forsake these wilds and hail a happier bower ?
And now consenting, with approving smiles,
Bid the young warrior tempt the daring toils ?   560
And, sweetly patient, wait the flight of days,
That crown our labours with immortal praise ?

* As the art of spinning is said to have been invented by
Oella, it is no improbable fiction, to suppose they first assumed
these white garments of cotton, as an emblem of the sun, in
order to inspire that reverence for their persons which was necessary to their success. Such a dress may likewise be supposed
to have been continued in the family, as a badge of royalty.

Silent

Silent the damfel heard; her moiftening eye
Spoke the full foul, nor could her voice reply;
Till fofter accents footh'd her anxious ear,   565
Compos'd her tumult and allay'd her fear:——
Think not, enchanting maid, my fteps would part,
While filent forrows heave that tender heart:
Oella's peace more dear fhall prove to me
Than all the realms that bound the raging fea;   570
Nor thou, bright Sun, fhould'ft bribe my foul to reft,
And leave one ftruggle in her lovely breaft.
Yet think in thofe vaft climes, my gentle Fair,
What haplefs millions claim our guardian care;
How age to age leads on their piteous gloom,   575
And rage and flaughter croud th'untimely tomb;
No focial ties their wayward paffions prove,
Nor peace nor pleafure treads the favage grove;
Mid thoufand heroes and a thoufand Fair,
No fond Oella meets her Capac there.   580
Yet, taught by thee domeftic joys to prize,
With fofter charms the virgin race fhall rife,
Awake new virtues, every grace improve,
And form their minds for happinefs and love.

   Behold, where future years, in pomp, defcend,   585
How worlds and ages on thy voice depend!

And,

And, like the Sun, whose all-delighting ray
O'er those mild borders sheds serenest day,
Diffuse thy bounties, give my steps to rove,
A few short months the noble task to prove, 590
And, swift return'd from glorious toils, declare
What realms submissive wait our fostering care.

And will my prince, my Capac, borne away,
Thro' those dark wilds, in quest of empire, stray?
Where tygers fierce command the howling wood, 595
And men like tygers thirst for human blood.
Think'st thou no dangerous deed the course attends?
Alone, unaided by thy fire and friends?
Ev'n chains and death may meet my rover there,
Nor his last groan could reach Oella's ear. 600
But chains, nor death, nor groans shall Capac prove,
Unknown to her, while she has power to rove.
Close by thy side where'er thy wand'rings stray,
My equal steps shall measure all the way;
With borrow'd soul each dire event I'll dare, 605
Thy toils to lessen, and thy dangers share.
Command, blest chief, since virtue bids thee go
To rule the realms and banish human woe,
Command these hands two snowy robes to weave,
The fun to mimic, and the tribes deceive; 610

Then

Then let us range, and spread the peaceful sway,
The radiant children of the power of day.

    The lovely counsel pleas'd.   The smiling chief
Approv'd her courage and dispell'd her grief;
Then to the distant bower in haste they move,   615
Begin their labours and prepare to rove.
Soon grow the robes beneath her forming care,
And the fond parents wed the princely pair;
But, whelm'd in grief, beheld th'approaching dawn,
Their joys all vanish'd, and their children gone.   620
Nine days they stray'd; the tenth effulgent morn
Beheld the steps that blifsful ifle adorn.
The toil begins; to every neighbouring band
They speak the message and their faith demand;
With various art superior powers display,   625
To prove their lineage and confirm their sway.
Th'aftonish'd tribes believe with glad surprise,
The gods descended from the fav'ring skies;
Adore their persons, rob'd in shining white,
Receive their laws, and leave each horrid rite;   630
Build, with affifting toil, the golden throne,
And hail and bless the sceptre of the Sun.

A DIS-

A
DISSERTATION

ON THE

GENIUS and INSTITUTIONS

OF

MANCO CAPAC.

ALTHOUGH the original inhabitants of America in general deſerve to be claſſed among the moſt unimproved ſavages that have ever been diſcovered; yet the Mexican and Peruvian governments exhibit remarkable inſtances of order and regularity. In the difference of national character between the people of theſe two empires we may diſcern the influence of political ſyſtems on the human mind, and infer the importance of the taſk which a legiſlator undertakes, in attempting to reduce a barbarous people under the controul of government and laws. The Mexican conſtitution was formed to render its ſubjeĉts brave and powerful; but, while it ſucceeded in this objeĉt, it tended to remove them farther from the real bleſſings of ſociety, than they were while in the rudeſt ſtate of nature. The hiſtory of the world affords no inſtance of men whoſe manners were equally ferocious, and whoſe ſuperſtition was more bloody and unrelenting. On the

F   contrary,

contrary, the eſtabliſhments of Manco Capac carry the marks
of a moſt benevolent and pacific ſyſtem ; they tended to hu-
manize the world, and render his people happy ; while his
ideas of the Deity were ſo perfect, as to bear a compariſon
with the enlightened doctrines of Socrates or Plato.

The moſt diſtinguiſhed characters in hiſtory, who have
been conſidered as legiſlators among barbarous nations, are
Moſes, Lycurgus, Solon, Numa, Mahomet, and Peter of
Ruſſia. Of theſe, only the two former and the two latter
appear really to deſerve that character. Solon and Numa
poſſeſſed not the means nor the opportunity of ſhewing their
talents in the buſineſs of original legiſlation. Athens and
Rome were conſiderably advanced in civilization, before
theſe perſons aroſe. The moſt they could do was to correct
and amend conſtitutions already formed. Solon, in particular,
may be conſidered as a wiſe politician ; but by no means as
the founder of a nation. The Athenians were too far advanced in ſociety to admit any radical alteration in their form
of government ; unleſs recourſe could have been had to
the repreſentative ſyſtem, by eſtabliſhing a perfect equality of
rank, and inſtructing all the people in their duties and their
rights ; a ſyſtem which was never underſtood by any ancient
legiſlator. The inſtitutions of Numa were more effective
and durable ; his religious ceremonies were, for many ages,
the moſt powerful check upon the licentious and turbulent
Romans, the greater part of whom were ignorant ſlaves.
By inculcating a remarkable reverence for the gods, and
making it neceſſary to conſult the auſpices, when any thing
important was to be tranſacted, he rendered the popular ſuperſtition

perſtition ſubſervient to the views of policy, and gave the
ſenate a ſteady check upon the extravagance of the plebeians.
But the conſtitutions of Rome and Athens, however the
ſubjeȼt of ſo much injudicious applauſe, were never fixed
upon any permanent principles; though the wiſdom of
ſome of their rulers, and the ſpirit of liberty that inſpired
the people, juſtly demand our admiration.

EACH of the other legiſlators above-mentioned deſerves
a particular conſideration, as having acted in ſtations ſome-
what ſimilar to that of the Peruvain lawgiver. Three ob-
jeȼts are to be attended to by the legiſlator of a barbarous
people. *Firſt*, That his ſyſtem be ſuch as is capable of reducing the greateſt number of men under one juriſdiction.
Secondly, That it apply to ſuch principles in human nature
for its ſupport, as are univerſal and permanent, in order to
enſure the duration of the government. *Thirdly*, That it
admit of improvements correſpondent to any advancement
in knowledge or variation of circumſtances that may happen
to its ſubjeȼts, without endangering the principle of government by ſuch innovations.—So far, therefore, as the ſyſtems
of thoſe legiſlators agree with theſe fundamental principles,
they are worthy of reſpeȼt; and ſo far as they deviate, they
may be conſidered as defeȼtive and imperfeȼt.

. To begin with Moſes and Lycurgus,—It is neceſſary in
the firſt place to obſerve, that, in order to judge of the merit
of any inſtitutions, we muſt take into view the peculiar cha-
raȼter of the people for whom they were framed. For want
of this attention, many of the laws of Moſes have been

                          ridiculed,

ridiculed, and many eſtabliſhments of Lycurgus have been cenſured. The Jews, who were led by Moſes out of Egypt, were not only uncivilized, but, having juſt riſen to independence from a ſtate of ſervitude, they united the manners of ſervants and of ſavages; and their national character is a compoſition of ſervility and contumacy, ignorance, ſuperſtition, filthineſs, and cruelty. Of their cruelty as a people, we need no other proof than the account of their avengers of blood, and the readineſs with which the whole congregation turned executioners and ſtoned to death the devoted offenders. The leproſy, a diſeaſe now wholly unknown, was undoubtedly produced by their total want of cleanlineſs, continued for ſucceſſive generations. In this view the frequent ablutions, the peculiar modes of trial, and many other inſtitutions, may be vindicated from ridicule, and proved to be not only wiſe, but even neceſſary regulations.

THE Spartan lawgiver has been equally cenſured for the toleration of theft and adultery. Among that race of barbarians, theſe crimes were too general to admit of total prevention or univerſal puniſhment. By veſting all property in the community, inſtead of encouraging theft, he removed the poſſibility of the crime; and, in a nation where licentiouſneſs was generally indulged, it was a great ſtep towards introducing a purity of manners, to puniſh adultery in all caſes, wherein the crime was not committed by the free conſent of all parties injured or intereſted.

UNTIL the inſtitution of repreſentative republics, which

ere of recent date, it was always a fact confirmed by experience, that those constitutions of government were best calculated for immediate energy and duration, which were interwoven with some religious system. The legislator, who appears in the character of an inspired person, renders his political institutions sacred, and interests the conscience, as well as the judgment, in their support. The Jewish lawgiver had this advantage over the Spartan : he appeared not in the character of a mere earthly governor, but as an interpreter of the divine will. By enjoining a religious observance of certain rites, he formed his people to habitual obedience ; by directing their cruelty against the breakers of the laws, he at least mitigated the rancour of private hatred ; by forbidding usury, and directing that real property should return to the original families in the year of Jubilee, he prevented too great an inequality of property ; and by selecting a particular tribe, to be the guardians and interpreters of religion, he prevented its mysteries from being the subject of profane and vulgar investigation. To secure the permanency of his institutions, he prohibited any intercourse with foreigners, by severe restrictions ; and formed his people to habits and a character disagreeable to other nations ; by which means any foreign intercourse was prevented, from the mutual hatred of both parties.

To these institutions the laws of Lycurgus bear a most striking resemblance. The features of his constitution were severe and forbidding ; it was, however, calculated to inspire the most enthusiastic love of liberty and martial honour. In no country was the patriotic passion more

F 3

energetic

energetic than in Sparta; no laws ever excluded the idea of
separate property in an equal degree, or inspired a more
thorough contempt for the manners of other nations. The
utter prohibition of money, commerce, and almost every
thing desirable to effeminate nations, entirely excluded
foreigners from Sparta; and, while it inspired the people
with contempt for others, it made them agreeable to each
other. By these means, Lycurgus rendered the nation
powerful and warlike; and, to insure the duration of his
government, he endeavoured to interest the consciences of
his people by the aid of oracles, and by the oath he is said
have exacted from them, to obey his laws till his return;
when he went into a voluntary and perpetual exile.

From this view of the Jewish and Spartan institutions,
applied to the principles before stated, they appear, in the
two first articles, considerably imperfect, and in the last,
totally defective. Neither of them was calculated to bring
any considerable territory or number of men under one
jurisdiction; from this circumstance alone, they could not
be rendered permanent, as they must be constantly exposed
to their more powerful neighbours. But the third object
of legislation, that of providing for the future progress of
society, which, as it regards the happiness of mankind, is
the most important of the three, was, in both instances,
entirely neglected. These systems appear to have been
formed with an express design to prevent all future improvement in knowledge, or enlargement of the human
mind; and to fix those nations for ever in a state of ignorance, superstition and barbarism. To vindicate their authors

from

from an imputation of weaknefs or inattention in this particular, it may be urged that they were each of them fur-
rounded by nations more powerful than their own ; it was
therefore impoffible for them to commence an eftablifhment upon any other plan.

THE inftitutions of Mahomet are next to be confidered.
The firft object of legiflation appears to have been better
underftood by the Arabian prophet, than by either of the
preceding fages ; his jurifdiction was capable of being en-
larged to any extent of territory, and governing any number
of nations that might be fubjugated by his powerful and
enthufiaftic armies; and to obtain this object, his fyftem of.
religion was admirably calculated. Like Mofes, he con-
vinced his people that he acted as the vicegerent of heaven ;
but with this capital advantage, adapting his religion to the
natural feelings and propenfities of mankind, he multiplied
his followers, by the allurements of pleafure, and the pro-
mife of a fenfual paradife. Thefe circumftances were likewife fure to render his conftitution permanent. His religious fyftem was fo eafy to be underftood, fo fplendid and
fo inviting, there could be no danger that the people would
lofe fight of its principles, and no neceffity of future
prophets, to explain the doctrines, or reform the nation.
To thefe advantages, if we add the exact and rigid military
difcipline, the fplendor and facrednefs of the monarch, and
that total ignorance of the people, which fuch a fyftem
will produce and perpetuate, the eftablifhment muft be
evidently calculated for a confiderable extent and duration.
But the laft and moft important end of government, that

of mental improvement and focial happinefs, was deplorably loft in the inftitution. And there was probably more learning and cultivated genius in Arabia, in the days of this extraordinary character, than can now be found in all the Turkifh dominions.

On the contrary, the enterprifing mind of the Ruffian monarch appears to have been wholly bent on the arts of civilization, and the improvement of fociety among his fubjects. Happy in a legal title to a throne, which already commanded a prodigious extent of country, he found that the firft object of government was already fecured; and by applying himfelf with great fagacity and perfeverance to the third object, he was fure that the fecond would be a necef-fary and invariable confequence. He effected his purpofes, important as they were, merely by the introduction of the arts, and the encouragement of politer manners. The great-nefs of his character appears not fo much in his inftitutions, which he copied from other nations, as in the extraordinary meafures he followed to introduce them, the judgment he fhowed in felecting and adapting them to the genius of his fubjects, and his furprifing affiduity and fuccefs, by which he raifed a favage people to a dignified rank among European nations. All his plans were formed to encourage the future progrefs of fociety; and their duration was enfured by their obvious value and importance.

To the nature and operation of the feveral forms of government above-mentioned, we will compare that of the Peruvian lawgiver. It is probable that the favages of Peru

before

before the time of Capac, among other objects of adoration, paid homage to the sun. By availing himself of this popular sentiment, he appeared, like Moses and Mahomet, in the character of a divine legiflator, endowed with fupernatural powers.   After impreffing thefe ideas ftrongly on the minds of the people, drawing together a number of the tribes, and rendering them fubfervient to his benevolent purpofes, he applied himfelf to forming the outlines of a plan of policy, capable of founding and regulating an extenfive empire, wifely calculated for perpetual duration, and exprefsly de-figned to improve the knowledge, peace, and happinefs of a confiderable portion of mankind.   In the apportionment of the lands, and the affignment of real property, he in-vented a mode fomewhat refembling the feudal fyftem of Europe : yet this fyftem was wifely checked in its opera-tion, by a law fimilar to that of Mofes, which regulated landed poffeffions in the year of Jubilee.   He divided the lands into three parts ; the firft was confecrated to the ufes of religion ; the fecond fet apart for the Inca and his family, to enable him to defray the expences of government, and to appear in the ftyle of a monarch ; the third, and much the largeft portion, was allotted to the people ; and this allotment was repeated every year, and varied according to to the number and exigencies of each family.

As the Incan race appeared in the character of divinities, it was neceffary that a fubordination of ranks fhould be eftablifhed, in order to render the diftinction between the monarch and his people more perceptible.   With this view

he

he created a band of nobles, who were diſtinguiſhed by per-
ſonal and hereditary honours. Theſe were united to the
monarch by the ſtrongeſt ties of intereſt; in peace they
acted as judges, and ſuperintended the police of the empire;
in war they commanded in the armies. The next order
of men were the reſpectable peaſantry of the country, who
compoſed the principal ſtrength of the nation. Below theſe
was a claſs of men who were the ſervants of the public,
who cultivated the public lands. They poſſeſſed no property, and their only ſecurity depended on their regular
induſtry and peaceable demeanour. Above all theſe orders
were the Inca and his family. He was poſſeſſed of abſolute
and uncontroulable power; his mandates were regarded as
the word of Heaven, and the double guilt of impiety and
rebellion attended on diſobedience. To impreſs the utmoſt
veneration for the Incan family, it was a fundamental
principle, that the royal blood ſhould never be contaminated
by any foreign alliance. The myſteries of religion were
preſerved ſacred by the high-prieſt of the royal family,
under the controul of the king; and celebrated with
rites, capable of making the deepeſt impreſſion on the
multitude. The annual diſtribution of the lands, while it
provided for the varying circumſtances of each family,
ſtrengthened the bands of ſociety, by preventing the different orders from interfering with each other; the peaſants
could not vie with their ſuperiors, and the nobles could not
be ſubjected by misfortune to a ſubordinate ſtation. A con-
ſtant habit of induſtry was inculcated upon all ranks by the
ſurpriſing force of example and emulation. The cultivation

of

of the foil, which in moſt other countries is conſidered as
one of the loweſt employments, was here regarded as a divine
art. Having had no knowledge of it before, and being
taught it by the children of their God, the people viewed it
as a ſacred privilege, and conſidered it as an honour, to
imitate and aſſiſt the ſun in opening the boſom of the earth
and producing vegetation. That the government might be
able to exerciſe the endearing acts of benevolence, the
produce of the public lands was reſerved in magazines, to
ſupply the wants of the unfortunate, as a depoſit for the
people in times of general ſcarcity, and as a reſource in caſe
of an invaſion.

THESE are the outlines of a government, the moſt ſimple
and energetic conceivable, and capable of reducing the
greateſt number of men under one juriſdiction; at the ſame
time, accommodating its principle of action to every ſtate
of ſociety, and every ſtage of improvement, by a ſingular
and happy application to the paſſions of the human mind,
it encouraged the advancement of knowledge, without being
endangered by ſucceſs. That ſuch a government has a fair
chance for duration is evident from this conſideration, that
a band of nobles are ever the firm ſupporters of regal authority; unleſs the monarch is ſo limited in his power that the
nobles deſpiſe his influence. This could not be the caſe in
Peru; the nobles were juſtly proud of their elevated ſtation,
though they could have no ambition to controul the Inca.
They were ſenſible that their intereſt was connected with
that of the monarch; and, ſuppoſing the influence of religion to be out of the queſtion, they would not attempt to

deſtroy

deſtroy an inſtitution on which their happineſs depended. A check equally effective was, by the conſtitution of human nature, impoſed on the Inca.   Elevated above the competition and rivalſhip which corrode and torment the boſoms of the great, he could have no ambition to gratify, and no motive to induce him to an improper exerciſe of arbitrary power.

In the traits of character which diſtinguiſh this inſtitution, we may diſcern all the great ſtrokes of each of the legiſlators above-mentioned.   The pretentions of Capac to divine authority were as artfully contrived, and as effectual in their conſequences, as thoſe of Mahomet; his exploding the worſhip of evil beings and objects of terror, forbidding human ſacrifices, inculcating more rational ideas of the Deity, and accommodating the rites of worſhip to a God of juſtice and benevolence, produced a greater change in the national character of his people, than any of the laws of Moſes: like Peter, he provided for the future improvement of ſociety, while his actions were never meaſured upon the ſmall and contracted ſcale, which limited the genius of Lycurgus.

Thus far we find the political ſyſtem of Capac at leaſt equal to thoſe of the moſt celebrated ancient or modern lawgivers.   But in one particular his character is placed beyond all compariſon; I mean for his religious inſtitutions, and the rational ideas he had formed of the nature and attributes of the Deity.

AND

AND here I shall premise, that idolatrous nations have never been guilty of those glaring absurdities with which they are usually charged by the Christian world. The Persian or Peruvian, when he directed his adoration to the Sun, considered it as the place of residence for the unknown Deity, whom he worshipped, and who communicated from thence the blessings of light, warmth, and vegetation; the Greek, who bowed at the statue of Jupiter, supposed it animated with the presence of his God; the Egyptian Apis, Isis, and Orus, the calf, the leek, and the onion, though the theme of universal ridicule to other nations, were, in their first consecration, like the Jewish cherubim, symbolical representations of the nature and attributes of their deities. No man ever erected a stock or a stone for a real object of worship; but all ignorant nations have paid their adoration before the symbol of the Deity, in some shape or other, and directed their homage to the place of his supposed residence. Even among enlightened nations, we find many traces of the same ideas; the Papist bows to the picture and the crucifix; and the Methodist rolls up his eyes in prayer to the sky. Perhaps unassisted wisdom can rise no higher; and the reason why idol worship was forbidden in the divine law, was not because of the erroneous ideas of the original institutors, but because the views of the vulgar, in process of time, are apt to stop short at the intermediate object, and to lose sight of the original essence. But the great crime of idolatrous nations consisted in their ascribing to the Deity the passions and attributes of the Devil, and in the horrid and murderous rites of their worship. Mankind are more inclined to consider the Deity as a

God

God of vengeance than a God of mercy. Even among Chriftians, moft perfons afcribe afflictions to the hand of Heaven, and profperity to their own merit and prudence. This principle operates in its full effect among favages. They ufually form no idea of a general fuperintending Providence; they confider not the Deity as the author of their beings, the creator of the world, and the difpenfer of the happinefs they enjoy; they difcern him not in the ufual courfe of nature, in the funfhine and in the fhower, the productions of the earth, and the bleffing of fociety; they find a Deity only in the ftorm, the earthquake, and the whirlwind; or afcribe to him the evils of peftilence and famine; they confider him as interpofing in wrath to change the courfe of nature, and exercifing the attributes of rage and revenge. They adore him with rites fuited to thefe attributes, with horror, with penance, and with facrifice; they imagine him pleafed with the feverity of their mortifications, with the oblations of blood, and the cries of human victims; and hope to compound for greater judgments, by voluntary fufferings and horrid facrifices, fuited to the relifh of his tafte.

Perhaps no fingle criterion can be given, which will determine more accurately the ftate of fociety in any age or nation, than their general ideas concerning the nature and attributes of the Deity.. In the moft enlightened periods of antiquity, only a very few of their wifeft philofophers, a Socrates, a Tully, or a Confucius, ever formed a juft idea on the fubject, or defcribed the Deity as a God of purity, juftice, and benevolence. Can any thing then be more

aftonifhing

astonishing than to view a savage native of the southern wilds of America, rising in an age, void of every trace of learning or refinement, and acquiring, by the mere efforts of reason, a sublime and rational idea of the parent of the universe !

HE taught the nation to confider him as the God of order and regularity; ascribing to his influence the rotation of the seasons, the productions of the earth, and the blessings of health; especially attributing to his inspiration the wisdom of their laws, and that happy constitution, which was the delight and veneration of the people.

THESE humane ideas of religion had a sensible effect upon the manners of the nation. They never began an offensive war with their savage neighbours: and, whenever their country was invaded, they made war, not to extirpate, but to civilize. The conquered tribes, and those taken captive, were adopted into the nation; and, by blending with the conquerors, forgot their former rage and ferocity.

A SYSTEM so just and benevolent, as might be expected, was attended with success. In about three centuries, the dominions of the Incas had extended fifteen hundred miles in length, and had introduced peace and prosperity through the whole region. The arts of society had been carried to a considerable degree of improvement, and the authority of the Incan race universally acknowledged; when an event happened, that disturbed the tranquillity of

the

the empire. Huana Capac, the twelfth monarch, had reduced the powerful kingdom of Quito, and annexed it to
his empire. To conciliate the affections of his new subjects,
he married a daughter of the ancient king of Quito. Thus,
by violating a fundamental law of the Incas, he left at his
death a disputed succession to the throne. Atabalipa, the son
of Huana, by the heirefs of Quito, being in possession of
the principal force of the Peruvian armies, which was left
at that place on the death of his father, gave battle to his
brother Huascar, who was the elder son of Huana by a
lawful wife, and legal heir to the crown. After a long and
destructive civil war, the former was victorious; and thus
was that flourishing and happy kingdom left a prey to civil
dissentions, and to the few soldiers of Pizarro, who happened
at that juncture to make a descent upon their coast. Thus
he effected an easy conquest and an utter destruction of that
unfortunate people. It is however extremely obvious, that
this deplorable event is not to be charged on Capac, as the
consequence of any defect in his institution. It is impossible
that any original legislator should effectually guard against
the folly of a future sovereign. Capac had not only removed every temptation that could induce a wife prince to
wish for a change in the constitution, but had connected
the ruin of his authority with the change; for he, who
disregards any part of institutions deemed sacred, teaches his
people to consider the whole as an imposture. Had he
made a law ordaining that the Peruvians should be absolved
from their allegiance to a prince, who should violate the
laws, it would evidently have implied possible error and im-
perfection in those persons whom the people were ordered to
regard

regard as Divinities : the reverence due to characters who made such high pretensions, would have been weakened ; and, instead of rendering the constitution perfect, such a law would have been its greatest defect.   Besides, it is probable the rupture might have been healed, and the succession settled, with as little difficulty as frequently happens with partial revolutions in other kingdoms, had not the descent of the Spaniards prevented it. And this event, to a man in that age and country, was totally beyond the possibility of human foresight.   But viewing the concurrence of these fatal accidents, which reduced this flourishing empire to a level with many other ruined and departed kingdoms, it only proves that no human system has the privilege to be perfect.

On the whole, it is evident, that the system of Capac is the most surprising exertion of human genius to be found in the history of mankind. When we consider him as an individual emerging from the midst of a barbarous people, having seen no possible example of the operation of laws in any country, originating a plan of religion and policy never equalled by the sages of antiquity, civilizing an extensive empire, and rendering religion and government subservient to the general happiness of mankind, there is no danger that we grow too warm in his praise, or pronounce too high an eulogium on his character. Had such a genius appeared in Greece or Rome, he had been the subject of universal admiration ; had he arisen in the favourite land of Turkey, his praises had filled a thousand pages in the diffusive writings of Voltaire.

G

THE

BOOK III.

ARGUMENT.

The actions of Capac. A general invasion threatened by the mountain savages. Rocha, the Inca's son, sent with a few companions to offer terms of peace. His embassy. His adventure with the worshippers of the Volcano. With those of the storm, on the Andes. Falls in with the savage armies. Character and speech of Zamor, their chief. Sacrifice of Rocha's companions. Death-song of Azonto. War-dance. March of the savage armies down the mountains to Peru. Incan army meets them. Battle joins. Peruvians routed by an eclipse of the sun. They fly to Cusco. Grief of Oella, supposing the darkness to be occasioned by the death of her son Rocha. Sun appears. Peruvian army assembles, and they discover Rocha on an altar in the savage camp. They march in haste out of the city and engage the savages. Exploits of Capac. Death of Zamor. Recovery of Rocha, and submission of the enemy.

THE

VISION of COLUMBUS.

BOOK III.

NOW, twice twelve years, the children of the skies
Beheld in peace their growing empire rife;
O'er happy realms display'd their generous care,
Diffus'd their arts, and sooth'd the rage of war;
Bade yon tall temple grace the fav'rite isle,   5
The gardens bloom, the cultur'd valleys smile,
Th'aspiring hills their spacious mines unfold,
Fair structures blaze, and altars burn, in gold,
Those broad foundations bend their arches high,
And rear imperial Cusco to the sky;   10
While wealth and grandeur bless'd th'extended reign,
From the bold Andes to the western main.
    When, fierce from eastern wilds, the savage bands
Lead fire and slaughter o'er the happy lands;
Thro' fertile fields the paths of culture trace,   15
And vow destruction io the Incan race.
The king, undaunted in defensive war,
Drives back their host and speeds their flight afar;

G 3

Till,

Till, fir'd with rage, they range the wonted wood,
And feaft their fouls on future fcenes of blood.   20

   Where yon blue fummits hang their cliffs on high,
Frown o'er the plains and lengthen round the fky ;
Where vales exalted thro' the breaches run,
And drink the purer fplendors of the fun,
The tribes innumerous meditate the blow,   25
To blend their force and whelm the world below.
Capac, with caution, views the dark defign,
From countlefs wilds what hoftile myriads join ;
And feeks the means, by proffer'd leagues of peace,
To calm their rage and bid the difcord ceafe.   30

   His eldeft hope, young Rocha, at his call,
Leaves the deep confines of the temple wall ;
In whofe fair form, in lucid garments dreft,
Began the facred function of the prieft.

   In early youth, ere yet the genial fun   35
Had twice fix changes o'er his childhood run,
The blooming prince, beneath his parents' hand,
Learn'd all the laws that fway'd the facred land ;
With rites myfterious * ferv'd the Power divine,
Prepar'd the altar and adorn'd the fhrine,   40

  * The high-prieft of the Sun was always one of the royal
family ; and, in every generation after the firft, was brother to
the king. This office probably began with Rocha, as he was
the firft who was capable of receiving it, and as it was neceffary,
in the education of the prince, that he fhould be initiated in the
facred myfteries.

Responsive hail'd, with still returning praise,
Each circling season that the God displays,
Sooth'd with funereal hymns the parting dead,
At nuptial feasts the joyful chorus led;
While evening incense, and the morning song,   45
Rose from his hand or trembled on his tongue.

  Thus, form'd for empire, ere he gain'd the sway;
To rule with reverence, and with power obey,
Reflect the glories of the parent Sun,
And shine the Capac of his future throne,   50
Employ'd his ripening years; till now, from far,
The distant fields proclaim approaching war;
Matur'd for active scenes he quits the shrine,
To aid the council or in arms to shine.

  Where the mild monarch courtly throngs enclose,   55
Sublime in modest majesty he rose,
With reverence bow'd, conspicuous o'er the rest,
Approach'd the throne, and thus the sire address'd:—
Great king of nations, heav'n-descended sage,
Guard of my youth and glory of my age,   60
These pontiff robes to my blest brother's hand
Glad I resign, and wait thy kind command.
Should war invade, permit thy son to wield
The shaft of vengeance through th'untempted field:

                    Led

Led by thy powerful arm, my foul fhall brave   65
The haughtieft foe, or find a glorious grave;
For this dread conflict all our force demands,
In one wide field to whelm the brutal bands,
Pour to the mountain gods their wonted food,
And fhield thy realms from future fcenes of blood.   70
Yet oh, may fovereign mercy firft ordain
Propounded compact to the favage train.
Fearlefs of foes their own dark wilds I'll trace,
To quell the rage and give the terms of peace,
Teach the grim tribes to bow beneath thy fway,   75
And tafte the bleffings of the Power of day.

   The fire return'd;—My earlieft wifh you know,
To fhield from flaughter and preferve the foe,
In bands of mutual peace all tribes to bind,
And live the friend and guardian of mankind.   80
Should ftrife begin, thy youthful arm fhall fhare
The toils of glory through the walks of war;
But o'er thofe hideous hills, thro' climes of fnow,
With reafon's voice to lure the favage foe,
To 'fcape their fnares, their jarring fouls combine, 85
Claims hardier limbs and riper years than thine.
Yet one of heav'nly race the tafk requires,
Whofe myftic rites controul th'etherial fires;

                                          So

So the sooth'd Godhead proves, to faithless eyes,
His sway on earth and empire of the skies.   90
Some veteran chief, in those rough labours try'd,
Shall aid the toil, and go thy faithful guide;
O'er dreary heights thy sinking limbs sustain,
Teach the dark wiles of each insidious train,
Through all extremes of life thy voice attend,   95
In council lead thee, or in arms defend;
While three firm youths, thy chosen friends, shall go
To learn the climes and meditate the foe;
That wars of future years their aid may find,
To serve the realm and save the savage kind.   100
Rise then, my son, bright partner of my fame,
With early toils to build thy sacred name;
In high behest these heav'nly tidings bear,
To bless mankind and ward the waste of war.
To those dark hosts, where shivering mountains run,   105
Proclaim the bounties of our sire the Sun.
On these fair plains, beneath his happier skies,
Tell how his fruits in boundless plenty rise;
How the bright Power, whose all-delighting soul
Taught round the courts of heav'n his stars to roll, 110
To us his peaceful sons hath kindly given
His purest laws, the fav'rite grace of heaven;
                                                      Bids

Bids every tribe the fame glad lawn attend,
His realms to widen and his fanes defend,
Confefs and emulate his bounteous fway,   115
And give his bleffings where he gives the day.
Yet, fhould the gathering legions ftill prepare
The fhaft of flaughter for the barb'rous war,
Tell them we know to tread the crimfon plain,
And heav'n's bright children never yield to man.   120
   But oh, my child, with fteps of caution go,
The ways are hideous, and enrag'd the foe ;
Blood ftains their altars, all their feafts are blood,
Death their delight, and darknefs reigns their God ;
Tygers and vultures, ftorms and earthquakes fhare   125
Their rites of worfhip and their fpoils of war.
Should'ft thou, my Rocha, tempt their vengeful ire,
Should thofe dear relics feed a favage fire,
Deep fighs would heave thy wretched mother's breaft,
The pale fun fink in clouds of darknefs dreft,   130
Thy fire and haplefs nations rue the day
That drew thy fteps from thefe fad walls away.
   Yet go ; 'tis virtue calls ; and realms unknown,
By thefe long toils, may blefs thy future throne ;
Millions of unborn fouls in time may fee   135
Their doom revers'd, and owe their joys to thee ;

                                              While

While favage fires, with murdering hands, no more
Dread the grim Gods that claim their children's gore;
But, fway'd by happier fceptres, here behold
The rites of freedom and the fhrines of gold.   140
Be wife, be mindful of thy realm and throne;
Heav'n fpeed thy labours, and preferve my fon !
  Soon the glad prince, in robes of white array'd,
Call'd his attendants, and the fire obey'd.
A diamond broad, in burning gold impreft,   145
Fix'd the fun's image on his royal breaft;
Fair in his hand appear'd the olive bough,
And the white lautu * grac'd his beauteous brow.
Swift o'er the hills that lift the walks of day,
Thro' parting clouds they took their eaftern way;   150
Height over height they gain'd, beyond the bound
Where the wide empire claims its utmoft round;
To numerous tribes proclaim'd the folar fway,
And hold, through various toils, their tedious way.
  At length, far diftant, thro' the darkening fkies,   155
Where hills o'er hills in rude diforder rife,
A dreadful groan, beneath the fhuddering ground,
Rolls down the fteeps and fhakes the world around.

* The lautu was a cotton fringe, worn by the Incas, as a
badge of royalty.

Columns

Columns of reddening smoke, above the height,

O'ercast the heav'ns and cloud their wonted light ;   160

From tottering tops descend the cliffs of snow,

The mountains reel, the valleys rend below,

The headlong streams forget their usual round,

And shrink and vanish in the gaping ground ;

The sun descends—Wide flames with livid glare   165

Break the red cloud and purple all the air ;

Above the gaping top, wild cinders driven,

Stream high and brighten to the midst of heaven ;

Deep from beneath, full floods of boiling ore

Burst the dread mount, and thro' the opening roar ;   170

Torrents of molten rocks, on every side,

Lead o'er the shelves of ice the fiery tide ;

Hills slide before them, skies around them burn,

Towns sink beneath, and heaving plains o'erturn ;

Thro' distant realms, the flaming deluge hurl'd,   175

Sweeps trembling nations from th' astonish'd world.

Meanwhile, at distance, through the livid light,

A busy concourse met their wondering sight ;

The prince drew near ; where lo ! an altar stood,

In form a furnace, fill'd with burning wood ;   180

There a fair youth in pangs expiring lay,

And the fond father thus was heard to pray :—

* Receive,

* Receive, O dreadful Power, from feeble age,
This laſt pure offering to thy fateleſs rage ;
Thrice has thy vengeance, on this hated land,   185
Claim'd a dear infant from my yielding hand ;
Thrice have thoſe lovely lips the victim preſs'd,
And all the mother torn that tender breaſt ;
When the dread duty ſtifled every figh,
And not a tear eſcap'd her beauteous eye.   190
The fourth, and laſt, now meets the fatal doom,
(Groan not, my child, thy God commands thee home)
Attend, once more, thou dark, infernal name,
From yon far-ſtreaming pyramid of flame ;
Snatch, from the heaving fleſh, th' expiring breath,   195
Sacred to thee and all the powers of death ;
Then, in thy hall, with ſpoils of nations crown'd,
Confine thy walks beneath the rending ground ;
No more on earth th' embowell'd flames to pour,
And ſcourge my people and my race no more.   200

     Thus Rocha heard ; and, tow'rd the trembling crowd,
Turn'd the bright enſign of his beaming God.

     * It is a fact, that the different tribes of thoſe mountain ſa-
vages worſhipped the various objects of terror that infeſted the
particular parts of the country where they dwelt ; ſuch as ſtorms,
volcanoes, rivers, lakes, and ſeveral beaſts and birds of prey ;
and all with this idea, that their forefathers deſcended from the
gods which they worſhipped.

Th'

Th' afflicted chief, with fear and grief oppress'd,
Beheld the sign, and thus the prince address'd :—
From what far land, O royal stranger, say,   205
Ascend thy wandering steps this nightly way ?
Com'st thou from plains like ours, with cinders fir'd ?
And have thy people in the flames expir'd ?
Or hast thou now, to stay the whelming flood,
No son to offer to the furious God ?   210
    From happier lands I came, the prince return'd,
Where no red vengeance e'er the concave burn'd ;
No furious God disturbs the peaceful skies,
Nor yield our hands the bloody sacrifice ;
But life and joy the Power delights to give,   215
And bids his children but rejoice and live:
Thou seest o'er heav'n the all-delighting sun,
In living radiance rear his golden throne ;
O'er plains and valleys shed his genial beams,
Call from yon cliffs of ice the winding streams ;   220
While fruits and flowers adorn th' indulgent field,
And seas and lakes their copious treasures yield,
He reigns our only God ; in him we trace
The friend, the father of our happy race.
Late the lone tribes, on those delightful shores,   225
With gloomy reverence serv'd imagin'd powers ;

Till

Till he, in pity to the roving race,
Difpens'd their laws, and form'd their minds for peace.
My heav'n-born parents firft the reign began,
Sent from his courts to rule the race of man,   230
To teach his arts, extend his bounteous fway,
And give his bleffings where he gives the day.

   The wondering chief reply'd : — Thy garb and face
Proclaim thy lineage of fuperior race ;
And our far-diflant fires, no lefs than thine,   235
Sprang from a God, and own a birth divine.
From that tremendous mount, the fource of flame,
In elder times, my great forefathers came ;
Where the dread Power conceals his dark abode,
And claims, as now, the tribute of a God.   240
This victim due when willing mortals pay,
His terrors leffen and his fires decay ;
While purer fleet regales th' untainted air,
And our glad hofls are fir'd for fiercer war.

   Yet know, dread chief, the pious youth rejoin'd,   245
One fov'reign Power produc'd all human kind ;
Some Sire fupreme, whofe ever-ruling foul
Creates, preferves, and regulates the whole.
That Sire fupreme muft lift his radiant eye
Round the wide concave of the boundlefs fky ;   250

That

That heav'n's high courts, and all the walks of men,
May rise unveil'd beneath his careful ken.
Could thy dark Power, that holds his drear abode
Deep in the bofom of that fiery flood,
Yield the glad fruits that diftant nations find?   255
Or praife, or punifh, or behold mankind?
When the bleft God, from glooms of changing night,
Shall gild his chambers with the morning light.
By myftic rites he'll vindicate his throne,
And own thy fervant for his duteous fon.   260
 Meantime, the chief reply'd, thy cares releas'd,
Share the poor relics of our fcanty feaft;
Which, driv'n in hafty rout, our train fupply'd,
When trembling earth proclaim'd the boiling tide.
They far'd, they refted; till approaching morn   265
Beheld the day-ftar o'er the mountain burn;
The prince arofe, an altar rear'd on high,
And watch'd the fplendors of the orient fky.
 When o'er the mountain flam'd the fun's broad ray,
He call'd the hoft his facred rites t'effay;   270
Then took the loaves of maize, the bounties brake,
Gave to the chief and bade them all partake;
The hallow'd relics on the pile he plac'd,
With tufts of flow'rs the fimple offering grac'd,

Held

Held to the sun the image from his breast, 275
Whose glowing concave all the God exprest;
O'er the dry'd leaves the rays concentred fly,
And thus his voice ascends the list'ning sky:—

O thou, whose splendors kindle heav'n with fire,
Great soul of nature, and the world's dread sire, 280
If e'er my father found thy sov'reign grace,
Or thy blest will ordain'd the Incan race,
Give these lone tribes to learn thine awful name,
Receive this offering, and the pile inflame:
So shall thy laws o'er these wide bounds be known, 285
And earth's unnumber'd sons be happy as thy own.

Thus pray'd the prince: the kindling flames aspire,
The tribes surrounding tremble and retire,
Gaze on the wonder, full conviction own,
And vow obedience to the sacred Sun. 290
The legates now their farther course descry'd,
A young cazique attending as a guide,
O'er craggy cliffs pursu'd their eastern way,
Where loftier champaigns meet the shivering day;
Saw timorous tribes, in those sublime abodes, 295
Adore the blasts, and turn the storms to gods;
While every cloud, that thunders thro' the skies,
Claims from their hands a human sacrifice.

H

Awhile

Awhile the youth, their better faith to gain,

Strives, with his usual art, but strives in vain;   300

In vain he pleads the mildness of the sun,

In those cold bounds where chilling whirlwinds run;

Where the dark tempests sweep the world below,

And load the mountains with eternal snow.

The sun's bright beam, the fearful tribes declare,   305

Drives all their evils on the tortur'd air;

He draws the vapours up the eastern sky,

That sail and centre tow'rd his dazzling eye;

Leads the loud storms along his mid-day course,

And bids the Andes meet their sweeping force;   310

Builds their bleak summits with an icy throne,

To shine through heav'n, a semblance of his own;

Hence the dire chills the lifted lawns that wait,

And all the scourges that attend their state.

Sev'n toilsome days, the virt'ous Inca strove,   315

To social joys their savage minds to move;

Then, while the morning glow'd serenely bright,

He led their footsteps to an eastern height;

The world, unbounded, stretch'd beneath them, lay,

And not a cloud obscur'd the rising day: 320

Broad Amazonia, with her star-like streams,

In azure drest, a heav'n inverted seems;

Dim

Dim Paraguay extends the aching sight;
Xaraya * glimmers like the moon of night;
The earth and skies, in blending borders stray,   325
And smile and brighten to the lamp of day.
When thus the prince: — What majesty divine!
What robes of gold! what flames around him shine!
There walks the God! his starry sons on high,
Draw their dim veil, and shrink behind the sky;   330
Earth with surrounding nature 's born a-new,
And tribes and empires greet the gladdening view!
Who can behold his all-delighting soul
Give life and joy, and heav'n and earth controul,
Bid death and darkness from his presence move—   335
Who can behold, and not adore and love?
Those plains, immensely circling, feel his beams,
He greens the groves, he silvers o'er the streams,
Swells the wild fruitage, gives the beast his food,
And mute creation hails the genial God.   340
But nobler joys his righteous laws impart,
To aid the life and mould the social heart,
His peaceful arts o'er happy realms to spread,
And altars grace with pure celestial bread;

* *Xaraya* is a large lake in the country of Paraguay, and is
the source of the river Paraguay.

H 2

Such

Such our diftinguifh'd lot, who own his fway,   345
Mild as his morning ftars, and liberal as the day.

    His unknown laws, the mountain chief reply'd,
In your far world your boafted race may guide ;
And yon low plains, that drink his genial ray,
At his glad fhrine their juft devotions pay.   350
But we, nor fear his frown, nor truft his fmile ;
He blafts our forefts and o'erturns our toil ;
Our bowers are bury'd in his whirls of fnow,
Or fwept and driv'n to fhade his tribes below.
Ev'n now his mounting fteps thy hopes beguile,   355
He lures thy raptures with a morning fmile ;
But foon (for fo thofe faffron robes proclaim)
Black ftorms fhall fail beneath his leading flame,
Thunders and blafts, againft the mountains driven,
Shall fhake the tott'ring tops, and rend the vault of heaven.

    He fpoke ; they waited, till th' afcending ray,
High from the noon-tide fhot the faithlefs day ;
When, lo ! far-gathering, round the eaftern fkies,
Solemn and flow, the dark-red vapours rife ;
Full clouds, convolving on the turbid air,   365
Move, like an ocean, to the watery war.
The hoft, fecurely rais'd, no dangers harm,
They fit unclouded, and o'erlook the ftorm ;

While,

While, far beneath, the fky-borne waters ride,
O'er the dark deep and up the mountain's fide;   370
The lightning's glancing wings, in fury curl'd,
Bend their long forky terrors o'er the world;
Torrents, and broken crags, and floods of rain,
From fteep to fteep roll down their force amain,
In dreadful cataracts; the crafhing found   375
Fills the wide heav'ns and rocks the fmouldering ground.
The blafts, unburden'd, take their upward courfe,
And, o'er the mountain top, refume their force:
Swift, thro' the long white ridges, from the north,
The rapid whirlwinds lead their terrors forth;   380
High rolls the ftorm, the circling furges rife,
And wild gyrations wheel the hovering fkies;
Vaft hills of fnow, In fweeping columns driven,
Deluge the air and cloud the face of heaven;
Floods burft their chains, the rocks forget their place, 385
And the firm mountain trembles to its bafe.

    Long gaz'd the hoft; when thus the ftubborn chief,
With eyes on fire, and fill'd with fullen grief:—
Behold thy carelefs God, fecure on high,
Laughs at our woes, and peaceful walks the fky,   390
Drives all his evils on thefe feats fublime,
And wafts his favours to a happier clime;

H 3   Sire

Sire of that joyous race thy words difclofe,
There glads his children, here afflicts his foes.
Hence! fpeed thy courfe! purfue him where he leads; 395
Left vengeance feize thee for thy father's deeds,
Thy immolated limbs affwage the fire
Of thofe curft powers, which now a gift require.

 The youth, in hafte, collects his fcanty train,
And, with the fun, flies o'er the weftern plain, 400
The fading orb with plaintive voice he plies,
To guide his fteps and light him down the fkies.
So, when the moon and all the hoft of even,
Hang, pale and trembling, on the verge of heaven,
While ftorms, afcending, threat their nightly reign, 405
They feek their abfent fire, and fettle down the main.

 Now, to the fouth he turns; where one vaft plain
Calls from the hills, a wide-extended train;
Of various drefs and various form they fhow'd;
Each wore the enfign of his local god. 410

 From eaftern fteeps, a grifly hoft defcends,
O'er whofe grim chief a tyger's hide depends;
The tufky jaws grin o'er his fhaggy brow,
The eye-balls glare, the paws depend below;
From his bor'd ears contorted ferpents hung, 415
And drops of gore feem'd rolling on his tongue.

          From

From northern wilds dark move the vulture-race;
Black tufts of quills their shaded foreheads grace;
The claws extend, the beak is op'd for blood,
And all the armour imitates the god.   420
The * condor, frowning, from a southern plain,
Borne on a standard, leads a numerous train:
Clench'd in his talons hangs an infant dead,
His long beak pointing where the squadrons tread;
His wings, far-stretching, cleave the yielding wind,   425
And his broad tail o'ershades the host behind.
From other plains, and other hills, afar,
The tribes throng dreadful to the promis'd war;
Some wear the crested furies of the snake,
Some show the emblems of a stream or lake;   430
All, from the Power they serve, assume their mode,
And foam and yell to taste the Incan blood.
The prince, incautious, with his train drew near,
Known for an Inca by his dress and air.
At once the savage bands to vengeance move,   435
Demand their arms, and chase them round the grove;
His scattering host in vain the combat tries,
While circling thousands from their ambush rise;

* The condor is suppofed to be the largeft bird in the world.
His wings, from one extreme to the other, are faid to meafure
twenty feet; and he is able to carry a child in his clutches.

H 4

Nor

Nor power to ſtrive, nor hope of flight remains,
They bow in ſilence to the victor's chains.   440
When, now the gathering ſquadrons throng the plain,
And echoing ſkies the rending ſhouts retain;
Zamor, the leader of the tyger-band,
By choice appointed to the firſt command,
Shrugg'd up his ſpotted ſpoils above the reſt,   445
And, grimly frowning, thus the crowd addreſs'd:—
    Warriors, attend; to-morrow leads abroad
Our ſacred vengeance for our brothers' blood.
On thoſe ſcorch'd plains for ever muſt they lie,
Their bones ſtill naked to the burning ſky;   450
Left in the field for foreign hawks to tear,
Nor our own vultures can the banquet ſhare?
But ſoon, ye mountain gods, yon dreary weſt
Shall ſate your vengeance with a nobler feaſt;
When the proud Sun, that terror of the plain,   455
Shall grieve in heav'n for all his children ſlain;
O'er boundleſs fields our ſlaught'ring myriads roam,
And your dark powers command a happier home.
Meanwhile, ye tribes, theſe men of ſolar race,
Food for the flames, your bloody rites ſhall grace: 460
Each to a different god his panting breath
Reſigns in fire; this night demands their death:

All but the Inca; him, reserv'd in state,
These conquering hands ere long shall immolate,
To that dread Power that thunders in the skies, 465
A grateful gift, before his mother's eyes.

    The savage ceas'd; the chiefs of every race
Lead the bold captives to their destin'd place;
The sun descends, the parting day expires,
And earth and heav'n display their sparkling fires. 470
Soon the rais'd altars kindle round the gloom,
And call the victims to the vengeful doom;
Led to the pile, in sovereign pomp they tread,
And sing, by turns, the triumphs of the dead.
Amid the crowd, beside his altar, stood 475
The youth devoted to the tyger-god:
A beauteous form he rose, of noble grace,
The only hope of his illustrious race;
His aged sire, through numerous years, had shone,
The first supporter of the Incan throne; 480
Wise Capac lov'd the youth, and grac'd his hand
With a fair virgin, from a neighbouring band;
And him the royal prince, in equal prime,
Had chose, t' attend him round the savage clime.
He mounts the pyre; the flames approach his breath, 485
And thus he wakes the dauntless song of death :—

O

O thou dark vault of heaven! his daily throne,
Where flee the absent glories of the sun?
Ye starry hosts, that kindle from his eye,
Can you behold him in the western sky?   490
Or if, unseen, beneath his watery bed,
The weary'd God reclines his radiant head,
When next his morning steps your courts inflame,
And seek on earth for young Azonto's name,
Then point these ashes, 'mark the smoky pile,   495
And say the hero suffer'd with a smile.
So shall th' avenging Power, in fury drest,
Bind the red * circlet o'er his changing vest,
Bid dire destruction, on these dark abodes,
Whelm the grim tribes and all their savage gods.   500
But oh! forbear to tell my stooping sire,
His darling hopes have fed a coward fire:
Why should he know the tortures of the brave?
Or fruitless sorrows bend him to the grave?
And may'st thou ne'er be told, my bridal Fair,   505
What silent pangs these panting vitals tear;
But, blooming still, th'impatient wish employ
On the blind hope of future scenes of joy.

* It is natural for the worshippers of the Sun to consider
any change in the atmosphere as indicative of the different
passions ascribed to their divinity. With the Peruvians, a sanguine appearance in the Sun denoted his anger.

Now hafte, ye ftrides of death; the Power of day,
In abfent flumbers, gives your vengeance way;   510
While fainter light thefe livid flames fupply,
And fhort-liv'd thoufands learn of me to die.......

  He ceas'd not fpeaking; when the yell of war
Drowns all their death-fongs in a hideous jar;
Round the far-echoing hills the yellings pour,   515
And wolves and tygers catch the diftant roar.
Now more concordant all their voices join,
And round the plain they form the feftive line;
When, to the mufic of the difmal din,
Indignant Zamor bids the dance begin.   520
Dim, thro' the fhadowy fires, each changing form
Moves like a cloud before an evening ftorm,
When, o'er the moon's pale face and ftarry-plain,
The fhades of heav'n lead on their broken train;
The mingling tribes their mazy circles tread,   525
Till the laft groan proclaims the victims dead:
Then part the fmoky flefh, enjoy the feaft,
And lofe their labours in oblivious reft.

  Now, when the weftern hills proclaim'd the morn,
And falling fires were fcarcely feen to burn,   530
Grimm'd by the horrors of the dreadful night,
The hofts woke fiercer for the diftant fight;

                                              And,

And, dark and silent, thro' the frowning grove,
The diff'rent tribes beneath their standards move.

But, round the blissful city of the Sun,   535
Since the young prince his foreign toils begun,
The prudent king collected, from afar,
His martial bands to meet th'expected war.
The various tribes, in one extended train,
Move to the confines of an eastern plain;   540
Where, from th'exalted kingdom's utmost end,
Sublimer hills and savage walks ascend.
High in the front, imperial Capac strode,
In fair effulgence like the beaming God;
A golden girdle bound his snowy vest,   545
A mimic sun hung trembling on his breast,
The lautu's circling band his temples twin'd,
The bow, the quiver, shade his waist behind;
Rais'd high in air, his golden sceptre burn'd,
And hosts surrounding trembled as he turn'd.   550

O'er eastern hills he cast his watchful eye,
Where op'ning breaches lengthen down the sky;
In whose blue clefts, wide-sloping alleys bend,
Where annual floods from melting snows descend;
Now, dry and deep, far up the dreary height,   555
Show the dark squadrons moving into sight;

They

They throng and thicken on the smoky air,
And every breach pours down the dusky war.
So when an hundred streams explore their way,
Down the same slopes, convolving to the sea ;   560
They boil, they bend, they urge their force amain,
Swell o'er obstructing crags, and sweep the distant plain.
    Capac beholds, and waits the coming shock,
Unmov'd, and gleaming, like an icy rock ;
And while for fight the arming hosts prepare,   565
Thus thro' the files he breathes the soul of war :—
Ye hosts, of every tribe and every plain,
That live and flourish in my father's reign,
Long have your flocks and rip'ning harvests shown
The genial smiles of his indulgent throne ;   570
As o'er surrounding realms his blessings flow'd,
And conquer'd all without the stain of blood.
But now behold, yon wide-collecting band,
With threat'ning war, demands the happy land :
Beneath the dark, immeasurable host,   575
Descending, swarming, how the crags are lost !
Already now their ravening eyes behold
Your star-bright temples and your gates of gold ;
And to their gods in fancied goblets pour,
The warm libation of your children's gore.   580
                                              Move

Move then to vengeance, meet the sons of blood,
Led by this arm, and lighted by that God ;
The strife is fierce, your fanes and fields the prize,
The warrior conquers or the infant dies.

Fill'd with his fire, the hosts, in squar'd array,   585
Eye the dark legions and demand th'affray ;
Their pointed arrows, rising on the bow,
Look up the sky and chide the lagging foe.
Fierce Zamor, frowning, leads the grisly train,
Moves from the clefts, and stretches o'er the plain ;   590
He gives the shriek ; the deep convulsing sound
The hosts re-echo ; and the hills around
Retain the rending tumult ; all the air
Clangs in the conflict of the clashing war.
But firm, undaunted, as a shelvy strand,   595
That meets the surge, the bold Peruvians stand ;
With steady aim the sounding bow-string ply,
And showers of arrows thicken thro' the sky ;
When each grim host, in closer conflict join'd,
Clench the dire ax, and cast the bow behind ;   600
Thro' broken ranks sweep wide the rapid course,
Now struggle back, now sidelong sway the force ;
Here, from grim chiefs is lopp'd the grisly head ;
All gride the dying, all deface the dead ;

There,

There, scattering o'er the field, in thin array,   605
Man strives with man, and stones with axes play ;
With broken shafts they follow and they fly,
And yells, and groans, and shouts invade the sky ;
Round all the plains and groves, the ground is strow'd
With sever'd limbs and corses bath'd in blood.   610
Long rag'd the strife ; and where, on either side,
A friend, a father, or a brother died,
No trace remain'd of what he show'd before,
Mangled with horrid wounds and smear'd with gore.

  Now the Peruvians, in collected might,   615
With one wide sweep had wing'd the savage flight ;
But heaven's bright splendor, in his mid day race,
With glooms unusual veil'd his radiant face.
By slow degrees a solemn twilight moves,
Browns the dim heav'ns and shades the conscious groves. 620
Th'observing Inca views, with wild surprise,
Deep glooms on earth, no cloud around the skies,
His host o'ershaded in the field of blood,
Gor'd by his foes, deserted by his God.
All, mute with wonder, cease the strife to wage,   625
Gaze at each other, and forget their rage ;
When pious Capac, to the listening croud,
Rais'd high his wand and pour'd his voice aloud :—

Ye

Ye chiefs and warriors of Peruvian race,
Some dire offence obscures my father's face ;   630
What moves the Godhead to desert the plain,
Nor save his children, nor behold them slain ?
Fly ! speed your course; and seek the friendly town,
Ere darkness shroud you in a deeper frown ;
The faithful walls your squadrons shall defend,   635
While my sad steps the sacred dome ascend ;
There learn the cause, and ward the woes we fear—
Haste, haste, my sons, I guard the flying rear.

The hero spoke ; the trembling tribes obey,
While deeper glooms obscure the source of day.   640
Sudden, the savage bands collect amain,
Hang on the rear and sweep them o'er the plain ;
Their shouts, redoubling o'er the flying war,
Drown the loud groans and torture all the air ;
The hawks of heav'n, that o'er the field had stood,   645
Scar'd by the tumult from the scent of blood,
Cleave the far gloom ; the beasts forget their prey,
And scour the waste, and give the war its way.

Zamor, elate with horrid joy, beheld
The sun depart, his children fly the field,   650
And rais'd his rending voice :—Thou darkening sky,
Deepen thy glooms, the Power of death is nigh ;

Behold

Behold him rising from his nightly throne,
To veil the heav'ns and drive the conquer'd sun !
The glaring Godhead yields to sacred night ;   655
And all his armies imitate his flight.
O dark, infernal Power, confirm thy reign ;
Give deadlier shades, and heap the piles of slain !
Soon the young captive Prince shall roll in fire,
And all his race accumulate the pyre.   660
Ye mountain vultures, here your vengeance pour,
Tygers and condors, all ye gods of gore,
In these dread fields, beneath your frowning sky,
A plenteous feast shall every god supply !—
Rush forward, warriors, hide the plains with dead ;   665
'Twas here our friends, in former combat, bled ;
Strow'd thro' the waste, their naked bones demand
This ample vengeance from our conquering hand.

He said ; and, high before the tyger-train,
With longer strides, hangs forward o'er the slain,   670
Bends, like a falling tree, to reach the foe,
And o'er tall Capac aims a deadly blow.
The king beheld the ax, and with his wand
Struck the rais'd weapon from his grasping hand ;
Then clench'd the falling helve, and whirling round, 675
Fell'd furious hosts of heroes to the ground :

I   Nor

Nor ftay'd, but follow'd, where the fquadrons run,
Fearing to fight, forfaken by the fun:
Till Cufco's walls falute their longing fight,
And the wide gates receive their rapid flight.   680
The folds are barr'd, the foes, in fhade conceal'd,
Like howling wolves, rave round th'affrighted field.

The monarch now afcends the facred dome,
Where the fun's image wore a faded gloom.
Thro' all the courts a folemn fhade prevail'd,   685
And female groans his liftening ear affail'd;
Deep from an inner fhrine, the burfting figh
Breathe forth awhile, and thefe fad accents rife :—
Was it for this, my fon to diftant lands
Muft trace the wilds, amid thofe favage bands?   690
And does the God obfcure his golden throne,
In mournful filence for my flaughter'd fon?
Oh, had his beam, ere that difaftrous day,
That fnatch'd the youth from thefe fond arms away,
Receiv'd my mounting fpirit to the fky,   695
That fad Oella might have feen him die!
Where flept thy fhaft of vengeance, O my God,
When thofe fell tygers drank his facred blood?
Did not the pious prince, with rites divine,
Feed the pure flame within thy hallow'd fhrine!   700

And

And early learn, beneath his father's hand,
To shed thy blessings round the favour'd land,
Form'd by thy laws the royal seat to grace,
Son of thy son, and glory of his race?
Where, dearest Rocha, rests thy beauteous head?   705
Where the rent robes thy hapless mother made?
I see thee, mid those hideous hills of snow,
Pursu'd and slaughter'd by the savage foe;
Or doom'd a feast for some infernal God,
Whose horrid shrine demands thy harmless blood.   710
Snatch me, O Sun, to happier worlds of light——
No, shroud me, shroud me, with thyself in night——
Thou hear'st me not; thou dread, departed Power,
Thy face is dark, and Rocha is no more.

Thus heard the silent king; his heaving heart   715
Caught all her grief, and bore a father's part.
The cause, suggested by her tender moan,
That veil'd the mid-day splendors of the sun,
And shouts insulting of the raging foe,
Fix'd him suspense, in all the strength of woe.   720
A doubtful moment held his changing choice;
Now would he sooth her; half assumes his voice;
But greater cares the rising wish controul,
And call forth all his dignity of soul.

I 2

Why

Why shoud he cease to ward the coming fate?   725
Or she be told the foes besiege the gate?
He turn'd in haste; and now the image-God,
High in the front, with kindling lustre glow'd:
Swift thro' the portal flew the hero's eye,
And hail'd the growing splendor in the sky.   730

    The troops courageous at return of light,
Pour round the dome, impatient for the fight;
The chief, descending, in the portal stood,
And thus address'd the all-delighting God:—

    O sovereign soul of heav'n; thy changing face   735
Makes or destroys the glory of thy race.
If, from the bounds of earth, my son be fled,
First of thy line that ever grac'd the dead;
If thy bright Godhead ceas'd in heav'n to burn,
For that lov'd youth, who never must return;   740
Forgive thine armies, when, in fields of blood,
They lose their strength, and fear the frowning God.
As now thy glory, with superior day,
Glows thro' the field and leads the warrior's way,
May our delighted souls, to vengeance driven,   745
Burn with new brightness in the cause of heaven;
For thy slain son see larger squadrons bleed,
We mourn the hero, but avenge the deed!

He

He faid ; and, from the battlements on high,
A watchful warrior rais'd an eager cry :   750
An Inca white on yonder altar tied——
'Tis Rocha's felf—the flame afcends his fide.,,
In fweeping hafte tho burfting gates unbar,
And flood the champaign with a tide of war ;
A cloud of arrows leads the rapid train,   755
They fhout, they fwarm, they hide the moving plain ;
The bows and quivers ftrow the field behind,
And the rais'd axes cleave the parting wind :
The prince, confeft to ev* ry warrior's fight,
Infpires each foul and centres all the fight ;   760
Each hopes to fnatch him from the kindling pyre,
Each fears his breath already flits in fire :
While Zamor fpread his thronging fquadrons wide,
Wedg'd like a wall—and thus the king defied :—
Hafte ! fon of Light, pour faft the winged war,   765
The prince, the dying prince, demands your care ;
Hear how his death-fong chides your dull delay,
Lift larger ftrides, bend forward to th'affray,
Ere folding flames prevent his ftifled groan,
Child of your beaming God, a victim to our own.   770
He faid ; and rais'd his fhaggy form on high,
And bade the fhafts glide thicker thro' the fky.

I 3

Like

Like the black billows of the lifted main,
Rolls into fight the long Peruvian train;
A white fail, bounding, on the billows toft,   775
Is Capac, ftriding o'er the furious hoft.
Now meet the dreadful chiefs, with eyes on fire;
Beneath their blows the parting ranks retire:
In whirlwind-fweep, their meeting axes bound,
Wheel, crafh in air, and plough the trembling ground; 780
Their finewy limbs, in fierce contortions, bend,
And mutual ftrokes, with equal force, defcend;
The king fways backward from the ftruggling foe,
Collects new ftrength, and with a circling blow
Rufh'd furious on; his flinty edge, on high,   785
Met Zamor's helve, and glancing, cleft his thigh.
The favage fell; when, thro' the tyger-train,
The driving Inca fwept a widening lane;
Whole ranks fall ftaggering, where he lifts his arm,
Or roll before him like a billowy ftorm;   790
Behind his fteps collecting legions clofe,
While, centred in a circling ridge of foes,
He drives his furious way; the prince unties,
And thus his voice:—Dread Sovereign of the fkies,
Accept my living fon, again beftow'd,   795
To grace with rites the temple of his God!—

Move,

Move, warriors, move, complete the work begun,
Crush the grim race, avenge the injur'd Sun.
    The savage host, that view'd the daring deed,
And saw deep squadrons with their leader bleed,   800
Rais'd high the shriek of horror; all the plain
Is trod with flight and cover'd with the slain.
The bold Peruvians circle round the field,
Confine their flight, and bid the relics yield:
While Capac rais'd his placid voice again—   805
Ye conquering hosts, collect the scatter'd train;
The Sun commands to stay the rage of war,
He knows to conquer, but he loves to spare.
    He ceas'd; and, where the savage leader lay
Welt'ring in gore, directs his eager way;   810
Unwraps the tiger's hide, and strives in vain
To close the wound, and mitigate the pain;
And, while soft pity mov'd his manly breast,
Rais'd the huge head, and thus the chief address'd :—
Too long, dread prince, thy raging arms withstood   815
The hosts of heav'n, and brav'd th'avenging God;
His sovereign will commands all strife to cease,
His realm is concord, and his pleasure, peace;
This copious carnage, spreading all the plain,
Insults his bounties, but confirms his reign.   820
Enough, 'tis past—thy parting breath demands
The last sad office from my yielding hands.

To ſhare thy pains, and feel thy hopeleſs woe,
Are rites ungrateful to a falling foe;
Yet reſt in peace; and know, a chief ſo brave,   825
When life departs, ſhall find an honour'd grave;
Theſe hands, in mournful pomp, thy tomb ſhall rear,
And tribes unborn thy hapleſs fate declare.

  Inſult me not with tombs, the ſavage cried,
Let cloſing clods thy coward carcaſe hide;   830
But theſe brave bones, unhury'd on the plain,
Touch not with duſt, nor dare with rites profane;
Let no curſt earth conceal this gory head,
Nor ſongs proclaim the dreadful Zamor dead.
Me, whom the hungry gods, from plain to plain,   835
Have follow'd, feaſting on thy ſlaughter'd train,
Me wouldſt thou cover ? no ! from yonder ſky,
The wide-beak'd hawk, that now beholds me die,
Soon, with his cowering train, my fleſh ſhall tear,
And wolves and tygers vindicate their ſhare   840
Receive, dread Powers (ſince I can ſlay no more)
My laſt glad victim, this devoted gore !

  Thus pour'd the vengeful chief his fainting breath,
And loſt his utterance in the gaſp of death.
The ſad remaining tribes confeſs the Power,   845
That ſheds his bounties round the fav'rite ſhore;
All bow obedient to the Incan throne,
And bleſt Oella hails her living ſon.

THE

VISION of COLUMBUS.

BOOK IV.

ARGUMENT.

Destruction of Peru foretold. Grief of Columbus. He is comforted by a promise of a vision of future ages. All Europe appears in vision. Effect of the discovery of America upon the affairs of Europe. Improvement in commerce—government. Revival of learning. Order of the Jesuits. Religious persecution. Character of Raleigh; who plans the settlement of North-America. Formation of the coast by the gulph-stream. Nature of the colonial establishments. Fleets of settlers steering for America.

THE

VISION of COLUMBUS.

BOOK IV.

IN one dark age, beneath a single hand,
Thus rose an empire in the savage land,
Her golden seats, with following years, increase,
Her growing nations spread the walks of peace,
Her sacred rites display the purest plan,   5
That e'er adorn'd th'unguided mind of man.

   Yet all the pomp th'extended climes unfold,
The fields of verdure and the towers of gold,
Those works of peace, and sov'reign scenes of state,
In short-liv'd glory hasten to their fate.   10
Thy followers, rushing like an angry flood,
Shall whelm the fields, and stain the shrines in blood;
Nor thou, Las Casas,* best of men, shall stay
The rav'ning legions from their guardless prey.

* Bartholomew de Las Casas was a Dominican priest, of a
most amiable and heroic character. He first went to Hispaniola
with Columbus in his second voyage, where he manifested an
ardent, but honest zeal, first in attempting to instruct the natives
in the principles of the catholic faith, and afterwards in defend-
ing

Oh! hapless prelate, hero, saint and sage,   15

Doom'd with hard guilt a fruitless war to wage,

To see, with grief (thy life of virtues run)

A realm unpeopled and a world undone!

While impious Valverde *, mock of priesthood stands,

Guilt in his heart, the gospel in his hands,   20

ing them against the insufferable cruelties exercised by the Spanish tyrants who succeeded Columbus in the discoveries and conquests in South America. He early declared himself the protector of the Indians; and he devoted himself, ever after, to the most indefatigable labours in their service. He made several voyages to Spain, to solicit, first from Ferdinand, then from cardinal Ximines, and finally from Charles V, some effectual restrictions against the horrid career of depopulation, which every where attended the Spanish arms. He followed these monsters of cruelty into all the conquered countries; where, by the power of his eloquence and that purity of morals which commands respect even from the worst of men, he doubtless saved the lives of many thousands of innocent people. His life was a continued struggle against that deplorable system of tyranny, of which he gives a description in a treatise addressed to Philip, prince of Spain, entitled *Brevissima relacion dela destruycion delas Indias.*

It is said by the Spanish writers, that the inhabitants of Hispaniola, when first discovered by the Spaniards, amounted to more than one million. This incredible population was reduced, in fifteen years, to sixty thousand souls.

* Vincent Valverde was a fanatical priest who accompanied Pizarro in his destructive expedition to Peru. If we were to search the history of mankind, we should not find another so extraordinary an example of the united efforts of ecclesiastical hypocrisy and military ferocity, of unresisted murder and insatiable plunder, as we meet with in the account of this expedition. Father Valverde, in a formal manner, gave the sanction of the church to the treacherous murder of Atabalipa and his relations; which was immediately followed by the destruction and almost entire depopulation of a flourishing empire.

Bids

Bids, in one field, their unarm'd thoufands bleed,
Smiles o'er the fcene and fanctifies the deed.
And thou, brave Gafca *, with thy virtuous train,
Shalt lift the fword and urge thy power in vain;
Vain the late ftrife, the finking land to fave,   25
Or call her flaughter'd millions from the grave.

    The Seraph fpoke. Columbus, with a figh,
Caft o'er the haplefs climes his moiften'd eye,
And thus return'd:—Oh, hide me in the tomb;
Why fhould I live to view th'impending doom?   30
If fuch dread fcenes the fcheme of Heav'n compofe,
And virt'ous toils induce redoubled woes,
Unfold no more; but grant a kind releafe,
Give me, 'tis all I afk, to reft in peace.

* Pedro de la Gafca was one of the few men whofe virtues form a fingular contraft with the vices which difgraced the age in which he lived, and the country in which he acquired his glory. He was fent over to Peru by Charles V, without any military force, to quell the rebellion of the younger Pizarro, and to prevent a fecond depopulation, by a civil war, of that country which had juft been drenched in the blood of its original inhabitants. He effected this great purpofe by the weight only of his perfonal authority, and the veneration infpired by his virtues. As foon as he had fupprefled the rebellion and eftablifhed the government of the colony, he haftened to refign his authority into the hands of his mafter; and, though his victories had been obtained in the richeft country upon earth, he returned to Spain as poor as Cincinnatus; having refifted every temptation to plunder, and refufed any emolument for his fervices.

Thy

Thy foul fhall reft in peace, the Power rejoin'd,   35
Ere thefe conflicting fhades involve mankind :
But nobler views fhall firft thy mind engage,
Where, far advanc'd beyond this darkfome age,
The happier fruits of thy unwearied care,
Thro' future years, a grateful world fhall fhare.   40
Europe's contending kings fhall foon behold
Thefe fertile plains and hills of opening gold ;
And in the path of thy advent'rous fail,
Their countlefs navies float in every gale,
For wealth and commerce, fearch the weftern fhore,   45
And load the ocean with the fhining ore.

    As, up the orient heav'n, the dawning ray
Smiles o'er the world and gives the promis'd day,
Drives fraud and rapine from their nightly fpoil,
And focial nature wakes to peaceful toil ;   50
So, from the blazing mine, the golden ftore
Mid warring ftates fhall fpread from fhore to fhore,
With new ambition fire their ravifh'd eyes,
O'er factious nobles bid the monarch rife,
Unite the force of realms, the wealth to fhare,   55
Lead larger hofts to milder walks of war ;
Wide o'er the world, while genius unconfin'd
Tempts happier flights, and opens all the mind,

                                        Diffolves

Diffolves the flavifh bands of monkifh lore,
Awakes the arts, and bids the Mufes foar.   60
Then fhall thy northern climes their charms difplay,
United nations there commence their fway;
O'er the new world exalt their peerlefs fame,
And pay juft tribute to thy deathlefs name.

Now caft thine eye o'er Europe's various coaft;   65
See factions wild their inland booty boaft;
The naked harbours, looking to the main,
Rear their kind cliffs and break the winds in vain,
The lab'ring tide no foreign treafures lade,
Nor fails nor cities caft a watery fhade;   70
Save, where yon opening gulph the ftrand divides,
Proud Venice bathes her in the broken tides,
Beholds her fcattering barks around her ftrown,
And, fovereign, deems the watery world her own.

But the firm bondage of the flavifh mind   75
Spreads deeper glooms, and fubjugates mankind;
The zealots fierce, whom local faiths enrage,
In caufelefs ftrife perpetual combat wage,
Support all crimes by full indulgence given,
Ufurp the power and wield the fword of Heaven.   80
But lo, where future years their fcenes unroll,
The rifing arts infpire the vent'rous foul.

Behold,

Behold, from all the opening ports of Spain,
New fleets afcending on the weftern main ;
From Tagus' banks, from Albion's rocky round,   85
Increafing fquadrons o'er the billows bound ;
Thro' Afric's ifles, obferve the fweeping fails,
Full pinions toffing in Arabian gales ;
Indus and Ganges, deep in canvafs, loft,
And navies crouding round each orient coaft ;   90
New nations rife, all climes and oceans brave,
And fhade with fheets th' immeafurable wave
See lofty Ximenes, with folemn gait,
Move from the cloifter to the walks of ftate,
And thro' the wafted realms of factious Spain,   95
Curb the fierce lords, and fix the royal reign.
Behold, dread Charles th' imperial feat afcends,
O'er Europe's climes his conquering arm extends ;
While wealthier fhores, beneath the weftern day,
Unfold their treafures and enlarge his fway.   100
See the brave Francis bear his banners round,
To guard the realms and give his rival bound ;
With equal zeal for boundlefs power contend,
Of arms the patron, and of arts the friend.
And fee proud Wolfey rife, fecurely great,   105
Kings at his call, and mitres round him wait ;

From monkifh walls, the hoards of wealth he draws,
To aid the tyrant and reftrain the laws,
Wakes Albion's genius, abler monarchs braves,
And fhares with them the empire of the waves.   110
Behold dark Solyman, from eaftern fkies,
With his grim hoft magnificently rife,
Extend his limits o'er the Midland fea,
And tow'rd Germania drive his conquering way,
Frown o'er the Chriftian powers with haughty air,   115
And teach the nations how to lead the war.
While powerful Leo wakes a nobler ftrife,
And, generous, calls the finer arts to life ;
New walls and ftruclures throng the Latian fhore,
The Pencil triumphs and the Mufes foar.   120
Snatch'd from the ground, where Gothic rage had trod,
And monks and prelates held their drear abode,
The Roman ftatues rife ; and wake to view
The fame bold tafte their ancient glory knew.

     O'er the dark world Erafmus cafts his eye,   125
·In fchoolmen's lore fees kings and nations lie,
With ftrength of judgment and with fancy warm,
Derides their follies, and diffolves the charm,
Draws the deep veil, that bigot zeal has thrown
O'er pagan books, and fcience long unknown,   130

K

From

From faith of pageant rites relieves mankind,
And feats bold virtue in the confcious mind.
But ftill the daring tafk, to brave alone
The rifing vengeance of the papal throne,
Reftrains his toil : he gives the conteft o'er,   135
And leaves his hardier fons to meet the threat'ning power;

See Luther rife in yon majeftic frame,
Fair light of heav'n, and child of deathlefs fame,
Born, like thyfelf, thro' toils and griefs to wind,
From flavery's chains to free the captive mind,   140
Brave adverfe realms, controul the papal fway,
And bring benighted nations into day.

And mark what crowds, his fame around him brings,
Schools, fynods, prelates, potentates, and kings,
All gaining knowledge from his boundlefs ftore,   145
And join'd to fhield him from the rage of power !

Firft of his friends, fee * Frederic's princely form
Ward from the fage divine the gathering ftorm ;
In learned Wittemburgh fecure his feat,
Where arts and virtues find a blcft retreat.   150

* Frederic of Saxony, furnamed *the wife*, was the firft fovereign prince who favoured the doctrines of Luther. He
became at once his pupil and his patron, defended him from the
perfecutions of the pope, and gave him an eftablifhment in the
univerfity of Wittemburgh.

There

There moves Melanchthon, mild as morning light,
And rage and strife are soften'd in his sight;
In terms so gentle flows his tuneful tongue,
Ev'n cloister'd bigots join the listening throng;
By foes and infidels he lives approv'd,   155
By monarchs courted, * and by Heav'n belov'd.
With stern deport, o'er all the circling band,
See Osiander lift his waving hand;
On others' faults he casts a haughty frown,
Nor their's will pardon, nor perceive his own;   160
A heart sincere his open looks unfold,
In virtue faithful, and in action bold.

   And lo, where Europe's utmost limits bend,
From this mild source what various lights ascend!

* Francis I, out of respect to the great learning and modera-
tion of Melanchthon, and disregarding the pretended danger of
discussing the dogmas of the church, invited him to come to
France and establish himself at Paris; but the intrigues of the
cardinal of Tournon prevented the king's intention from taking
effect.

If every leader of religious sects had possessed the amiable
qualities of Melanchthon, and every monarch who wished to
oppose the introduction of new opinions had partook of the
wisdom of Francis, the blood of many hundreds of millions of
the human species, which has flowed at the shrine of fanaticism,
would have been spared. This circumstance alone would have
made of human society by this time a state totally different from
what it is at present; and its influence on the progress of improvement in national happiness would have been beyond our
calculation.

K 2

See

See haughty Henry, from the papal tie   165
His realms difmember, and the power defy ;
While Albion's fons difdain a foreign throne,
And bravely bound th' oppreffion of his own.

There ftarts fierce Loyola, an unknown name,
By paths unfeen to reach the goal of fame;   170
Thro' courts and camps, by fecret fkill, to wind,
To mine whole ftates and over-reach mankind.
Train'd to his lore, a bold and artful race,
Range thro' the world, and every fect embrace;
All creeds, and powers, and policies explore,   175
Their feats of fcience raife on every fhore,
Till a wide empire gains a wond'rous birth,
Built in all empires o'er the peopled earth.
Led by thy followers to the weftern day,
O'er native tribes they form a fov'reign fway,   180
Where Paraguay's mild realms their wealth increafe,
And happy millions learn the arts of peace.

Thus all the race of men, beneath thy view,
Improve their ftate and nobler toils purfue ;
Unwonted deeds, in rival greatnefs, fhine,   185
Call'd into life, and firft infpir'd by thine.
So, while imperial Homer tunes the lyre,
The living lays unnumber'd bards infpire,

From

From realm to realm the kindling fpirit flies,
Sounds thro' the earth and echoes to the fkies.   190
   Now move, in rapid hafte, the years of time,
When, borne afar from Europe's cultur'd clime,
Thy fav'rite fons fhall reach the weftern ftrand,
Where a new empire waits their forming hand.
To fpeed their courfe, the fons of bigot rage,   195
In perfecution whelm th' enquiring age;
Millions of martyr'd heroes mount the pyre,
And blind devotion lights the facred fire.
Led by the dark Inquifitors' of Spain,
See defolation mark her dreary reign!   200
See Jews and Moors, that crowd the fatal ftrand,
Roll in the flames, or flee the hated land!
See, arm'd with power, the fame tribunal rife,
Where haplefs Belgia's fruitful circuit lies;
What wreaths of fmoke roll heavy round the fhore!   205
What fhrines and altars flow with Chriftian gore!
Where the flames open, lo! their arms, in vain,
Reach out for help, diftorted with the pain!
Till, folded in the fires, they difappear,
And not a found invades the ftartled ear.   210
See Philip, thron'd in infolence and pride,
Enjoy their wailings, and their pangs deride;

K 3

While,

While, scattering death round Albion's crimson isles,
O'er the same scenes his cruel consort smiles.
Amid the strife, a like destruction reigns,   215
With wider sweep, o'er Gallia's fatal plains;
There factious nobles pour the slaughtering tide,
Grim death unites whom sacred creeds divide;
Each dreadful victor bids the flames arise,
And waft a thousand murders to the skies.   220

    Now cease the factions, with the Valois line,
And the great Bourbon's liberal virtues shine;
Quell'd by his voice, the furious sects accord,
And distant empires tremble at his sword.
Britannia smiling views, with glad surprise,   225
A rival reign, in blest Eliza, rise;
While Belgia's hosts to independence soar,
And curb the vengeance of th' Iberian power.

    Now from all realms, where shaded plains extend,
See the bent forests to the shores descend.   230
From Albion's strand, behold the navies heave,
Stretch in a line, and thunder o'er the wave;
There toils brave Howard, master of the main,
And moves in triumph o'er the force of Spain.

    The Seraph spoke; when fair beneath their eye,   235
A new form'd squadron rose along the sky;

High

High on the tallest deck majeſtic ſhone
Great Raleigh, pointing tow'rd the weſtern ſun;
His eye, bent forward, ardent and ſublime,
Seem'd piercing nature and evolving time;   240
Beſide him ſtood a globe, whoſe figures trac'd
A future empire in each wilder'd waſte;
All former works of men behind him ſhone,
Grav'd by his hand in ever-during ſtone;
On his mild brow a various crown diſplays   245
The hero's laurel and the ſcholar's bays;
His graceful limbs in ſteely mail were dreſt,
The bright ſtar burning on his manly breaſt;
His ſword high-beaming, like a waving ſpire,
Illum'd the ſhrouds and flaſh'd the ſolar fire;   250
The ſmiling crew roſe reſolute and brave,
And the glad ſails hung bounding o'er the wave.

Far on the main they held their rapid flight,
And weſtern coaſts ſalute their longing ſight:
Glad Cheſapeak unfolds a paſſage wide,   255
And leads their ſtreamers up the freſh'ning tide;
Where a mild region and delightful ſoil,
And groves and ſtreams, allure the ſteps of toil.
Here, lodg'd in peace, they tread the welcome land,
An inſtant harveſt waves beneath their hand,   260

K 4   Spontaneous

Spontaneous fruits their eafy cares beguile,
And op'ning fields in living culture fmile.

   With joy Colombus view'd ; when thus his voice :
Ye beauteous fhores and generous hofts, rejoice !
Here ftretch the water'd plains and midland tide,   265
And nature blooms in all her virgin pride ;
And now the years advance, fo long foretold,
When the deep wilds their promis'd change behold,
Be thou, my Seer, the people's guardian friend,
Protect their virtues, and their lives defend ;   270
May wealth and wifdom, with their arts, unfold,
Yet fave, oh, fave them from the thirft of gold !
May the poor natives, round the guardlefs climes,
Ne'er feel their rage, nor groan beneath their crimes ;
But learn the various bleffings, that extend,   275
Where civil rights and focial virtues blend,
In thefe brave leaders find a welcome guide,
And rear their fanes and empires by their fide.
Smile, happy region, fmile ; the ftar of morn
Illumes thy heav'ns, and bids thy day be born ;   280
Thy op'ning forefts fhow the work begun,
Thy plains, unfhaded, drink a purer fun ;
Unwonted navies on thy currents glide,
And new-found treafures roll on every tide ;

                        Yield

Yield now thy bounties, load the distant main,   285
Give birth to nations, and begin thy reign.

   The Hero spoke ; when thus the Power rejoin'd,
Approv'd his joy, and feasted still his mind :—
To thy warm wish, beneath these opening skies,
The pride of earth-born empires soon shall rise.   290
My powerful arm, to which the task was given,
On this fair globe to work the will of Heaven,
To rear the mountain, spread the subject plain,
Lead the long stream, and roll the billowy main,
In every clime prepar'd the seats of state,   295
Design'd their limits and prescrib'd their date.
To meet these tides, I stretch'd the level strand,
Heav'd the green banks, and taught the groves to stand,
Strow'd the wild fruitage, gave the beasts their place,
And form'd the region for thy kindred race.   300
At nature's birth when first the watery round,
And solid lands their blending borders found ;
Back to those distant hills, whose vapour shrouds,
A reek-rais'd world in Alleganian clouds,
Th'Atlantic wave its coral kingdoms spread,   305
And scaly nations here their gambols led.
By slow degrees, thro' following years of time,
I bar'd these realms * and rais'd the sedgy clime ;

   * Among the various mutations, which appear to have taken
place in different parts of the earth, the formation of the coast
                                                            of

As, from retiring feas, the rifing fand
Stole into light, and gently drew to land.   310
   Mov'd by the winds, that fweep the flaming zone,
The waves roll weftward with the conftant fun,
Meet the firm Ifthmus, fcoop that gulphy bed,
Wheel tow'rd the north, and here their currents fpread.
Thofe ravag'd banks, that move beneath their force,   315
Borne on the tide and loft along the courfe,
Have form'd this beauteous fhore, by Heav'n defign'd
The happieft empire that awaits mankind.
   Think not the luft of gold fhall here annoy,
Enflave the nations, and the race deftroy.   320
No ufelefs mine thefe northern hills enclofe,
No ruby ripens, and no diamond glows;

of North-America by the gulph-ftream, is one of the moft remarkable. The rifing of fand-banks, which are perpetually
increafing along the fhores of Virginia and the Carolinas—the
layers of fea-fhells and pieces of wood, which are found at the
depth of forty or fifty feet below the furface, at the diftance of
a hundred miles from the fea, in the middle and fouthern
States—the level and uniform appearance of the country, from
New-Jerfey to Faft-Florida—and the vaft cavity which appears
to have been fcooped out of the earth, to form the gulph of
Mexico, are circumftances which eftablifh the above as an un-
doubted faft. It is evident, that, not only the ifland of New-
foundland, Cape-Cod, &c. but the greater part of the fettled
country, from the river Delaware to Cape St. Auguftine, is an
accretion of earth, worn off from the Ifthmus of Darien, and
brought hither by that ftrong current of water which follows the
trade winds; and, which, meeting the obftruction of the
Ifthmus, takes a northern direction, and fweeps the coaft as
far as the river St. Laurence.

                          But

But richer ftores, and rocks of ufeful mould,
Repay, in wealth, the penury of gold.
Freedom's unconquer'd fons, with healthy toil,   325
Shall lop the grove, and warm the furrow'd foil,
From iron ridges break the rugged ore,
And plant with men the man-enobling fhore ;
While fails, and towers, and temples round them heave,
Shine o'er the realms, and fhade the diftant wave.   330
Nor think the native tribes, thefe wilds that trace,
A foe fhall find in this exalted race ;
In fouls like theirs, no mean ungenerous aim
Can fhade their glories with the deeds of fhame ;
Nor low deceit, weak mortals to enfnare,   335
Nor bigot zeal to urge the barb'rous war.
From eaftern tyrants driv'n, and nobly brave,
To build new ftates, or feek a diftant grave,
The generous hoft with proffer'd leagues of peace,
Approach thefe climes, and hail the favage race ;   340
Pay the juft purchafe for th'uncultur'd fhore,
Diffufe their arts, and fhare the friendly power ;
While the dark tribes in focial aid combine,
Exchange their treafures and their joys refine.

   O'er Europe's wilds, when firft the nations fpread,   345
The pride of conqueft every legion led.

Each powerful chief, by servile crowds ador'd,
O'er conquer'd realms assum'd the name of lord,
Built the proud castle, rang'd the savage wood,
Fir'd his grim host to frequent fields of blood,   350
With new-made honours lur'd his subject bands,
Price of their lives, and purchase of their lands;
For names and titles bade the world resign
Their faith, their freedom, and their rights divine.

Thus haughty baronies their terrors spread,   355
And slavery follow'd where the standard led;
Till, little tyrants by the great o'erthrown,
Contending nobles give the regal crown;
Wealth, wisdom, virtue, every claim of man,
Unguarded fall to form the finish'd plan: 360
Ambitious cares, that nature never gave,
Warm the starv'd peasant, fire the sceptred slave;
Thro' all degrees, in gradual pomp, ascend,
Honour, the name, and Tyranny, the end.

But nobler honours here the breast inflame;   365
Sublimer views, and deeds of happier fame;
A new creation waits the western shore,
And reason triumphs o'er the pride of power.
Thy free-born sons, with genius unconfin'd,
Nor sloth can poison, nor a tyrant bind;   370

With

With felf-wrought fame and worth internal bleft,
No venal ftar fhall brighten on their breaft ;
No king-created name or courtly art
Damp the bold thought, or fway the changing heart.
Above all fraud, beyond all titles great,   375
Heav'n in their foul, and fceptres at their feet,
Like fires of unborn realms, they move fublime,
Look empires thro', and pierce the veil of time,
Hold o'er the world, that men may choofe from far
The palm of peace, or fcourge of barb'rous war ;   380
Till arts and laws in one great fyftem bind,
By leagues of peace, the labours of mankind.
    But flow proceeds the plan.   Long toils remain,
Ere thy bleft children can begin their reign.
That daring leader, whofe exalted foul   385
Pervades all fcenes that future years unroll,
Muft yeild the palm ; and at a courtier's fhrine,
His fame, his freedom, and his life refign.
That feeble train, the lonely wilds who tread,
Their fire, their genius, in their Raleigh dead,   390
Shall pine and perifh in the frowning gloom,
Or mount the wave and feek their ancient home.
Succeeding hofts in vain the tafk purfue,
The dangers tempt, and all the ftrife renew ;

While

While kings and courtiers still neglect the plan,   395
The slaves of ease and enemies of man.

At last brave Delaware his hardy host
Leads in full triumph to the well-known coast,
Aids with a liberal hand the patriot cause,
Begins the culture, and defigns their laws ;   400
Till o'er Virginia's plains they fix their sway,
And spread their hamlets tow'rd the setting day.

While impious Laud, on England's wasted shore,
Renews the flames that Mary rear'd before,
Unnumber'd fects his sullen fury fly,   405
To feek new seats beneath another sky ;
Where faith and freedom spread th'alluring charm,
And toils and dangers every bosom warm.
Amid th'unconquer'd, venerable train,
Whom tyrants press and seas oppose in vain,   410
See virtuous Baltimore ascend the wave,
See heav'n-taught Penn its unknown terrors brave,
Sweeds, Belgians, Gauls, their various flags display,
Full pinions crowding on the watery way ;
All from their diff'rent shores, their fails unfurl'd,   415
Point their glad streamers to the western world

THE

THE
VISION of COLUMBUS.

BOOK V.

ARGUMENT.

Vision confined to North America. Progress of the settlements. General invasion of the natives. Their defeat. Settlement of Canada. Invasion of the French. Braddock's defeat. Washington saves the English army. Actions of Abercrombie, Amherst, and Wolfe. Peace. Darkness overshades the continent. Apprehensions of Columbus from that appearance. Cause explained. Cloud bursts away in the centre. View of Congress. Invasion of the English. Conflagration of towns, from Falmouth to Norfolk. Battle of Bunker-hill, viewed through the smoke. American army assembles. Speech of Washington. Actions and death of Montgomery. Actions of Washington. Approach and capture of Burgoyne.

THE
VISION of COLUMBUS.

BOOK V.

COLUMBUS hail'd them with a father's smile,
Fruits of his cares and children of his toil;
With tears of joy while still his eyes descried
Their course advent'rous o'er the distant tide.
Thus, when o'er delug'd earth her Seraph stood,   5
The tost ark bounding on the shoreless flood,
The sacred treasure claim'd his guardian view,
While climes unnotic'd in the wave withdrew.

He saw his fav'rites reach the rising strand,
Leap from the wave, and share the joyous land;   10
Receding forests yield the heroes room,
And opening wilds with fields and gardens bloom.
Fill'd with the glance ecstatic, all his soul
Now seems unbounded with the scene to roll,
And now, impatient, with retorted eye,   15
Perceives his station in another sky :—

L

Waft

Waft me, O winged Angel, waft me o'er,
With those blest heroes, to the happy shore;
There let me live and die!—but all appears
A fleeting vision! these are future years.   20
Yet grant in nearer view the climes may spread,
And my glad steps may seem their walks to tread;
While eastern coasts and kingdoms, wrapp'd in night,
Arise no more to intercept the sight.

The hero spoke; the Angel's powerful hand   25
Moves bright'ning o'er the visionary land;
The height, that bore them, still sublimer grew,
And earth's whole circuit settled from their view :
A dusky deep, serene as breathless even,
Seem'd vaulting downward like another heaven ;   30
The sun, rejoicing on his western way,
Stamp'd his fair image in th'inverted day :
When now th' Atlantic shores arose more nigh,
And life and action fill'd the Hero's eye.
Where the dread Laurence breaks his passage wide,   35
Where Missisippi's milder currents glide,
Where midland realms their swelling mountains heave,
And slope their champaigns to the distant wave,
On the green banks, and o'er the woodland plain,
Move into sight the happiest walks of man.   40

The

The placid ports, that break the billowing gales,
Rear their tall masts and stretch their whitening sails;
Full harvests wave, the groves with fruitage bend,
And bulwarks heave, and spiry domes ascend;
All the rich works of peace in splendor rise,   45
And grateful earth repays the bounteous skies.
Till war invades; when opening vales disclose,
In moving crowds, the savage tribes of foes;
High-tufted quills their painted foreheads press,
Dark spoils of beasts their shaggy shoulders dress,   50
The bow bent forward, for the combat strung,
The ax, the quiver, on the girdle hung;
The deep discordant yells convulse the air,
And the wild waste resounds approaching war.

    The Hero look'd; and every darken'd height   55
Pours down the dusky squadrons to the fight.
Where Kennebec's high source forsakes the sky,
Where deep Champlain's extended waters lie,
Where the bold Hudson leads his strad'wy tide,
Where Kaatskill-heights the azure vault divide,   60
Where the dim Alleganies range sublime,
And give their streams to every distant clime,
The swarms descended, like an evening shade,
And wolves and vultures follow'd where they spread.

L 2

Thus when a ftorm, on eaftern pinions driven,   65
Meets the firm Andes in the midft of heaven,
The clouds convulfe, the torrents pour amain,
And the black waters fweep the fubject plain.

   Thro' cultur'd fields the bloody myriads fpread,
Sack the lone village, ftrow the ftreets with dead;   70
The flames afpire, the fmoky volumes rife,
And fhrieks and fhouts redouble round the fkies;
Fair babes and matrons in their domes expire,
Or burft their paffage thro' the folding fire;
O'er woods and plains promifcuous rave along   75
The yelling victors and the driven throng;
The ftreams run purple; all the peopled fhore
Is wrapp'd in flames and trod with fteps of gore.
Till numerous hofts, collecting from afar,
Exalt the ftandard and oppofe the war,   80
Point their loud thunders on the fhouting foe,
And brave the fhafted terrors of the bow.
When, like a broken wave, the favage train
Lead back the flight and fcatter o'er the plain,
Slay their weak captives, leave their fhafts in hafte, 85
Forget their fpoils, and fcour the diftant wafte,
From wood to wood in wild confufion hurl'd,
Sweep o'er the heights and lakes, far thro' the wilder'd world.

Now

Now move secure the cheerful toils of peace,
New temples rise and fruitful fields increase.   90
Where Delaware's wide waves behold with pride
Penn's beauteous town ascending on their side,
The crossing streets in just arrangement run,
The walls and pavements sparkle to the sun.
Like that fam'd city rose the beauteous plan,   95
Whose spacious bounds Semiramis beg.n;
Long ages finish'd what her hand design'd,
The pride of kings and wonder of mankind.

Where lab'ring Hudson's glassy current strays,
York's growing walls their splendid turrets raise;   100
Albania towering o'er the distant wood,
Rolls her rich treasures on his parent flood;
Blest in her circling streams young Newport laves,
And Boston opens o'er the subject waves;
On southern shores, where warmer currents glide,   105
The banks bloom gay, and cities grace their side;
Like morning clouds, that tinge their skirts with day,
Bright Charleston's domes their rising roofs display.

Thro' each extended realm, in wisdom great,
Elected sires assume the cares of state;   110
Long robes of purest white their forms infold,
And rights and charters flame in figur'd gold.

L 3   Dispensing

Difpenfing juftice to the train below,
Peace in their voice and firmnefs on their brow,
They ftretch o'er all the fame paternal hand,   115
Drive titled flavery from the joyous land,
Bid arts and culture, wealth and wifdom, rife,
Friends of mankind and fav'rites of the fkies.

   Now round the glade where lordly Laurence ftrays,
Great Gallia's fons their forts & villas raife,   120
Thro' cold Canadia ftretch a growing fway,
And, circling far beneath the weftern day,
Bid Louifania's milder clime prepare
New arts to prove, and infant ftates to rear;
While the far lakes, that thro' the midland fpread,   125
Unfold their channels to the paths of trade,
Ohio's wave its deftin'd honours claim,
And fmile, as confcious of approaching fame.

   But foon their warlike barks arife in fight,
White flags difplay'd, and armies rob'd in white,   130
Through midland wilds extend their toils afar,
And threat th' Atlantic realms with wafting war.
Where proud Quebec exalts her rocky feat,
They range their camp and fpread the frowning fleet,
Ofwego rifes o'er his frighted flood,   135
And wild Ontario fwells beneath his load.

And

And now a friendly hoft, from Albion's ftrand,
Arrives to aid the young colonial band;
They join their force; and, tow'rd the falling day,
Impetuous Braddock leads their dreadful way;   140
O'er Allegany-heights, like ftreams of fire,
The red flags wave and glittering arms afpire,
To meet the favage hordes, who there advance,
Their wafting bands to join the arms of France.

Near broad Ohio, where, its flag unfurl'd,   145
A Gallic fortrefs awes the weftern world,
The Britons bend their march; the hofts within
Behold their danger, and the ftrife begin.
From the full burfling gates the fweeping train,
Pour forth the war and hide the founding plain;   150
The batteries blaze, the moving volleys pour,
The fhuddering vales and echoing mountains roar;
Clouds of convolving fmoke the welkin fpread,
The champaign fhrouding in fulphurious fhade.
Loft in the rocking thunder's loud career,   155
No fhouts or groans invade the Hero's ear,
Nor val'rous feats are feen, nor flight, nor fall;
While deep-furrounding darknefs buries all.

'Till, driv'n by rifing winds, the clouds withdrew;
The fpreading flaughter open'd to his view.   160

L 4

He

He saw the British leader borne afar,
In dust and gore, beyond the wings of war ;
Saw the long ranks of foes his host surround,
His chiefs confus'd, his squadrons press the ground ;
As, hemm'd on every side, the trembling train,   165
Nor dare the fight, nor can they flee the plain.
But, while conflicting tumult thinn'd the host,
Their flags, their arms, in wild confusion tost,
Bold in the midst a blooming warrior strode,
And tower'd undaunted o'er the field of blood,   170
In desp'rate toils, with rising vengeance burn'd,
And the pale Britons brighten'd where he turn'd.
So, when thick vapours veil the evening sky,
And starry hosts in half-seen lustre fly,
Bright Hesper shines o'er all the twinkling crowd,   175
And gives new splendor thro' the opening cloud.
    Fair on a fiery steed sublime he rose,
Wedg'd the firm files to pierce the line of foes ;
Then wav'd his gleamy sword, that flash'd the day,
And thro' dread legions hew'd the rapid way :   180
His hosts roll forward, like an angry flood,
Sweep ranks away, and smear their paths in blood ;
The hovering foes pursue the strife afar,
And shower their balls along the flying war ;

                                        When

When the brave leader turns his sweeping force,   185
Points the flight forward, speeds his backward course;
The French fly scattering where his arm is wheel'd,
And the glad Britons quit the fatal field.

   While these fierce toils the pensive chief descried,
With anxious thought he thus address'd the Guide:—
Why combat here the trans-atlantic bands,
And strow their corses o'er these pathless lands?
Can Europe's realms, the seat of endless strife,
Afford no trophies for the waste of life!
Can monarchs there no proud applauses gain,   195
No living laurel for their subjects slain?
Nor Belgia's plains, so fertile made with gore,
Hide heroes' bones nor feast the vultures more;
Danube and Rhine no more their currents stain,
Nor sweep the slaughter'd myriads to the main,   200
That infant empires here the rage must feel,
And these pure streams with foreign carnage swell?

   The Power reply'd:—In each successive age,
Their different views thy varying race engage.
Here roll the years, when Albion's parent hand,   205
Leagu'd with thy children, guards th' invaded land;
That growing states their veteran force may train,
And nobler toils in later fields sustain,

When

When foes more furious cross the well-known wave,
The realms to ravage and the race enslave.   210
Here toils dread Albion with the sons of Gaul;
Here hapless Braddock finds his destin'd fall;
Brave Washington, in that young martial frame,
From yon lost field begins a life of fame.
'Tis he, in future strife and darker days,   215
Desponding states to sovereign rule shall raise,
When the weak empire in his arm, shall find
The sword, the shield, the bulwark of mankind.

    The Seraph spoke; when thro' the purpled air
The northern armies spread the flames of war: 220
O'er dim Champlain, and thro' surrounding groves,
Rash Abercrombie, mid his thousands, moves
To fierce unequal strife; the batteries roar,
Shield the strong foes, and rake the banner'd shore;
Britannia's troops again the contest yield,   225
And heaps of carnage strow the fatal field.

    But happier Amherst, on Acadia's isle,
Leads a bold squadron, and renews the toil;
Young Wolfe, beside him, points the lifted lance,
The boast of Albion and the scourge of France.   230
The tide of vict'ry here the heroes turn,
And Gallic navies in their harbours burn;

High

High flame the ships, the billows swell with gore,
And the red standard shades the conquer'd shore.

    And lo, a British host, unbounded spread,   235
O'er sea-like Laurence, casts a moving shade ;
They stem the lessening tide ; till Abr'ham's height
And dread Quebec rose frowning into sight.
They tread the shore, the arduous conflict claim,
Rise the tall mountain, like a rolling flame,   240
Stretch their wide wings in circling onset far,
And move to fight, as clouds of heav'n at war.
The smoke falls folding thro' the downward sky,
And shrouds the mountain from the Hero's eye ;
While on the burning top, in open day,   245
The flashing swords, in fiery arches, play.
As on a ridgy storm, in terrors driven,
The forky flames curl round the vault of heaven,
The thunders break, the burstling torrents flow,
And flood the air, and whelm the hills below ;   250
Or, as on plains of light, when Michael strove,
And swords of Cherubim to combat move ;
Ten thousand fiery forms together play,
And flash new lightning on empyreal day.

    Long rag'd promiscuous combat, half conceal'd,   255
When sudden parle suspended all the field ;

                                        Thick

Thick groans fucceed, the fmoke forfakes the plain,
And the high hill is topp'd with heaps of flain.
Now, proud in air, the Britifh ftandard wav'd,
And fhouting hofts proclaim'd a country fav'd ;   260
While, calm and filent, where the ranks retire,
He faw brave Wolfe, in pride of youth, expire.
So the pale moon, when morning beams arife,
Veils her lone vifage in the-filent fkies ;
Requir'd no more to drive the fhades away,   265
Nor waits to view the glories of the day.

    Again the towns afpire, the cultur'd field
And blooming vale their copious treafures yield ;
The grateful hind his cheerful labour proves,
And fongs of triumph fill the warbling groves ;   270
The confcious flocks, returning joys that fhare,
Spread thro' the midland, o'er the walks of war :
When, borne on eaftern winds, dark vapours rife,
And fail and lengthen round the weftern fkies,
Veil all the vifion from the hero's fight,   275
And wrap the climes in univerfal night.

    Columbus griev'd, and thus befought the Power :—
Why finks the fcene ? or muft I view no more ?
Muft here the fame of that fair world defcend,
And my brave children find fo foon their end ?   280

                                              Where

Where then the word of Heaven, "thy foul fhall fee
" That half mankind fhall owe their blifs to thee ?"
    The Power replied :—Ere long, in happier view,
The realms fhall brighten, and thy joys renew.
The years advance, when, round the thronging fhore,   285
They rife confus'd to change the fource of power ;
When Albion's Prince, who fway'd the happy land,
Shall ftret..h, to lawlefs rule, the foveretgn hand ,
To bind in flavery's chains the peaceful hoft,
Their rights unguarded, and their charters loft.   290
Now raife thine eye ; from this delufive claim,
What glorious deeds adorn their growing fame !
    Columbus look'd ; and ftill around them fpread,
From fouth to north, th'immeafurable fhade ;
At laft the central fhadows burft away,   295
And rifing regions open'd on the day.
Once more, bright Delaware's delightful ftream,
And Penn's throng'd city caft a cheerful gleam ;
The dome of ftate, that met his eager eye,
Now heav'd its arches in a loftier fky ;   300
The burfting gates unfold ; and lo, within,
Th' affembled ftates, in youthful glory, fhine.
    High on the foremoft feat, in living light,
Majeftic Randolph caught the Hero's fight :

                                                    He

He opes the caufe, and points in profpect far,   305
Thro' all the toils that wait th'impending war—
But, haplefs fage, thy reign muft foon be o'er,
To lend thy luftre and to fhine no more.
So the bright morning-ftar, from fhades of even,
Leads up the dawn, and lights the front of heaven,   310
Points to the waking world the fun's broad way,
Then veils his own, and fhines above the day.
And fee great Wafhington behind thee rife,
Thy following fun, to gild our morning fkies;
O'er fhadowy climes to pour th' enlivening flame,   315
The charms of freedom and the fire of fame.
For him the patriot bay beheld, with pride,
The hero's laurel fpringing by its fide;
His fword hung ufelefs on his graceful thigh,
On Britain ftill he caft a filial eye;   320
But fovereign fortitude his vifage bore,
To meet their legions on th' invaded fhore.

Sage Franklin next arofe, in cheerful mien,
And fmil'd, unruffled, o'er the folemn fcene;
High on his locks of age a wreath was brac'd,   325
Palm of all arts, that e'er a mortal grac'd;
Beneath him lies the fceptre kings have borne,
And crowns and laurels from their temples torn.

Nafh,

Nash, Rutledge, Jefferson, in council great,
And Jay and Laurens, op'd the rolls of fate ;   330
O'er climes and kingdoms turn'd their ardent eyes,
Bade all th' opprefs'd to fpeedy vengeance rife ;
All powers of ftate, in their extended plan,
Rife from confent, to fhield the rights of man.
Bold Wolcott urg'd the all-important caufe ;   335
With fteady hand the folemn fcene he draws ;
Undaunted firmnefs with his wifdom join'd,
Nor kings nor worlds could warp his ftedfaft mind.

Here, graceful rifing from his purple throne,
In radiant robes, immortal Hofmer fhone ;   340
Morals and laws expand his liberal foul,
Beam from his eyes, and in his accents roll.
But lo, an unfeen hand the curtain drew,
And fnatch'd the patriot from the hero's view ;
Wrapp'd in the fhroud of death, he fees defcend   345
The guide of nations and the Mufes' friend.
Columbus dropp'd a tear ; the Angel's eye
Trac'd the freed fpirit mounting thro' the fky.

Each generous Adams, Freedom's fav'rite pair,
Unfhaken ftood the tyrant's rage to dare ;   350
Each in his hand colonial charters bore,
And lawlefs acts of minifterial power ;

Some

Some injur'd right in every page appears,
A king in terrors and a land in tears;
From all the guileful plots the veil they drew,   355
With eye retortive look'd creation thro',
Op'd the wide range of nature's boundless plan,
Trac'd all the steps of liberty and man;
Crowds rose to vengeance while their accents rung,
And INDEPENDENCE thunder'd from their tongue.   360
     The Hero turn'd.   And tow'rd the crowded coast
Rose on the wave a wide-extended host,
They shade the main and spread their sails abroad,
From the wide Laurence to the Georgian flood,
Point their black batteries to the peopled shore,   365
And bursting flames begin the hideous roar.
Where guardless Falmouth, looking o'er the bay,
Beheld, unmov'd, the stormy thunders play,
The fire begins; the shells o'er-arching fly,
And shoot a thousand rainbows thro' the sky;   370
On Charlestown spires, on Bristol roofs, they light,
Groton and Fairfield kindle from the flight,
Fair Kingston burns, and York's delightful fanes,
And beauteous Norfolk lights the neighb'ring plains,
From realm to realm the smoky volumes bend,   375
Reach round the bays, and up the streams extend;

                                                  Deep

Deep o'er the concave heavy wreaths are roll'd,
And midland towns and diftant groves infold.
Thro' the dark curls of fmoke the winged fires
Climb in tall pyramids above the fpires;   380
Cinders, high-failing, kindle heav'n around,
And falling ftructures fhake the fmouldering ground.

   Now, where the fheeted flames thro' Charleftown roar,
And lafhing waves hifs round the burning fhore,
Thro' the deep folding fires, dread Bunker's height   385
Thunders o'er all and fhows a field of fight.
Like fhad'wy phantoms in an evening grove,
To the dark ftrife the clofing fquadrons move;
They join, they break, they thicken thro' the air,
And blazing batteries burft along the war;   390
Now, wrapp'd in reddening fmoke, now dim in fight,
They fweep the hill or wing the downward flight;
Here, wheel'd and wedg'd, Britannia's veterans turn,
And the long lightnings from their mufquets burn;
There fcattering ftrive the thin colonial train,   395
And broken fquadrons ftill the field maintain;
Britons in frefh battalions rife the height,
And, with increafing vollies, give the fight.
Till, fmear'd with clouds of duft, and bath'd in gore,
As growing foes their rais'd artillery pour,   400

               M   Columbia's

Columbia's hoft moves o'er the field afar,
And faves, by flow retreat, the fad remains of war.
There ftrides bold Putnam, and from all the plains
Calls the tir'd troops, the tardy rear fuftains,
And, mid the whizzing deaths that fill the air,   405
Waves back his fword and dares the foll'wing war.

   Thro' falling fires, Columbus fees remain
Half of each hoft in heaps promifcuos flain ;
While dying crowds the lingering life-blood pour,
And flippery fteeps are trod with prints of gore.   410
There, glorious Warren ! thy cold earth was feen,
There fpring thy laurels in immortal green ;
Deareft of chiefs, that ever prefs'd the plain,
In freedom's caufe, with early honours, flain,
Still dear in death, as when, in fight you mov'd,   415
By hofts applauded, and by Heav'n approv'd ;
The faithful Mufe fhall tell the world thy fame,
And unborn realms refound th' immortal name.

   Now, from all plains, as fmoky wreaths decay,
The free-born myriads ftarted into day ;   420
Tall, thro' the leffening fhadows, half conceal'd,
They throng and gather in a central field ;
There, ftretch'd immenfe, their unform'd fquadrons ftand,
Eye the ftrong foe, and eager ftrife demand.

                                                  In

In front great Wafhington exalted fhone,   425
His eye directed tow'rd the half-feen fun ;
As thro' the mift the burfling fplendors glow,
And light the paffage to the diftant foe.
His waving fteel returns the living day,
Clears the broad plains, and marks the warrior's way ; 430
The forming columns range in order bright,
And move impatient for the promis'd fight.

When great Columbus faw the chief arife,
And his bold blade caft lightning on the fkies,
He trac'd the form that met his view before,   435
On drear Ohio's defolated fhore.
Matur'd with years, with nobler glory warm,
Fate in his eye, and vengeance on his arm,
The great Obferver here with joy beheld
The hero moving in a broader field.   440

There rofe brave Greene, in all the ftrength of arms,
Unmov'd and brightening as the danger warms ;
In counfel great, in every fcience fkill'd,
Pride of the camp and terror of the field.
With eager look, confpicuous o'er the crowd,   445
The daring port of great Montgomery ftrode ;
Bar'd the bright blade, with honour's call elate,
Claim'd the firft field, and haften'd to his fate.

M 2

Calm —

Calm Lincoln next, with unaffected mien,
In dangers daring, active and serene,   450
Carelefs of pomp, with fteady greatnefs fhone,
Sparing of others' blood and liberal of his own.
Heath, for th' impending ftrife, his falchion draws;
And fearlefs Woofter aids the facred caufe.
Mercer advanc'd, an early fate to prove,   455
And Wayne and Mifflin fwift to combat move.
There ftood ftern Putnam, feam'd with many a fcar,
The veteran honours of an earlier war;
Undaunted Stirling, dreadful to his foes,
And Gates and Sullivan to vengeance rofe;   460
While brave M'Dougall, fteady and fedate,
Stretch'd the nerv'd arm to ope the fcene of fate.
Howe mov'd with rapture to the toils of fame,
Laurens adorn'd a father's honour'd name;
Parfons and Smallwood lead their daring bands,   465
St. Clair alert in front of thoufands ftands.
There gallant Knox his moving engines brings,
Mounted and grav'd, * *the laft refort of kings*;

* *Ultima ratio regum*; a device of Louis XIV, engraved on
his ordnance. The fame device has fince been adopted by
other nations. Many pieces of foreign cannon, ufed in America
in the courfe of former wars, had been left in the country at the
conclufion of the laft peace. Thefe compofed the American
                                                    artillery

The long black rows in dreadful order wait,
Their grim jaws gaping, foon to utter fate ;   470
When, at his word, the red-wing'd clouds fhall rife,
And the deep thunders rock the fhores and fkies.
Beneath a waving fword, in blooming prime,
Fayette moves graceful, ardent and fublime ;
In foreign guife, in freedom's noble caufe,   475
His untry'd blade the youthful hero draws ;
On the great chief his eyes in tranfport roll,
And fame and Wafhington infpire his foul.
Steuben advanc'd, in veteran armour dreft,
For Pruffian lore diftinguifh'd o'er the reft ;   480
From rank to rank, in eager hafte, he flew,
And marfhall'd hofts in dread arrangement drew.
Wadfworth, to aid their generous ardour, ftood,
The friend, the patron of the brave and good.
While other chiefs and heirs of deathlefs fame   485
Rife into fight, and equal honours claim ;
But who can tell the dew-drops of the morn ?
Or count the rays that in the diamond burn ?

  Now, the broad field as untry'd warriors fhade,
The fun's glad beam their fhining ranks difplay'd ;   490

artillery at the commencement of the war of Independence;
which accounts for the circumftance of this device being found
on the cannon of a republican army.

M 3   The

The glorious Leader wav'd his glittering steel,
Bade the long train in circling order wheel ;
And, while the banner'd hoft around him prefs'd,
With patriot ardour thus the ranks addrefs'd :—

    Ye generous bands, behold the tafk to fave,   495
Or yield whole nations to an inftant grave.
See headlong myriads crowding to your fhore,
Hear, from all ports, their boafted thunders roar ;
From Charleftown-heights their bloody ftandards play,
O'er far Champlain they lead their northen way,   500
Virginian banks behold their ftreamers glide,
And hoftile navies load each fouthern tide.
Beneath their fteps your towns in afhes lie,
Your inland empires feaft their greedy eye ;
Soon fhall your fields to lordly parks be turn'd,   505
Your children butcher'd, and your villas burn'd ;
While following millions, thro' the reign of time,
Who claim their birth in this indulgent clime,
Bend the weak knee, to fervile toils confign'd,
And floth and flavery overwhelm mankind.   510
Rife then to war, to noble vengeance rife,
Ere the grey fire, the helplefs infant dies ;
Look thro' the world where endlefs years defcend,
What realms, what ages on your arms depend !

Reverfe

Reverſe the fate, avenge th' inſulted ſky ;   515
Move to the ſtrife—we conquer or we die.
    So ſpoke the chief; and with his guiding hand
Points the quick toil to each ſurrounding band.
At once the different lines are wheel'd afar,
In different realms, to meet the gathering war.   520
    With his young hoſt Montgomery iſſues forth,
And lights his paſſage thro' the duſky north ;
O'er ſtreams and lakes his conqu'ring banners play,
Navies and forts, ſurrend'ring, mark his way ;
Thro' deſert wilds, o'er rocks and fens, they go,   525
And hills before them loſe their crags in ſnow ;
Unbounded toils they brave ; when riſe in ſight
Quebec's dread walls, and Wolfe's ſtill cheerleſs height ;
With ſkillful glance he eyes the turrets round,
Briſtled with pikes, with dark artillery crown'd,   530
Reſolves with naked ſteel to ſcale the towers,
And ſnatch a realm from Britain's hoſtile powers.
    Now drear December's boreal blaſts ariſe,
A roaring hail-ſtorm ſwept the ſhuddering ſkies,
Night with condenſing horrors ſhroudcd all,   535
And trembling watch-lights glimmer'd from the wall.
He points th' aſſault, and thro' the howling air,
O'er rocky ramparts leads the dreadful war.

M 4

Swift

Swift rife the rapid hoft ; the walls are red
With flafhing flames ; down roll the heaps of dead.   540
Till back recoiling from the ranks of flain,
They leave their leader with a feeble train,
Begirt with foes within the founding wall,
While round his arm fucceffive Britons fall ;
But fhort the ftrife ; new fquadrons gather'd round,   545
And brave Montgomery preft the gory ground.
Another Wolfe Columbus here beheld,
In youthful charms, a foul undaunted yield ;
While loft, o'erpower'd, his hardy hoft remains,
Stretch'd by his fide, or led in captive chains.   550
    And now the Angel turn'd the Hero's eye,
To other realms, where other ftandards fly ;
Where Wafhington amid furrounding foes,
Still greater rifes as the danger grows ;
And wearied ranks, o'er welt'ring warriors flain,   555
Attend his courfe thro' many a crimfon'd plain.
From Hudfon's banks to Trenton's dreary ftrand,
He guards in firm retreat his feeble band ;
While countlefs foes with Britifh Howe advance,
Bend o'er his rear, and point the lifted lance ;   560
O'er Del'ware's frozen wave, with fcanty force,
He lifts the fword, and points the backward courfe,

Wings

Wings the dire vengeance on the shouting train,
And leads whole squadrons in the captive chain ;
Where vaunting foes to half their numbers yield,   565
Tread back the flight, or press the fatal field,
Twas there in furious strife, brave Mercer strode,
And seal'd the vict'ry with his streaming blood.

Where the broad Laurence mingles with the main,
Rose into sight a wide extended train :   570
From shore to shore, along th' unfolding skies,
Beneath full sails, imbanded nations rise ;
Britain and Brunswick here their flags unfold ;
Here, Heffia's hordes, for toils of slaughter sold,
Hibernian hosts and Hanoverian slaves,   575
Move o'er the decks and shade the conscious waves.
Tall, on the boldest bark, superior shone,
A warrior, ensign'd with a various crown ;
Myrtles and laurels equal honours join'd,
Which arms had purchas'd and the Muses twin'd ;   580
His sword wav'd forward, and his ardent eye
Seem'd sharing empires in the southern sky.
Beside him rose a herald, to proclaim
His various honours, titles, feats, and fame ;
Who rais'd an op'ning scroll, where proudly shone   585
Burgoyne and vengeance from the British throne.

Champlain

Champlain receives the congregated hoſt,
And his dark waves, beneath the ſails, are loſt;
St. Clair beholds; and, with his feeble train,
In firm retreat, o'er many a fatal plain,   590
Lures their wild march.—Wide moves their furious ſorce,
And flaming hamlets mark their waſting courſe;
Thro' pathleſs realms their ſpreading ranks are wheel'd
O'er Mohawk's weſtern wave and Bennington's dread field;
Till, where deep Hudſon's winding waters ſtray,   595
A yeoman hoſt oppos'd their rapid way;
There on a towery height brave Gates aroſe,
Wav'd the blue ſteel and dar'd the headlong foes;
Undaunted Lincoln, moving at his ſide,
Urg'd the dread ſtrife, and ſwell'd the ſlaughtering tide. 600
Now roll, like winged ſtorms, the lengthening lines,
The clarion thunders and the battle joins;
Thick flames, in vollied flaſhes, fill the air,
And ſhuddering mountains give the noiſe of war;
Sulphurious clouds riſe reddening round the height,   605
And veil the ſkies and wrapt the ſounding fight.
Now, in the ſkirt of ſmoke where thouſands toil,
Ranks roll away and into light recoil;
The rout increaſes, all the Britiſh train
Tread back their ſteps and ſcatter o'er the plain;   610

To

To the glad holds precipitate retire,
And wide behind them streams the flashing fire.
  Scarce mov'd the smoke above the gory height,
And op'd the slaughter to the Hero's fight;
Back to their fate, when baffled squadrons flew,   615
Refum'd their rage, and pour'd the strife anew;
Again the batteries roar, the lightnings play,
Again they fall, again they roll away.
And now Columbia, circling round the field,
Points her full force—Britannia's thousands yield;   620
When bold Burgoyne, in one disastrous day,
Sees future crowns and former wreaths decay;
While two illustrious armies shade the plain,
The mighty victors and the captive train.

ARGUMENT.

Coast of France rises in Vision. Louis, to humble the British power, forms an alliance with the American states. This brings France, Spain, and Holland into the war, and rouses Hyder Ally to attack the English in India. The Vision returns to America, where the military operations continue with various success. Battle of Monmouth. Actions of Lincoln. Movements of Cornwallis. Actions of Greene. French army arrives, and joins the American. They march and besiege the English army under Cornwallis in York-town. Naval action of De Grasse and Graves. Capture of the English army.

THE
VISION OF COLUMBUS.

BOOK VI.

THUS view'd the Sage; when, lo, in eastern skies,
From glooms unfolding Gallia's coasts arise.
Bright o'er the scenes of state a golden throne,
Instarr'd with gems and hung with purple, shone;
Young Bourbon there in sovereign splendor sate,   5
And fleets and moving armies round him wait.
For now the contest, with increas'd alarms,
Fill'd every clime, and rous'd the world to arms;
While Heav'n's high will, that light from darkness brings,
And good to nations from the scourge of kings,   10
In this dread hour bade all the plan unfold,
And the new world illuminate the old.
   Thro' Europe's realms unnumber'd sages trace
Th' expanding dawn that waits the reas'ning race;
O'er western climes they turn their ardent eyes,   15
Thro' glorious toils where struggling nations rise;

Where

Where each firm deed, each new illuſtrious name
Calls into light a field of nobler fame.
They mark beyond, thro' wilder'd walks of day,
Where abſent ſuns their unknown beams diſplay,   20
What fires of unborn nations claim their birth,
And aſk their empires in that waſte of earth.
While o'er the eaſtern world, with painful eye,
In ſlavery ſunk they ſee the kingdoms lie,
Whole realms exhauſted to-enrich a throne,   25
Their fruits untaſted, and their rights unknown;
Thro' tears of grief that ſpeak the melting mind,
They hail the era that relieves mankind.

   Of theſe the firſt, the Gallic ſages ſtand,
And urge their king to liſt an aiding hand.   30
The generous cauſe their glowing breaſts inſpir'd,
Columbia's wrongs their indignation fir'd;
To ſhare her glorious toils their counſel mov'd,
In juſtice founded and by faith approv'd.
Surrounding heroes wait the monarch's word,   35
In foreign fields to draw the glittering ſword,
Prepar'd with joy to join thoſe infant powers,
Who build new empires on the weſtern ſhores.
  By honeſt guile the royal ear they bend,
And lure him on, fair freedom to defend;   40

That

That, once recognis'd, once eſtabliſh'd there,
The world might learn the proffer'd boon to ſhare;
While artful arguments the plan diſguiſe,
Garb'd in the gloſs that ſuits a monarch's eyes.

By arms to humble Britain's haughty power,   45
From her to ſever that extended ſhore,
Contents his utmoſt wiſh.   For this he lends
His powerful aid, and calls th' oppreſs'd his friends.
The league propos'd, he lifts his arm to ſave,
And ſpeaks the borrow'd language of the brave: 50

Ye ſtates of France, and ye of riſing name,
Who work thoſe diſtant miracles of fame,
Hear and attend; let heav'n the witneſs bear,
We draw the ſword, we aid the righteous war.
Let leagues eternal bind each friendly land,   55
Giv'n by our voice, and 'ſtabliſh'd by our hand;
Let yon extenſive empire fix her ſway,
And ſpread her bleſſings with the bounds of day.
Yet know, ye nations, hear, ye Powers above,
Our purpos'd aid no views of conqueſt move;   60
In that vaſt world revives no ancient claim
Of regions peopled by the Gallic name;
Our envied bounds, already ſtretch'd afar,
Nor aſk the ſword, nor fear the rage of war;

N

But

But virtue, ſtruggling with the vengeful Power,   65
That ſtains yon fields, and deſolates that ſhore,
With nature's foes bids former compact ceaſe ;
We war reluctant, and our wiſh is peace ;
To ſuffering nations be the ſuccour given,
The cauſe of nations is the cauſe of Heaven.   70

   He ſpoke ; his moving armies ſhade the plain,
His fleets rode bounding on the weſtern main ;
O'er lands and ſeas the loud applauſes rung,
And *war* and *union* dwelt on every tongue.

   The other Bourbon caught the ſplendid ſtrain,   75
And rous'd in haſte the naval force of Spain.
Swift o'er the tide, where Gallic flags advance,
He bids his own in wonted union dance ;
And while dread Elliott ſhakes the Midland wave,
They ſtrive in vain the Calpian rock to brave.   80
The Belgian powers with equal ſpeed prepare
Thro' weſtern iſles to meet the watery war ;
Where ſtill proud Albion ſweeps the ſhuddering main,
And foils the force of Holland, France and Spain.

   Where Indian borders ſkirt the orient ſkies,   85
To furious ſtrife unwonted myriads riſe ;
Great Hyder there, unconquerably bold,
Bids vengeance move and freedom's flag unfold,

                       Fires

Fires the wide realms t'affert their ancient fway,
And fcourge fierce Britons from their lawlefs prey.   90
   Now Europe's northern powers, their counfels blend,
The laws of trade to foften and extend ;
An arm'd Neutrality the way prepares,
To check the horrors of all future wars ;
Till by degrees the wafting fword fhall ceafe,   95
And commerce lead to univerfal peace.
   Thus all the ancient world with ardent eyes
Enjoy the lights that gild th' Atlantic fkies,
Wake to new life, affume a borrow'd flame,
Enlarge the luftre and partake the fame.   100
So mounts of ice, that polar heav'ns invade,
Unheeded ftand beneath the night's long fhade,
Yet when the morning lights their glaring throne,
Give back the day, and imitate the fun.
   But ftill Columbus, o'er the weftern fhore,   105
Sees Albion's fleets her new battalions pour ;
The realms unconquer'd ftill their terrors wield,
And ftain with mingled gore th' embattled field.
O'er Schuylkill's wave to various fight they move,
And adverfe nations equal flaughter prove ;   110
Till, where dread Monmouth lifts a frowning height,
Parading armies caft a glaring light.

N 2

There

There ſtrode the Britiſh Clinton o'er the field,
And marſhall'd hoſts for ready combat held.
As the dim ſun, beneath the ſkirts of even,   115
Crimſons the clouds that ſail the weſtern heaven;
So, in red wavy rows, where ſpread the train
Of men and ſtandards, ſhone the fateful plain.
  But now dread Waſhington aroſe in ſight,
And the long ranks roll forward to the fight;   120
He points the charge, the mounted thunders roar,
And plough the plain, and rock the diſtant ſhore.
Above the folds of ſmoke, that veil'd the war,
His guiding ſword illum'd the fields of air;
The vollied flames, that burſt along the plain,   125
Break the deep clouds, and ſhow the piles of ſlain;
Till flight begins; the ſmoke is roll'd away,
And the red ſtandards open into day.
Britons and Germans hurry from the field,
Now wrapp'd in duſt, and now to ſight reveal'd;   130
Behind, great Waſhington his falchion drives,
Thins the pale ranks, and copious vengeance gives.
Hoſts captive bow, and move behind his arm,
And hoſts before him wing the driven ſtorm;
When the glad ſhore ſalutes their fainting ſight,   135
And thundering navies ſcreen their rapid flight.

Thro'

Thro' plains of death, that gleam with hoftile fires,
Brave Lincoln now to fouthern climes retires ;
Where o'er her ftreams beleagur'd Charlefton rofe,
The hero moves to meet th' affembled foes.   140
Around the pointed ftrand, on either flood,
Red ftandards wav'd and floating batteries rode ;
While, braving death, his fcanty hoft remains,
And the dread ftrife with various fate fuftains.

High from the fable decks the burfting fires   145
Sweep the full firgets, and cleave the glittering fpires.
The flying flames, that vault the burning air
Strow their crackt fhells and pour th' etherial war ;
And all the tented plain, where heroes tread,
Is torn with crags and cover'd with the dead.   150
Each fhower of flames renews the townfmen's woe,
They wail the ftrife, they dread th' infuriate foe.
Th' afflicted Fair, while tears bedew their charms,
Babes at their fide and infants in their arms,
With piercing fhrieks his guardian hand implore,   155
To fave them trembling from the victor's power.
He fhares their anguifh with a moift'ning eye,
And bids the balls rain thicker thro' the fky ;
But vain the ftrife ; while crowding to the fhore,
The foes in frefh battalions round him pour.   160

N 3   He

He yields at laft the long-contefted prize,   ·
And freedom's banners quit the fouthern fkies.

   The conqu'ring legions now the champaign tread,
And tow'rd the north their fire and flaughter fpread ;
Thro' towns and realms, where arming peafants fly,   165
The bold Cornwallis bears his ftandard high ;
O'er many a field difplays his wafting force,
And thoufands fall, and thoufands aid his courfe ;
While in his march thro' all the wide domain,
Colonial daftards join his fplendid train.   ·   170
So mountain ftreams o'er climes of melting fnow,
Spread with increafing waves, and flood the world below.

   The great Columbus, with an anxious figh,
Saw Britifh enfigns reaching round the fky,
Saw defolation whelm his fav'rite coaft,   175
His children fcatter'd, and their vigour loft,
De Kalb in furious combat prefs the plain,
Morgan and Smallwood various fhocks fuftain ;   ·
When Greene, in lonely greatnefs, rofe to view,
A few firm patriots to his ftandard drew ;   180
And, moving ftately to a rifing ground,   ·
Bade the loud trump to fpeedy vengeance found ;
Fir'd by the voice, new fquadrons, from afar,
Crowd to the hero and demand the war.

Round

Round all the shores and plains he turn'd his eye,   195
Saw forts arise, and conquering banners fly:
The saddening scene suspends his ardent soul,
And fates of empires in his bosom roll.
With slender force where should he lift the steel,
While hostling foes immeasurably wheel?   190
Or how behold the boundless slaughter spread,
Himself stand idle and his country bleed?

A silent moment thus the hero stood,
And held his warriors from the field of blood;
Then points the British legions where to roll,   195
Marks out their progress, and designs the whole.
He lures their chief, o'er yielding realms to roam,
To build his greatness, and to find his doom;
With gain and grandeur feeds his sateless flame,
And leaves the vict'ry to a nobler name;   200
Gives to great Washington, to meet his way,
Nor claims the glories of so bright a day.

Then to the conquer'd south, with gathering force,
O'er sanguine plains he shapes his rapid course;
Forts fall around him, hosts before him fly,   205
And captive bands his growing train supply.
At length, far spreading thro' a fatal field,
Britannia's chiefs their circling armies wheel'd;

N 4

Near Eutaw's fount, where, long renown'd for blood,
Pillars of ancient fame in triumph flood,   210
The ready fquadrons, rang'd in order bright,
Stand, like a fiery wall, and wait the fhock of fight.
    When o'er the neighb'ring hill, brave Greene arofe,
Ey'd the far plain, and view'd the glittering foes;
Difpos'd for combat each compacted train,   215
To lead the charge, or the wide wings fuftain,
Rous'd all their rage, fuperior force to prove,
Wav'd the bright blade, and bade the onfet move.
As hovering clouds, when morning beams arife,
Hang their red curtains round the eaftern fkies,   220
Unfold a fpace to hail the promis'd fun,
And catch their fplendors from his rifing throne;
Thus glow'd th'approaching fronts, whofe fteely glare
Glanc'd o'er the hideous interval of war.
Now roll with kindling hafte the rapid lines,   225
From wing to wing the founding battle joins;
Batteries and foffes wide, and ranks of fire,
In mingled fhocks, their thundering blafts expire:
Beneath the fmoke, when firm advancing bands,
With piked arms bent forward in their hands,   230
In dreadful filence tread.   As, wrapp'd from fight,
The nightly ambufh moves to fecret fight;

So

So rush the raging files, and sightless close,
In plunging strife, with fierce conflicting foes;
They reach, they strike, they struggle o'er the slain,   235
Deal doubtful blows, and strow with death the plain;
Ranks crush on ranks, with equal slaughter gor'd,
While dripping streams, from every lifted sword,
Stain the thin, carnag'd hosts; who still maintain,
With mutual shocks, the vengeance of the plain.   240
Till, where brave Williams strove and Campbell fell,
Unwonted strokes the British force repel:
The rout begins; the shatter'd wings, afar,
Roll back in haste and scatter from the war;
They drop their arms, they scour the marshy field;   245
Whole squadrons fall and faint battalions yield.

    O'er all the great Observer fix'd his eye,
Mark'd the whole strife, beheld them fall and fly;
He saw where Greene thro' all the combat drove,
And death and vict'ry with his presence move;   250
Beneath his arm saw Marion pour the strife,
Pickens and Sumner, prodigal of life;
He saw young Washington, the child of fame,
Preserve in fight the honours of his name;
Brave Lee, in pride of youth and veteran might,   255
Swept the dread field, and put whole troops to flight;

While numerous chiefs, that equal trophies raife,
Wrought, not unfeen, the deeds of deathlefs praife.
  Columbus now his gallant fons beheld
In triumph move thro' many a banner'd field;   260
When o'er the main, from Gallia's friendly fhore,
To the glad ftrife a hoft of heroes pour.
On the tall fhaded decks the leaders ftand,
View leffening waves, and hail the crowded ftrand.
Brave Rochambeau, in gleamy fteel array'd,   265
Th'afcending fcenes with eager joy furvey'd;
Saw Wafhington, amid his thoufands, ftride,
And long'd to toil and conquer by his fide.
Two brother chiefs, in rival luftre, rofe,
Rear'd the long lance, and claim'd the field of foes;   270
The bold Viominils, of equal fame,
And eager both to grace the honour'd name.
Lauzon, beneath his fail, in armour bright,
Frown'd o'er the wave, impatient for the fight;
A fiery fteed befide the hero ftood,   275
And his broad blade wav'd forward o'er the crowd.

  And now, with eager hafte, they tread the coaft;
Thro' grateful regions march their veteran hoft;
Join the great Chief, where allied banners lead,
Demand the foe, and bid the war proceed.   280

Again

Again Columbus caſt his anxious eye,
Where Britain's ſtandard wav'd along the ſky;
And, grac'd with ſpoils of many a field of blood,
The bold Cornwallis on a bulwark ſtood.
O'er conquer'd provinces, and towns in flame,   285
He mark'd his recent monuments of fame;
High-rais'd in air his hands ſecurely hold,
With conſcious pride, a ſheet of cypher'd gold;
There, in deluſive haſte, his ſkill had grav'd
A clime ſubdu'd, a flag in triumph wav'd: 290
A middle realm, by fairer figures known,
Adorn'd with fruits, lay bounded for his own;
Deep thro' the centre ſpreads a beauteous bay,
Full ſails aſcend and golden rivers ſtray;
Bright palaces ariſe, reliev'd in gold,   295
And gates and ſtreets the croſſing lines unfold;
O'er all the mimic ſcene, his fingers trace
His future ſeat and glory of his race.
     While thus the Britiſh chief his conqueſts view'd,
And gazing thouſands round the ramparts ſtood,   300
Whom future eaſe and golden dreams employ,
The ſongs of triumph and the feaſt of joy;
Sudden great Waſhington aroſe in view,
And union'd flags his ſtately ſteps purſue;

                                        Great

Great Gallia's hoft and young Columbia's pride,   305
Bend the long march and glitter at his fide.

   Now on the wave the warring fleets advance,
And rival enfigns o'er their pinions dance ;
Graves, from the north, dread Albion's flag unfurl'd
That wav'd defiance to the watery world ;   310
De Graffe, from fouthern ifles, conducts his train, .
And fhades with Gallic fheets the billowy main.

   The fwelling fails, as far as eye can fweep,
Look thro' the fkies and awe the fhuddering deep.
As, when the winds of heav'n, from each far pole,   315
Their adverfe ftorms acrofs the concave roll,
The floecy vapours thro' th'expanfion run,
Veil the blue vault, and tremble o'er the fun ;
Till the dark folding wings together drive,
And, ridg'd with fires and rock'd with thunders, ftrive ; 320
So, bearing thro' the void, at firft appear
White clouds of canvafs floating on the air ;
Then frown th' approaching fronts ; the fails are laid,
And the black decks extend a dreadful fhade ;
While rolling flames and tides of fmoke arife,   325
And thundering cannons rock the feas and fkies.
Where the long burfting fires the cloud difclofe,
Hofts heave in fight and blood the decks o'er-flows ;

                                             Here

Here from the strife tost navies rise to view,
Drive back to vengeance, and the toil renew,   330
There shatter'd barks in squadrons move afar,
Led thro' the smoke, and struggling from the war;
While hulls half seen, beneath a gaping wave,
And plunging heroes fill the watery grave.

Now the dark smoky volumes roll'd away,   335
And a long line ascended into day;
The pinions swell'd, Britannia's flag arose,
And flew the vengeance of triumphing foes.
When up the bay, Virginian lands that laves,
The Gallic line its conquering standard waves: 340
Where still dread Washington directs his way,
And fleets and moving realms his voice obey;
While the brave Briton, mid the gathering host,
Perceives his glories and his empire lost.

The heav'n-taught Sage in this broad scene beheld   345
His fav'rite sons the fates of nations wield;
There joyous Lincoln shone in arms again,
Nelson and Knox mov'd ardent o'er the plain;
Unconquer'd Scammel, mid the closing strife,
In sight of vict'ry pour'd his gallant life;   350
While Gallic thousands eager toils sustain,
And death and danger hearten every train.

                                                    Where

W'here Tarleton turns with hopes of flight elate,
Brave Lauzon moves, and drives him back to fate.
In one dread view two chosen bands advance,   355
Columbia's veterans and the pride of France;
These bold Viominil exalts to fame,
And those Fayette's conducting guidance claim.
They lift the sword, with rival glory warm,
O'er piked ramparts pour the flaming storm,   360
The mounted thunders brave, and lead the foe,
In captive squadrons, to the plain below.
O'er all great Washington his arm extends,
Points every movement, every toil defends,
Bids closer strife and bloodier strokes proceed,   365
New batteries blaze and heavier squadrons bleed;
Round the pent foe approaching breastworks rise,
And shells like meteors vault the flaming skies.
With dire dismay the British chief beheld
The foe advance, his veterans quit the field;   370
Despair and slaughter when he turns his eye,
No hope in combat, and no power to fly;
De Graffe victorious shakes the shuddering tide,
Imbody'd nations all the champaign hide;
Fosses and batteries, growing on the sight,   375
Still pour new thunders and increase the fight,

Shells

Shells rain before him, rock the shores around,
And crags and balls o'erturn the tented ground ;
From post to post the driven ranks retire,
The earth in crimson and the skies on fire.   380

    Now grateful truce suspends the burning war,
And groans and shouts, promiscuous, load the air ;
When the tir'd Britons, where the smokes decay,
Resign their arms and move in open day.
Columbus saw th' immeasurable train,   385
Thousands on thousands, redden all the plain ;
Beheld the glorious Leader stand sedate,
Hosts in his chain, and banners at his feet ;
Nor smile o'er all, nor chide the fallen chief,
But share with pitying eye his manly grief.   390
Thus thro' th' extremes of life, in every state,
Shines the clear soul, beyond all fortune great ;
While smaller minds, the dupes of fickle chance,
Slight woes o'erwhelm, and sudden joys entrance.
So the full sun, through all the changing sky,   395
Nor blasts, nor overpowers, the naked eye ;
Tho' transient splendors, borrow'd from his light,
Glance on the mirror and destroy the sight.

    He bids brave Lincoln, as they move along,
Conduct the triumph of the vanquish'd throng ;   400
Who sees, once more, two armies shade the plain,
The mighty victors and the captive train.

THE

VISION of COLUMBUS.

———

BOOK VII.

ARGUMENT.

*Hymn to Peace. Progress of Arts in America. Fur-trade.
Fisheries. Productions and Commerce. Education. Philosophical discoveries. Painting. Poetry.*

BOOK VII.

HAIL facred Peace, who claim'ft thy bright abode
Mid circling faints that grace the throne of God !
Before his arm, around the fhapelefs earth,
Stretch'd the wide heav'ns, and gave to nature birth ;
Ere morning-ftars his glowing chambers hung,   5
Or fongs of gladnefs woke an angel's tongue,
Veil'd in the brightnefs of th'Almighty's mind,
In bleft repofe thy placid form reclin'd.
Borne through the heav'ns with his creating voice,
Thy prefence bade th'unfolding worlds rejoice,   10
Gave to feraphic harps their founding lays,
Their joys to angels, and to men their praife.

   From fcenes of blood, thefe beauteous fhores that ftain,
From gafping friends that prefs the fanguine plain,
From fields, long taught in vain thy flight to mourn,   15
I rife, delightful Power, and greet thy glad return.

O 2

Too

Too long the groans of death, and battle's bray,
Have rung difcordant through th'unpleafing lay:
Let pity's tear its balmy fragrance fhed,
O'er heroes' wounds and patriot warriors dead ;   20
Accept, departed fhades, thefe grateful fighs,
Your fond attendants to th'approving fkies.

   And thou, my earlieft friend, my brother dear,
Thy fall untimely wakes the tender tear.
In youthful fports, in toils, in blood allied,   25
My kind companion and my hopeful guide,
When Heav'n's fad fummons, from our infant eyes,
Had call'd our laft, lov'd parent to the fkies.
Tho' young in arms, and ftill obfcure thy name,
Thy bofom panted for the deeds of fame,   30
Beneath Montgomery's eye, when, by thy fteel,
In northern wilds, the frequent favage fell.
Yet, haplefs Youth ! when thy great leader bled,
Thro' the fame wound thy parting fpirit fled.

   But now th'untuneful trump fhall grate no more,   35
Ye filver ftreams, no longer fwell with gore ;
Bear from your beauteous banks the crimfon ftain,
With yon retiring navies, to the main.
While other views unfolding on my eyes,
And happier themes bid bolder numbers rife :   40

Bring,

Bring, bounteous Peace, in thy celestial throng,
Life to my soul, and rapture to my song;
Give me to trace, with pure unclouded ray,
The arts and virtues that attend thy sway;
To see thy blissful charms, that here descend,   45
Through distant realms and endless years extend.

   To cast new glories o'er the changing clime,
The Seraph now revers'd the flight of time;
Roll'd back the years that led their course before,
And stretch'd immense the wild uncultur'd shore;   50
The paths of peaceful Science rais'd to view,
And show'd th' ascending crowds that useful arts pursue.

   As o'er the canvass, when the master's mind
Glows with a future landscape, well design'd,
While gardens, vales, and streets and structures rise,   55
A new creation to his kindling eyes;
He smiles o'er all; and, in delightful strife,
The pencil moves and calls the whole to life.
So, while the great Columbus stood sublime,
And saw wild nature clothe the trackless clime;   60
The green banks heave, the winding currents pour,
The bays and harbours cleave the yielding shore,
The champaigns spread, the solemn groves arise,
And the rough mountains lengthen round the skies;

Through all the scene he trac'd, with skillful ken,   65
The unform'd seats and future walks of men ;
Mark'd where the fields should bloom, the streamers play,
And towns and empires claim their peaceful sway ;
When, sudden waken'd by the Angel's hand,
They rose in pomp around the cultur'd land.   70

   In western wilds, where still the natives tread,
From sea to sea an inland commerce spread ;
O'er the dim streams, and thro' the gloomy grove,
The trading bands their cumb'rous burdens move ;
Where furs, and skins, and all th' exhaustless store   75
Of midland realms, descended to the shore.

   Where summer's suns, along the northern coast,
With feeble force dissolve the chains of frost,
Prolific waves the scaly nations trace,
And tempt the toils of man's laborious race.   80
Though rich Peruvian strands, beneath the tide,
Their rocks of pearl and sparkling pebbles hide ;
Lur'd by the gaudy prize, a vent'rous train
Plunge the dark deep and brave the surging main ;
Whole realms of slaves the dangerous labours dare,   85
To stud a sceptre or emblaze a star :
Yet wealthier stores these genial tides display,
And busy throngs with nobler spoils repay.

                         The

The Hero faw the hardy hofts advance,
Caft the long line and aim the barbed lance ;   90
Load the deep floating barks, and bear abroad
To each far clime the life-fuftaining food ;
While growing fwarms by nature's hand fupplied,
People the fhoals and fill the fruitful tide.

   Where fouthern ftreams thro' broad favannahs bend, 95
The rice-clad vales their verdant rounds extend ;
Tobago's plant its leaf expanding yields,
The maize luxuriant clothes a thoufand fields ;
Steeds, herds and flocks o'er northern regions rove,
Embrown the hill, and wanton thro' the grove ;   100
The wood-lands wide their fturdy honours bend,
The pines, the live-oaks, to the fhores defcend ;
Along the ftrand the crooked keels arife,
The huge hulls heave, and mafts afcend the fkies ;
Launch'd in the deep o'er eaftern waves they fly,   105
Feed fouthern ifles, and Europe's realms fupply.

   Silent he gaz'd : when thus the guardian Power :—
While ufeful toils like thefe adorn the fhore,
The liberal arts with more diftinguifh'd praife,
Shall crown their labours and thy rapture raife.   110
Each orient realm, the former pride of earth,
Where menand fcience drew their ancient birth,

O 4   Shall

Shall foon behold, on this enlighten'd coaft,
Their fame tranfcended, and their glory loft.
That train of arts, that grac'd mankind before,   115
Warm'd the glad Sage or taught the Mufe to foar,
Here with fuperior fway their progrefs trace,
And aid the triumphs of thy filial race;
While rifing crowds, with genius unconfin'd,
Thro' deep inventions lead th' aftonifh'd mind,   120
Wide o'er the world their name unrivall'd raife,
And bind their temples with immortal bays.

In youthful minds to wake a virtuous flame,
To nurfe the arts, and point the paths of fame,
Behold their liberal fires, with guardian care,   125
Thro' all the realms their feats of fcience rear.
Great without pomp the modeft manfions ftand,
Harvard and Yale and Princeton grace the land,
Penn's peaceful dome his youths with ruptnre greet,
On James's bank Virginian mufes meet,   130
York's beauteous town her college walls command,
Bofom'd in groves, fee growing Dartmouth ftand;
While, o'er the realm reflecting folar fires,
On yon tall hill, Rhode-Ifland's feat afpires.

O'er all the fhore, with fails and cities gay,   135
And where rude hamlets ftretch their inland fway,

With

With humbler walls unnumber'd schools arise,
And home-bred freemen seize the solid prize.
In no blest land has Science rear'd her fane,
And fix'd so firm her peace-diffusing reign ;   140
Each rustic here, that turns the furrow'd soil,
The maid, the youth, that ply mechanic toil,
In freedom nurst, in useful arts inur'd,
Know their just claims, and see their rights secur'd.

 And lo ! descending from the seats of art,   145
The growing throngs for active scenes depart ;
In various garbs they tread the welcome land,
Swords at their side or statutes in their hand,
With healing powers bid dire diseases cease,
Or sound the tidings of eternal peace.   150

 In no blest land has fair religion shone,
And fix'd so firm her everlasting throne.
Where o'er the realms those spacious temples shine,
Frequent and full the throng'd assemblies join ;
There, fir'd with virtue's animating flame,   155
The preacher's task persuasive sages claim ;
The task, for angels great—in early youth,
To lead whole nations in the walks of truth,
To shed the beams of knowledge on the mind,
In bands of peace to harmonize mankind,   160

To

To life, to happiness, to joys above,
The soften'd soul with ardent zeal to move.
For this the voice of Heav'n, in early years,
Tun'd the glad songs of life-inspiring seers;
For this confenting seraphs leave the skies,   165
Reveal the path of life, and teach them how to rise.

   Tho' different faiths their various orders show,
That seem discordant to the train below ;
They tread the same bright steps, and smoothe the road,
Lights of the world and messengers of God.   170
So the galaxy broad o'er heav'n displays
Of various stars the same unbounded blaze ;
Where great and small their mingling rays unite,
And earth and skies repay the friendly light.

   While thus the Hero view'd the sacred band,   175
Mov'd by one voice and guided by one hand,
He saw the heav'ns unfold, a form descend,
Down the dim skies his arm of light extend,
From God's own altar bear a living coal,
Touch their glad lips and brighten every soul ;   180
To listening crowds from each accordant tongue,
O'er the wide clime these welcome accents rung :—

   Ye darkling race of poor distress mankind,
For bliss still groping and to virtue blind,

Hear from on high th' Almighty's voice defcend ;   185
Ye heav'ns, be filent, and thou earth, attend.
I reign the Lord of life ; I fill the round
Where ftars and fkies and angels know their bound ;
Before all years, beyond all thought I live,
Light, form and motion, time and fpace I give ;   190
Touch'd by this hand, all worlds within me roll,
Mine eye their fplendor, and my breath their foul.
Earth, with her lands and feas, my power proclaims,
There moves my fpirit, there defcend my flames ;
Grac'd with the femblance of the Maker's mind,   195
Rofe from the darkfome duft the reas'ning kind,
With powers of thought to trace th' eternal caufe,
That all his works to one great fyftem drawn,
View the full chain of love, th' all-ruling plan,
That binds the God, the angel, and the man,   200
That gives all hearts to feel, all minds to know
The blifs of harmony, of ftrife the woe.
This heav'n of concord, who of mortal ftrain
Shall dare oppofe—he lifts his arm in vain ;
Th' avenging univerfe on him fhall roll   205
Th' intended wrong, and whelm his guilty foul.
Then lend your audience ; hear, ye fons of earth,
Rife into life, behold the promis'd birth ;

From

From pain to joy, from guilt to glory rife,
Be babes on earth, be feraphs in the fkies.   210
O'er mortal fcenes exalt the deathlefs mind,
And feize the bleffings of a nobler kind,
That wait your choice, that crown, in worlds above,
The fainted hoft, the firft-born fons of love.
View the glad throng, the glorious triumph join,   215
Their paths purfue, and in their fplendor fhine,
Hail, with feraphic fmiles, the bleft abode,
Affume their fpotlefs robes, and reign befide your God.

   Thus heard the Hero—while his roving view
Trac'd other crowds that liberal arts purfue ;   220
When thus the Seraph :—Lo, a fapient band,
The torch of fcience flaming in their hand !
Thro' nature's range their ardent fouls afpire,
Or wake to life the canvafs and the lyre.
Fixt in fublimeft thought, behold them rife,   225
Superior worlds unfolding to their eyes ;
Heav'n in their view unveils th' eternal plan,
And gives new guidance to the paths of man.

   See on yon dark'ning height bold Franklin tread,
Heav'n's awful thunders rolling o'er his head ;   230
Convolving clouds the billowy fkies deform,
And forky flames emblaze the black'ning ftorm.

See

See the defcending ftreams around him burn,
Glance on his rod, and with his guidance turn ;
He bids conflicting heav'ns their blafts expire,   235
Curbs the fierce blaze and holds th' imprifion'd fire.
No more, when folding ftorms the vault o'erfpread,
The livid glare fhall ftrike thy race with dread ;
Nor towers nor temples, fhuddering with the found,
Sink in the flames and fpread deftruction round.   240
His daring toils, the threat'ning blaft that wait,
Shall teach mankind to ward the bolts of fate ;
The pointed fteel o'er-top the lofty fpire,
And lead from trembling walls the harmlefs fire ;
In his glad fame while diftant worlds rejoice,   245
Far as the lightnings fhine or thunders raife their voice.
    See the fage Rittenhoufe, with ardent eye,
Lift the long tube and pierce the ftarry fky ;
Clear in his view the circling fyftems roll,
And broader fplendors gild the central pole.   250
He marks what laws th' eccentric wand'rers bind,
Copies creation in his forming mind,
And bids, beneath his hand, in femblance rife,
With mimic orbs, the labours of the fkies:
Here wond'ring crowds with raptur'd eye behold   255
The fpangled heav'ns their myftic maze unfold ;

While

While each glad sage his splendid hall may grace,

With all the spheres that cleave th' etherial space.

　To guide the sailor in his wandering way,

See Godfrey's * toils reverse the beams of day.　　　260

His lifted quadrant to the eye displays

From adverse skies the counteracting rays;

And marks, as devious sails bewilder'd roll,

Each nice gradation from the stedfast pole.

　See, West with glowing life the canvass warms;　　265

His sovereign hand creates impassion'd forms,

Spurns the cold critic rules, to seize the heart,

And boldly bursts the former bounds of Art.

No more her powers to ancient lore confin'd,

He opes her liberal aid to all mankind;　　　　270

And calls to life each patriot, chief, or sage,

Garb'd in the dress and drapery of his age.

Again bold Regulus to death returns,

Again her falling Wolfe Britannia mourns;

* It is less from national vanity, than from a regard to truth and a desire of rendering personal justice, that the author wishes to rectify the history of Science in the circumstance here alluded to.　The instrument, known by the name of Hadley's Quadrant, now universally in use and generally attributed to Dr. Hadley, was invented by Mr. Godfrey of Philadelphia. *See Jefferson's Notes on Virginia.*

Edward

Edward in arms to frowning combat moves,   275
Or, won to pity by the queen he loves,
Spares the devoted Six, whose deathless deed
Preserv'd the town his vengeance doom'd to bleed.
     With rival force, see Copley's pencil trace
The air of action and the charms of face.   280
Fair in his tints unfold the scenes of state,
The senate listens and the peers debate ;
Pale consternation every heart appals,
In act to speak, while death-struck Chatham falls.
He bids dread Calpe cease to shake the waves,   285
While Elliott's arm the host of Bourbon saves ;
O'er the wing'd batteries sinking in the flood,
Mid flames and darkness, drench'd in hostile blood,
Britannia's sons extend their generous hand,
To snatch their foes from death, and bear them to the land.
     Fir'd with the martial toils, that bath'd in gore
His brave companions on his native shore,
Trumbull with daring hand the strife recalls,
He shades with night Quebec's beleagur'd walls,
Mid flashing flames, that round the turrets rise,   295
Blind carnage raves and great Montgomery dies.
On Charlestown's height, thro' floods of rolling fire,
Brave Warren falls, and sullen hosts retire ;

While

While other plains of death, that gloom the Ikies,
And chiefs immortal, o'er his canvaſs riſe.   300
    See rural ſeats of innocence and eaſe,
High-tufted towers and walks of waving trees,
The white waves daſhing on the craggy ſhores,
Meand'ring ſtreams and meads of ſpangled flowers,
Where nature's ſons their wild excurſions lead,   305
In juſt deſign, from Taylor's pencil ſpread.
    Steward and Brown the moving portrait raiſe,
Each rival ſtroke the force of life conveys;
See circling Beauties round their tablets ſtand,
And riſe immortal from their plaſtic hand;   310
Each breathing form preſerves its wonted grace,
And all the ſoul ſtands ſpeaking in the face.
    Two kindred arts the ſwelling ſtatue heave,
Wake the dead wax, and teach the ſtone to live.
While the bold chiſſel claims the rugged ſtrife,   315
To rouſe the ſceptred marble into life;
See Wright's fair hands the livelier fire controul,
In waxen forms ſhe breathes th' impaſſion'd ſoul;
The pencil'd tint o'er moulded ſubſtance glows,
And different powers th' unrivall'd art compoſe.   .   320
Grief, rage and fear beneath her fingers ſtart,
Roll the wild eye and pour the burſting heart,

While

While slumbering heroes wait her wakening call,
And diftant ages fill the ftory'd hall.

  To equal fame afcends thy tuneful throng,   325
The boaft of genius and the pride of fong ;
Warm'd with the fcenes that grace their various clime,
Their lays fhall triumph o'er the lapfe of time.

  With keen-ey'd glance thro' nature's walks to pierce,
With all the powers and every charm of verfe,   330
Each fcience opening in his ample mind,
His fancy glowing and his tafte refin'd,
See Trumbull lead the train.   His fkilful hand
Hurls the keen darts of Satire thro' the land ;
Pride, knavery, dullnefs, feel his mortal ftings,   335
And lift'ning virtue triumphs while he fings ;
Proud Albion's fons, victorious now no more,
In guilt retiring from the wafted fhore,
Strive their curft cruelties to hide in vain—
The world fhall learn them from his deathlefs ftrain.   340

  On glory's wing to raife the ravifh'd foul,
Beyond the bounds of earth's benighted pole,
For daring Dwight the epic Mufe fublime
Hails her new empire on the weftern clime.

Fir'd with the themes by feers feraphic fung,   345
Heav'n in his eye, and rapture on his tongue,

P

His

His voice divine revives the Promis'd Land,
The Heav'n-taught Leader and the chosen band.
In Hanniel's fate, proud faction finds her doom,
Ai's midnight flames light nations to their tomb,   350
In visions bright supernal joys are given,
And all the dread futurities of heaven.

While freedom's cause his patriot bosom warms,
In counsel sage, nor inexpert in arms,
See Humphreys glorious from the field retire,   355
Sheathe the glad sword and string the sounding lyre ;
That lyre which erst, in hours of dark despair,
Rous'd the sad realms to urge th' unfinish'd war.
O'er fallen friends, with all the strength of woe,
His heart-felt sighs in moving numbers flow ;   360
His country's wrongs, her duties, dangers, praise,
Fire his full soul and animate his lays ;
Immortal Washington with joy shall own
So fond a fav'rite and so brave a son.

THE

VISION of COLUMBUS.

BOOK VIII.

ARGUMENT.

The vision suspended. Causes of the slow progress that Science has hitherto made in the world, and of its frequent interruptions. Its ancient compared with its modern establishment. Consequences of the latter. Causes of the apparent uncertainty in matters of theology. Superstition built on the passions; scepticism on the reasoning power. Necessity and happy effect of the united force of reason and the passions in the discovery of truth.

VISION of COLUMBUS.

BOOK VIII.

AND now the Angel, from the trembling fight,
Veil'd the wide world—when fudden fhades of night
Move o'er th' etherial vault ; the ftarry train
Paint their dim forms beneath the placid main ;
While earth and heav'n, around the Hero's eye,   5
Seem arch'd immenfe, like one furrounding fky.
Still, from the Power fuperior fplendors fhone,
The height emblazing like a radiant throne ;
To converfe fweet the foothing fhades invite,
And on the Guide the Hero fix'd his fight.   10

     Kind meffenger of Heav'n, he thus began,
Why this progreffive lab'ring fearch of man ?
If man, by wifdom form'd, hath power to reach
Thefe opening truths that following ages teach,
Step after ftep, thro' devious paths to wind,   15
And fill at laft the meafure of the mind,

P 3

Why

Why did not Heav'n, with one unclouded ray,
All human arts and reason's powers display ?
That mad opinions, and sectarian strife
Might find no place t' imbitter human life.   20
     To whom th' Angelic Power :—To thee 'tis given
To hold high converse and enquire of Heaven,
To mark untravers'd ages, and to trace
The promis'd truths that wait thy kindred race.
Know then, the counsels of the Maker's mind,   25
Thro' nature's range, progressive paths design'd.
Progressive works at every step we trace,
Thro' all duration and around all space ;
Till power and wisdom all their parts combine,
And full perfection speaks the work divine.   30
     So the first week beheld the progress rise,
Which form'd the earth and arch'd the ambient skies.
Dark and imperfect first, the formless frame
From vacant night to crude existence came ;
Light stair'd the heav'ns and suns were taught their bound,
Winds woke their force, and floods their centre found ;
Earth's kindred elements, in joyous strife,
Warm'd the glad glebe to vegetable life,
Till sense and power and action claim'd their place,
And godlike reason crown'd th' imperial race.   40

Ta

'Tis thus meek Science, from creation's birth,
With time's long circuit treads the darksome earth,
Leads in progressive march th' enquiring mind,
To curb its passions and its bliss to find,
To guide the reas'ning power, and smoothe the road, 45
That leads mankind to nature and to God.

In elder times, when savage tribes began,
A few strong passions sway'd the wayward man;
Envy, revenge, and fateless lust of power
Fir'd the dark soul, and stain'd the fields with gore; 50
Till growing bands superior strength supply'd,
And wall'd their cities with the towers of pride.
And when by force the infant arts arose,
They lur'd the envy of surrounding foes;
Some savage band would seize the peaceful prey, 55
And blast the learning, to obstruct the sway.

Thus, at the Muse's call, when Thebes arose,
And Science dawn'd where nurt'ring Nilus flows,
Rich with the toils of art, bold structures blaz'd,
And barb'rous nations envy'd as they gaz'd; 60
The wond'rous pyramid, the tempting store,
The charm of conquest, and the grasp of power,
Lur'd the dark world, with envious pride elate,
To whelm fair Science in the wrecks of state;

Till

Till Thebes and Memphis nameless ruins lie,   65
And crush the race that rais'd them to the sky.

O'er Chaldea's plains her sons began to stray,
To count the stars, and trace their wand'ring way;
Where the glad shepherd learn'd the skies to read,
His loves to cherish and his flocks to feed;   70
Till haughty Babel stretch'd an envy'd sway,
And furious millions warr'd the arts away.

Iliffus' banks display'd a happier seat,
Where every Muse and all the virtues meet,
To grace the Grecian states; then, steering far,   75
Driv'n by the close pursuit of vengeful war,
She wings her flight, a western region gains,
And finds a home on Latium's friendly plains.

But force and conquest follow where she leads,
Her labours changing to heroic deeds.   80
Rome's haughty Genius, taught by her to soar,
With pride of learning swell'd the pride of power,
From Brits, from Scythians pluck'd the laurel crown,
And deem'd by right th' unletter'd world his own.
Till, fir'd by insult, vengeful myriads rose,   85
And all the north pour'd forth the swarming foes;
Like sweeping tempests in embattled heaven,
When fire and blackness streak the sails of even,

The

The grifly Goths' imbodied nations rife,
The toils of ages fpread the tempting prize ;   90
Spain, Latium, Afric, feed the furious flame,
And haplefs Science mourns her buried name.

  As when the fun moves o'er the flaming zone,
Careering clouds attend his fervid throne,
Superior fplendors, in his courfe difplay'd,   95
Proclaim the progrefs of a heavier fhade ;
Thus where the Power her ancient circuit held,
Her fhining courfe fucceeding darknefs veil'd.
Fear, intereft, envy bound her narrow reign,
A coaft her walk, the Hellefpont her main,   100
Ere Goya's magnet pointed to the pole,
Or taught thy bark o'er wider worlds to roll.

  At length the fcene a nobler pomp affumes,
A milder beam difpels the Gothic glooms ;
In fober majefty, and charms of peace,   105
The goddefs moves, and cheers her filial race,
Lifts bolder wings, with furer flight to foar,
No more to reft, till heav'n illumes no more.

  At once, confenting nations rife to fame ;
Here Charles's genius wakes the Gallic name,   110
There Alfred aids the univerfal caufe,
And opes the fource of liberty and laws ;

                                                    She

She claims in Greece her long deserted home,
In wild Germania rears her Gothic dome;
Extends her sway o'er blest Arabian plains   .   115
Where her own Caliph, liberal Rachid, reigns,
While all the climes confess her spreading power,
From farthest Ganges to th' Atlantic shore.

   Ev'n horrid war, that erst her course withstood,
And whelm'd, so oft, her peaceful shrines in blood,   120
Now leads thro' paths unseen her glorious way,
Widens her limits, and secures her sway.
From Europe's realms the Christian zealots pour
In crowding millions to the Asian shore;
Mankind their prey, th' unmeaning Cross their pride,   125
And sacred vengeance their delusive guide.
Zeal points their way thro' famine, toil and blood,
To aid with arms th' imagin'd cause of God;
Till fields of slaughter whelm the broken host,
Their pride appall'd, their countless myriads lost,   130
The sad remains to Europe's shores return,
And there transplant the arts that eastern climes adorn.

   The rival barons, whom ambition draws
Their wealth to lavish in the Holy Cause,
In peace retiring, yield the kingly crown,   135
And blend their counsels to exalt the throne.

While

While slaves, no longer purchas'd with the soil,
Half wake to freedom and protected toil,
Exchange the feudal for the regal reign,
In quest of commerce tempt the friendly main,   140
Find in the magnet's power a faithful guide,
And stretch the sail o'er every distant tide.

See Rome once more the finer arts attend,
Her groves rewarble and her walls afcend;
Bologna's * learned feats arife to fame,   145
And, Paris, thine fuperior honours claim;
In rival fplendor fair Oxonia fmiles,
And fpreads her bleffings o'er the Britifh ifles;
There, like the ftar that leads the orient day,
Chaucer directs his tuneful fons their way.   150
See bold Copernicus with ardent foul
Explore the ftars and teach their orbs to roll;
And Fauftus, † with a happier ftretch of mind,
Awakes th' unbounded genius of mankind:

* The univerfities of Bologna, Paris and Oxford, as to the
dates of their inftitution, are placed in this order by Dr. Robert-
fon in his introduction to the hiftory of Charles V.

† Perhaps there is no fubject in the hiftory of art, on which
the affertions of writers have been fo various with refpect to the
name of the inventer, as on that of printing. I have afcribed
this invention to John Fauftus; though I can fcarcely recollect
on which of the numerous authorities I grounded my opinion.
One would think a difcovery of this nature would have been
                                                      more

Wide o'er the world his letter'd types diſplay   155
The works of Science, and confirm her ſway.

   Bold chivalry romantic aids her cauſe ;
In honour's name the knight his falchion draws ;
Lur'd by the charms that grace the guardleſs Fair,
To virtue's cries he bends his generous care,   160
Thro' toil and pain in queſt of glory roves,
Braves death and danger for the maid he loves ;
While fir'd by gallantry, the generous art
Improves the manners and amends the heart.

   When pride and rapine held their vengeful ſway,   165
And praiſe purſu'd where conqueſt led the way,
Nature's ſereneſt grace, the female mind,
By rough-brow'd power neglected and confin'd.
Unheeded ſigh'd, mid empire's rude alarms,
Unknown its virtues, and enſlav'd its charms.   170
So the lone wild-roſe opes the ſweeteſt bloom,
To ſcent th' unconſcious thorn, and wither round the tomb.

more likely than any other to have thrown a ſplendor upon
its own origin, and to have perpetuated its own hiſtory.
But the obſcurity in which it is involved is probably
owing to this circumſtance, that the art was at firſt conſidered as diabolical; thoſe who firſt practiſed it were perſe-
cuted; and as they fled from one country to another, they were
probably obliged to change their names. The man who firſt
carried the art into France, was taken up as a ſorcerer, and a
proſecution was carried on againſt him as ſuch, by the doctors
of law.

Bleſt

Bleſt Science then, to rugged toils confin'd,
Roſe but to conquer and enſlave mankind,
O'er gentle paſſions ſpread a harſh controul,   175
And wak'd the glare of grandeur in the ſoul.
She taught the lance to thirſt for human gore,
She taught pale avarice to ſwell the ſtore,
Taught milder arts the peaceful prize to yield,
Her Muſe to thunder thro' th' embattled field;   180
In ruin'd realms to build the ſhrine of fame,
And call celeſtial aid to raiſe a tyrant's name.
In chains and darkneſs mourn'd the hapleſs Fair,
The price of gold, th' inſulted prize of war,
While ſires, unfeeling, claim'd the ſordid dower,   185
And nymphs were ſold the ſlaves of luſt and power.

A happier morn now brightens in the ſkies,
Superior arts, in peaceful glory, riſe;
While ſofter virtues claim the public care,
And crowns of laurel grace the riſing Fair.   190
While ſtates and empires, policies and laws,
Lure the firm patriot in the bolder cauſe,
To ſtem the tide of power or guide the war,
Like thee to ſuffer and like thee to dare—
With equal honour, as with ſofter grace,   195
The well-taught matron guides the infant race.

On

On this broad bafe while Science rears her fane,
New toils and triumphs fill her glorious train,
Thro' fairer fields fhe leads th' expanding mind,
Glads every clime, and dignifies mankind.   200
Tho' ftill the pride of kings the ftrife maintains,
Their hofts wide fweeping o'er the feas and plains;
With engines new they rend the harmlefs air,
And lofe the horrors in the pomp of war.

While the glad fage to ufeful labours foars,   205
Tempts other feas and unknown worlds explores,
Bids feeble tribes difplay their powers abroad,
And regions fmile without the wafte of blood.

Then, while the daring Mufe, from heav'nly quires,
With life divine the raptur'd bard infpires,   210
With bolder hand he ftrikes the trembling ftring,
Virtues and loves and deeds like thine to fing.
No more with vengeful chiefs and furious gods,
Old Ocean crimfons and Olympus nods,
Nor heav'ns, convulfive, rend the dark profound,   215
Nor Titans groan beneath the heaving ground;
But milder themes fhall wake the poets fong,
Life in the foul and rapture on the tongue;
To moral charms he bids the world attend,
Fraternal nations focial ties extend,   220

Thro'

Thro' union'd realms the rage of conquest cease,
War sink in night, and nature smile in peace.
Then shall he soar sublimer heights, and rove
O'er brighter walks, and purer climes of love ;
Rapt into vision of the blest abode,   225
From Angel-harps to catch th' inspiring God ;
Thro' heav'ns o'er-canopy'd by heav'ns, behold
New suns ascend and other skies unfold,
Seraphs and system'd worlds around him shine,
And lift his mortal strains to harmony divine.   230

   To these superior flights, the Chief rejoin'd,
If future years shall raise the roving mind ;
Progressive arts exalt the soul on high,
Peace rule the earth, and faith unfold the sky ;
Say, how shall truths like these to man be given,   235
Or Science find the limits mark'd by Heaven ?

   In every age since reas'ning pride began,
And heav'n's dread Sire reveal'd himself to man,
What different faiths the changing race inspire !
What blind devotions and unhallow'd fire !   240
What gods of human form and savage power
Cold fear could fashion or mad zeal adore !
These crowd their temples, those their names despise,
In each dire cause th' exulting martyr dies ;

Till,

Till, sense renounc'd, and virtue driv'n afar,   245
Rage fires the realms, religion sounds to war;
And the first blessing Heav'n for earth design'd,
Proves the severest curse that waits mankind.

   Say then, my Guide,—if heav'nly wisdom gave
To erring man a life beyond the grave—   250
If one creative Power, one living soul
Produc'd all beings and preserves the whole;
Who, thron'd in light, with full perfection blast,
Mid changing worlds, enjoys eternal rest;
While man, still grov'ling, passionate, and blind,   255
Wars with his neighbour and destroys his kind—
Say, what connecting chain, in endless line,
Links earth to heav'n, and mortal with divine,
Applies alike to every age and clime,
And lifts the soul beyond the bounds of time;   260
And when shall Science trace th' immortal way,
And hail religion in her native day;

   The Power return'd :—Thy race shall soon behold
Reason expand and moral lights unfold;
While Science rises, freed from pedant pride,   265
Of truth the standard and of faith the guide.

   The passions wild, that sway the changing mind,
The reasoning powers, her watchful guides design'd,

                                                     Each,

Each, unreftrain'd, alike fubvert the plan,
Miflead the judgment, and betray the man ;   270
Hence raging zeal or fceptic fcorn prevails,
And arms decide the faith, where wifdom fails.
Of human paffions, one above the reft,
Fear, love, or envy, rules in every breaft ;
And, while it varies with the changing clime,   275
Now ftoops to earth, now lifts the foul fublime,
Forms local creeds of fuperftitious lore,
Creates the god, and bids the world adore.

    Lo ! at the Lama's feet, as lord of all,
Age following age in dumb devotion fall !   280
The youthful god, mid fuppliant kings enfhrin'd,
Difpenfing fate and ruling half mankind,
Sits, with contorted limbs, a filent flave,
An early victim of a fecret grave.
And, where the mofque's dim arches bend on high,   285
Mecca's dead prophet mounts the mimic fky ;
While pilgrim hofts, o'er tracklefs deferts come,
Crowd the deep fhrine, and worfhip round his tomb !
See Memphian altars reek with human gore,
Gods hifs from caverns, or in cages roar ;   290

                    Q   Nile

Nile pours from heav'n a tutelary flood,
And vales produce the vegetable god ! *
Two rival Powers the Magian faith infpire,
The fire of Darknefs, and the fource of Fire :
Evil and Good, in thefe contending rife,   295
And each, by turns, the fovereign of the fkies !
Sun, ftars, and planets round the earth behold
Their fanes of marble and their fhrines of gold ;
The fea, the grove, the harveft and the vine
Spring from their gods, and claim a fource divine ;   300
While heroes, kings, and fages of their times,
Thofe gods on earth, are gods in happier climes,
Minos in judgment fits, and Jove in power,
And Odin's friends are feafted ftill with gore.

Yet wifdom's eye with juft contempt defcries   305
Thefe rites abfurd, and bids the world defpife :
Then reas'ning powers o'er paffion gain the fway,
And fhroud in deeper glooms the mental ray.
See the proud fage, with philofophic eye,
Rove thro' all climes, and trace the ftarry fky,   310
The fyftems mark, their various laws purfue,
The God ftill rifing to his raptur'd view !

: * O fan&tas gentes, quibus hæc nafcuntur in hortis
      Numina !   *Juv. Sat.* 15.

But what this God ? and what the great defign,
Why creatures live, or worlds around him fhine ?
If all perfection dwelt in him alone,   315
If power, he cries, and wifdom were his own,
No pain, no guilt, no variance could annoy
The realm of peace, the univerfe of joy.

    Yet reafon here, with homeward ken, defcries
From jarring parts what dark diforders rife !   320
From froft and fire what ftorms untemper'd rave !
What plagues, what earthquakes crowd the gaping grave !
Pain, toil, and torture give the infant breath,
His life is mis'ry and his portion death.
From moral ills a like deftruction reigns,   325
War founds the trump, and flaughter dyes the plains ,
While wrath divine proclaims a heavier doom,
And guilt, aftonifh'd, looks beyond the tomb.
Whence thefe unnumber'd caufelefs ills ? he cries
Could wifdom form them, or could love devife ?   330
No love, no wifdom, no confiftent plan,
No God in heav'n, nor future life to man !

    While thus, thro' nature's walks, he foars on high,
Acquits all guilt, difpeoples all the fky,
Denies unfeen exiftence, and believes   335
No form beyond what human fenfe perceives,

Q 2

An

An anxious search impels th' inquiring mind,

Its own bright essence and its powers to find,

From conscious thought * his reas'ning force he plies,

And deep in search the active soul descries ;   340

* *Ego cogito; ergo sum.* Metaphysical writers in general
may be divided into two classes : The first class, *against the
dictates of their reason*, reject a proposition, because. it is contrary to the opinions of the age, and to the traditions handed
down from their ancestors; when, for the most part, these traditions are the fruit of an original deception imposed upon the
senses, or of an artful fable contrived by interested men. The
other class, *against the evidence of their senses*, reject a proposition, because it cannot be proved by an abstract theory previ-
ously settled in their own minds, and supposed to have been
established by a chain of reasoning.

It is difficult to say which of these classes deviates the most
from that *moral sense*, which is the result of rational information,
and the only criterion of truth that we are able to obtain. The
first class has been in all ages the supporters of the religion of
the country where they have lived; whatever may have been
the absurdities of that religion, and whatever degree of wickedness may have been enjoined in its practice. The second class,
not only overturns all religion, but strikes at the root of morals,
destroys the obligations of society, opposes the common principles of prudence in the physical concerns of life and the preserva-
tion of the species. The former system has done the most mischief
in the world, because its doctrines are always calculated to gain
the belief of the great body of mankind, and to keep them in perpetual contention about the particular modes of faith that happen to predominate in different societies. The latter is less per-
nicious, because its absurdities are too glaring to impose upon
the common sense of men.

The general happiness of mankind is doubtless to be attained
by pursuing a middle course, and making use of all the aids that
arise from our physical senses, from our reason, and from the
experience of former ages, in rectifying and enlightening the
consciences of men, or the *moral sense*, which is the portion of
every human creature.

Yet sense and substance no relation claim,
That dupes the reason, this exists a name :
All matter, mind, sense, knowledge, pleasure, pain,
Seem the wild phantoms of the vulgar brain ;
Reason, collected, sits above the scheme, 345
Proves God and Nature but an idle dream,
In one great learned doubt involopes all,
And whelms its own existence in the fall !

    These wide extremes of passion and of pride
A while on earth thy changing race divide ; 350
That man may find his limits and his laws,
Where zeal inflames, or coward caution awes;
And learn, by these, the happier course to steer,
Nor sink too low, nor mount beyond his sphere.
And soon that happier course thy race shall gain, 355
And zealots rave, and sceptics doubt, in vain ;
While reason, sense, and passion aid the soul,
Science her guide, and truth th' eternal goal.

    First, his own powers the man, with care, descries,
What nature gives, and various art supplies ; 360
Rejects the ties of controversial rules,
The pride of names, the prejudice of schools ;
The sure foundation lays, on which to rise,
To look thro' earth and meditate the skies :

Q 3

And

And finds fome general laws in every breaft, .   365
Where ethics, faith, and politics may reft.
  Of human powers, the Senfes always chief,
Produce inftruction or enforce belief ;
Reafon, as next in fway, the balance bears,
Receives their tidings, and with fkill compares,   370
Reftrains wild fancy, calms th' impaffion'd foul,
Illumes the judgment, and refines the whole.
Senfe, the great fource of knowledge, . ever juft,
High in command, but faithful to its truft,
Aid of this life, and fuited to its place,   375
Giv'n to fecure, but not exalt the race—
Defcries no God, nor claims fuperior birth,
And knows no life beyond the bounds of earth.
Reafon, tho' taught by Senfe to range on high,
To trace the ftars and meafure all the fky ;   380
Tho' fancy, mem'ry, forefight, fill her train,
And o'er the beaft fhe lifts the pride of man,
Yet, ftill to matter, form, and fpace confin'd,
Or calculations that amufe mankind,
Could ne'er, unaided, pierce the mental gloom,   385
Explore new fcenes beyond the clofing tomb,
Reach with immortal hope the bleft abode,
Or raife one thought of Spirit, or of God.

                                            Yet

Yet names of God, and powers of heav'nly strain

All nations reverence and all tongues contain ;　　390

Thro' every age the conscious mind perceives,

Reason pronounces, and the Sense believes.

What cause mysterious could the thought impart,

Not taught by nature nor acquired by art ?

It speaks of nature's God—no matter when　　395

The Name was caught, 'tis never lost by men ;

From clime to clime, from age to age it flies,

Sounds thro' the world, and echoes to the skies.

It proves him, *self-reveal'd* ; and all the plan

On this connexion rests, of God and man.　　400

　　Observe, in man, desires immortal given,

To range o'er earth and climb the heights of heaven ;

Yet fear and conscious guilt his flight restrain,

His God offended, and his wishes vain :

The wrath divine, impending on his breast,　　405

Precludes the hope of refuge and of rest ;

He seeks the fane, obtests th' avenging skies,

Pours the full tear, and yields the sacrifice ;

Some foreign aid, some mediating grace,

He seeks to shield him from his Maker's face.　　410

　　All forms of worship that engage mankind,

In different climes to various Names confin'd,

Require

Require of fuppliants fome external aid,
Some victim offer'd, or fome penance paid,
Some middle name, or reconciling plan,   415
To footh the Godhead and abfolve the man.
This thought, fo wide diffus'd thro' all mankind,
Rofe not from earth, or force of human mind ;
From heav'n reveal'd, it fhows fome fov'reign fcheme,
To link this nature with the Power fupreme,   420
From guilt and pain to lift the foul on high,
And ope a happier fcene, a world beyond the fky.

  Thus in clear light to philofophic eyes,
While books on books, and creeds on creeds arife,
Reafon refin'd with liberal glance furveys   425
Th' oppofing faiths and various modes of praife ;
Yet finds in all, what nature might approve,
A God of juftice reconcil'd by love ;
With joy beholds th' accordant fcheme of Heaven,
Dire vengeance footh'd, a rule of action given,   430
Man freed from pain, the ftains of guilt remov'd,
To angels liken'd, and by Heav'n approv'd,
Death bound in chains, from his old empire hurl'd,
And peace and union promis'd to the world.

  In this harmonious round, united rife   435
Power to create, and Wifdom to devife ;

While

While love ſupreme before all action flow'd,
The firſt, the laſt, the chain of general good,
Thro' nature's range to ſpread the ſway divine,
And heav'n and earth in mild accordance join ;   440
To one great Moral Senſe all ſenſe to draw,
Strong as neceſſity, and fixt as law.
    This Moral Senſe thro' all the ſyſtem known,
Image and brightneſs of th' eternal throne,
By whom all Wiſdom ſhines, all Power extends,   445
God ſtands reveal'd, and heav'n with nature blends,
Thro' earth and ſkies proclaim'd th' indulgent plan,
And ſpoke the law to angel and to man.
It taught how pain and death and all their woes
From wayward ſtrife and breach of order roſe ;   450
How each diſcordant wiſh, the ſoul that ſwells
'Gainſt human bliſs and heav'nly power rebels.
While one clear rule diſplays th' eternal code,
To love the neighbour, is to pleaſe the God.
    Here the laſt flights of ſcience ſhall aſcend,   455
To look thro' life, and ſenſe with reaſon blend,
View the great ſource of love, that flows abroad,
Spreads to all creatures, centres ſtill in God,
Lives thro' the whole, from nature's compact ſprings,
Orders, reverſes, fills the ſum of things,   460

Commands

Commands all fenfe to feel, all life to prove
Th' attracting force of univerfal love.

    Here ends the toilfome fearch ; in this may reft
The doubts and fears that move the lab'ring breaft.
As, on an arch of ftone, fome temple ftands,   465
Looks thro' the clouds, and fhines to diftant lands ;
The firm foundations, open to the fight,
Crowd, as it grows, and ftrengthen with the weight ;
Thus, on the characters of God and Man,
By Heav'n reveal'd in this conformant plan,   470
The beauteous fyftem refts ; and tho' awhile
Mad zeal o'erload it, and cold fcorn revile,
Stands, felf-exalted, fill'd with native light,
Firm to the faith, and growing on the fight.
It fpeaks one fimple, univerfal caufe,   475
Which time and fpace from one great centre draws ;
Whence this unfolded, that began its flight,
Worlds fill'd the fkies, and nature roll'd in light ;
Whither all beings tend ; and where, at laft,
Their progrefs, changes, imperfections, paft,   480
Matter fhall turn to light ; to pleafure, pain,
Strife end in union, angel form in man ;
From ftage to ftage, from life to life, refin'd,
All centre, whence they fprang, in one eternal Mind.

THE

VISION OF COLUMBUS.

———

BOOK IX.

ARGUMENT.

The vision resumed, and extended over the whole earth. Present character of different nations. Future progress of society with respect to commerce, discoveries, the opening of canals, philosophical, medical, and political knowledge, the assimilation and final harmony of all languages. Cause of the first confusion of tongues explained, and the effect of their union described. View of a general council of all nations assembled to establish the political harmony of mankind. Conclusion.

THE

VISION of COLUMBUS.

BOOK IX.

NOW, round the yielding canopy of shade,
Again the Guide his heav'nly power display'd.
Sudden the stars their trembling fires withdrew,
Returning splendors burst upon the view ;
Floods of unfolding light the skies adorn,   5
And more than mid-day glories grace the morn.
So shone the earth, as if the starry train,
Broad as full suns, had sail'd th' etherial plain ;
When no distinguish'd orb could strike the sight,
But one clear blaze of all-surrounding light   10
O'erflow'd the vault of heav'n.   For now in view
Remoter climes and future ages drew ;
While deeds of happier fame, in long array,
Call'd into vision, fill the new-born day.

   Far as th'angelic Power could lift the eye,   15
Or earth or ocean bend the yielding sky,

Or

Or circling funs awake the breathing gale,
Drake lead the way, or Cook extend the fail;
All lands, all feas, that boaft a prefent name,
And all that unborn time fhall give to fame,   20
Around the Chief in fair expanfion rife,
And earth's whole circuit bounds the level'd fkies.

    He faw the nations tread their different fhores,
Ply their own toils and claim their local powers.
He mark'd what tribes ftill rove the favage wafte,   25
What cultur'd realms the fweets of plenty tafte;
Where arts and virtues fix their golden reign,
Or peace adorns, or flaughter dyes the plain.
He faw the reftlefs Tartar, proud to roam,
Move with his herds, and fpread his tranfient home;   30
Thro' the vaft tracts of China's fix'd domain,
The fons of dull contentment plough the plain;
The gloomy Turk afcends the blood-ftain'd car,
And Ruffian banners fhade the plains of war;
Brazilia's wilds and Afric's burning fands   35
With bickering ftrife inflame the furious bands;
On bleft Atlantic ifles, and Europe's fhores,
Proud wealth and commerce heap their growing ftores;
While his own weftern world, in profpect fair,
Calms her brave fons, now breathing from the war,   40

Unfolds

Unfolds her harbours, fpread the genial foil,
And welcomes freemen to the cheerful toil.

   When thus the Power :—In this extended view,
Behold the paths thy changing race purfue.
See, thro' the whole, the fame progreffive plan,   45
That draws, for mutual fuccour, man to man,
From friends to tribes, from tribes to realms afcend,
Their powers, their int'refts, and their paffions blend ;
Adorn their manners, focial virtues fpread,
Enlarge their compacts, and extend their trade ;   50
While chiefs like thee, with perfevering foul,
Bid vent'rous barks to new difcoveries roll.
High in the north, and tow'rd the fouthern fkies,
New ifles and nations greet the roving eyes ;
Till each remoteft realm, by friendfhip join'd,   55
Links in the chain that binds all human kind,
United banners rife at laft unfurl'd,
And wave triumphant round th' accordant world.

   As fmall, fwift ftreams their furious courfe impel,
Till meeting waves their winding currents fwell ;   60
Then widening fweep thro' each defcending plain,
And move majeftic to the boundlefs main ;
'Tis thus fociety's fmall fources rife ;
Through paffions wild their devious progrefs lies ;

Int'reft

Int'reft and faith and pride and power withftand,   65

And mutual ills the growing views expand ;

Till tribes, and ftates, and empires find their place,

* And one wide int'reft fways the peaceful race.

* Since finifhing the Poem (the whole of which, except a fmall part of the feventh Book, was written previous to the conclufion of the late war) the Author is happy to find that his general ideas, refpecting the future progrefs and final perfection of human fociety, are fupported by thofe of fo refpectable a writer as Dr. Price. That amiable Philofopher, in his *Obfervations on the importance of the American Revolution,* remarks, " That Reafon, as well as Tradition and Revelation, leads us " to expect that a more improved and happy ftate of human " affairs will take place before the final confummation of all " things. The world has been hitherto gradually improving ; " light and knowledge have been gaining ground, and human " life at prefent, compared with what it once was, is much the " fame that a youth approaching to manhood is, compared " with an infant. "

It has long been the opinion of the Author, that fuch a ftate of peace and happinefs as is foretold in fcripture, and commonly called the millennial period, may be rationally expected to be introduced without a miracle. *Nec deus interfit nifi dignus vindice nodus,* is a maxim, as ufeful to a Philofopher as to a Poet. Although, from the hiftory of mankind, it appears, that the progrefs of improvement has been flow and often interrupted, yet it gives pleafure to obferve the caufes of thefe interruptions, and to difcern the end they were defigned in the courfe of Providence to anfwer, in accelerating the fame events, which they feemed for awhile to retard. The ftate of the Arts and Sciences among the ancients, viewed with reference to the event under confideration, was faulty or rather unfortunate, in two particulars ; *firft,* in their comparative eftimation ; and *fecondly,* in their not flourifhing in more than one nation at a time. Thefe circumftances were highly favourable to the exertions of individual genius, and may be affigned both as caufes of the univerfal deftruction of the arts by the Gothic conqueft, and

as

And ſee, in haſte, the deſtin'd hour advance,
Secur'd by leagues, commercial navies dance ;   70

as reaſons why we ſhould not greatly lament that deſtruction. From the ſituation of mankind in the days of ancient literature, it was natural that thoſe arts which depend on the imagination, ſuch as Architecture, Statuary, Painting, Eloquence, and Poetry, ſhould claim the higheſt rank in the eſtimation of a people. In ſeveral, and perhaps all of theſe, the ancients remain unrivalled. But theſe are not the arts which tend greatly to the general improvement of mankind. The man, who in thoſe days ſhould have aſcertained the true figure of the earth, would have rendered more ſervice to the world, than he that could originate a heaven and fill it with all the Gods of Homer ; and, had the expences of the Egyptian pyramids been employed in furniſhing fleets of diſcovery, to be ſent out of the Mediterranean, the civilized world would probably never have been overrun by Barbarians. But the ſciences of Geography, Navigation, and Commerce, with all their conſequential improvements in natural philoſophy and humanity, could not, from the nature of things, be objects of great encouragement or enterpriſe among the ancients. They therefore turned their attention to the cultivation of arts more ſtriking to the ſenſes ; ſuch as require the ſtrongeſt exertion of the human genius, and would be entitled to the higheſt rank in any age of univerſal refinement. As theſe arts were adapted to gratify the vanity of a prince, to fire the ambition of a hero, or to gain a point in a popular aſſembly, they were carried to a degree of perfection, which prevented their being reliſhed or underſtood by barbarians. The literature of the world therefore deſcended with the line of conqueſt from one nation to another, till the whole was ſwallowed up in the Roman Empire. There its tendency was to inſpire a contempt for nations leſs civilized, and to induce the Romans to conſider all mankind as the objects of their inſult, and all countries as the ſcenes of their military parade. Theſe circumſtances, through a courſe of ages, prepared and finally opened a ſcene of wretchedneſs, at which the human mind has been taught to ſhudder ; but it was wiſely calculated to reduce mankind

R

In views fo juft all Europe's Powers combine,

And the wide world approves the bleft defign.

kind to a fituation, capable of commencing regular and extenfive improvements. And, however novel the affertion may
appear, the Author will venture to fay, that, as to the profpect
of univerfal civilization, mankind were in a much more eligible
fituation in the time of Charlemagne than they were in the days
of Auguftus. The final deftruction of the Roman empire left
the nations of Europe in circumftauces fimilar to each other;
and their confequent rivalfhip prevented any difproportionate
refinement from appearing in any particular region. The feeds
of government, firmly rooted in the principles of the feudal
fyftem, laid the foundation of that balance of power, which dif-
courages the Cæfars and Alexanders of mankind from attempting the conqueft of the world.

It feems neceffary, that the arrangement of events in civilizing
the world fhould be in the following order : *Firft*, all parts of it
muft be confiderably peopled ; *fecondly*, the different nations
muft be known to each other ; and *thirdly*, their imaginary wants
muft be increafed, in order to infpire a paffion for commerce.
The firft of thefe objects was probably not accomplifhed till a
late period. The fecond, for three centuries paft, has been
greatly accelerated, but is now very far from being completely
obtained. The third is always a neceffary confequence of the
two former. The fpirit of commerce is happily calculated to
open an amicable intercourfe between all countries, to foften the
horrors of war, to enlarge the field of fcience and fpeculation,
and to affimilate the manners, feelings, and languages of all nations. This leading principle, in its remoter confequences, will
produce a thoufand advantages in favour of government and
legiflation, give Patriotifm the air of Philanthropy, induce all men
to regard each other as brethren and friends, eradicate all kinds
of literary, religious, and political fuperftition, prepare the minds
of all mankind for the rational reception of truth, and finally
evince that fuch a fyftem of Providence, as appears in the unfolding of thefe events, is the beft poffible fyftem to produce the
happinefs of men. I conceive it is no objection to this plan,
that

Tho' inland realms awhile the combat wage,

And hold in ling'ring ftrife th' unfettled age ;

Yet no rude war, that fweeps the crimfon plain,   75

Shall dare difturb the labours of the main.

For Heav'n impartial fpread the watery way,

Liberal as air and unconfin'd as day ;

hat the progrefs has hitherto been flow ; when we confider the vaft magnitude of the object, the obftructions to be removed, and the great length of time that will probably be taken to ac- complifh it. To refume the comparifon of Dr. Price, perhaps the world can hardly be faid as yet to be "approaching to man- hood ; " probably we are rather ftill in our infancy ; we have not yet been able to wander over the whole houfe and obferve upon the furniture. It is poffible that fome confiderable revo- lutions are yet to happen, before the progrefs will be entirely free from embarraffments. But the general fyftem appears fo rational and complete, that it furnifhes a new fource of fatisfaction, in contemplating the apparent difpenfations of Heaven.

The author firft ventured upon thefe ideas, in the courfe of the Poem, with all the timidity of youth ; determining not to rifk a ferious illuftration of the fentiment in profe. But finding that a theory fo pleafing to himfelf has not been unnoticed by others, he feels a greater confidence in the fubject, and hopes the importance of it will apologize to the reader for fo long a note.

☞ The forgoing remarks were written and publifhed in the firft edition of this poem in the year 1787. Since that period, the great event of the French revolution has doubtlefs induced the friends of humanity, in Europe as well as in America, to partake the opinions of the author with refpect to the future progrefs of fociety ; and to look forward with a degree of cer- tainty to the general eftablifhment of republican principles, univerfal civilization, and perpetual peace.

R 2

That

That every diſtant land the wealth might ſhare,
Exchange their fruits, and fill their treaſures there;   80
Their ſpeech aſſimilate, their empires blend,
And mutual int'reſt fix the mutual friend.

  The Hero look'd: beneath his wondering eyes
Bright ſtreamers lengthen round the ſeas and ſkies;
The countleſs nations open all their ſtores,   85
Load every wave and crowd the maſted ſhores;
The ſails, in mingling mazes, ſweep the air,
And commerce triumphs o'er the rage of war.

  From Baltic ſtreams, that ſwell in lonely pride,
From Rhine's long courſe, and Texel's lab'ring tide,   90
From Gallia's coaſt, from Albion's hoary height,
And fair Hibernia, cloth'd in purer light,
Hiſpania's ſtrand, that two broad oceans lave,
From Senegal's and Tagus' winding wave,
The loaded barks, in peaceful ſquadrons, riſe,   95
And wave their cloudly curtains to the ſkies.
Thro' the deep ſtrait that leads the Midland tide,
The ſails look forth, and ſwell their beauteous pride;
Where Aſia's iſles and utmoſt ſhores extend,
Like riſing ſuns the ſheeted maſts aſcend,   100
And join with peaceful toil the friendly train,
No more to combat on the liquid plain.

                                        In

In diftant glory, where the watery way
Spreads the blue borders of defcending day,
Unfolding flags from every current fweep,   105
Pride of the world and daughters of the deep.
From arctic heav'ns, and deep in fouthern fkies,
Where froft recedes as blooms of culture rife—
Where eaftern Amur's lenth'ning current glides,
Where California breaks the billowy tides,   110
Peruvian ftreams their golden margins boaft,
And fpreading Chili leads the channell'd coaft,
The pinions fwell; till all the cloud-like train,
From pole to pole o'erfhades the whitening main.
So fome imperial Seraph, plac'd on high,   115
From heav'n's fublimeft tower o'erlook'd the fky;
When fpace unfolding heard the voice of God,
And funs and ftars and fyftems roll'd abroad,
Caught their firft fplendors from th' all-beaming Eye,
Began their years, and vaulted round the fky: 120
Their mingling fpheres in bright confufion play,
Exchange their beams; and fill the new-born day.

He faw, as widely fpreads th' unchannell'd plain,
Where inland realms for ages bloom'd in vain,
Canals, long-winding, ope a watery flight,   125
And diftant ftreams and feas and lakes unite.

R 3

Where Darien hills o'er look the gulphy tide,
By human art the ridgy banks divide ;
Afcending fails the opening pafs purfue,
And waft the fparkling treafures of Peru.   130
Janeiro's ftream from Plata winds his way,
Madera greets the waves of Paraguay.
From rich Albania, tow'rd the falling fun,
Back thro' the midland numerous channels run,
Meet the far lakes, their beauteous towns that lave,   135
And Hudfon join to broad Ohio's wave.
From dim fuperior, whofe unfathom'd fea
Drinks the mild fun-beams of the fetting day,
New paths, unfolding, lead their watery pride,
And towns and empires rife along their fide,   140
To Miffifippi's fource the paffes bend,
And to the broad Pacific main extend.
From the red banks of bleft Arabia's tide,
Thro' the dread Ifthmus, waves unwonted glide ;
From Europe's crowded fhores while bounding fails   145
Look through the pafs and call the Afian gales.
Volga and Obi diftant oceans join,
And the long Danube meets the rolling Rhine ;
While other ftreams, that cleave the midland plain,
Spread their new courfes to the diftant main.   150
Ile

He saw th' aspiring genius of the age,
Soar in the bard and strengthen in the sage;
With daring thought, thro' time's long flight extend,
Rove the wide earth, and with the heav'n ascend;
Bid each fond wish, that leads the soul abroad, 155
Breathe to all men, to nature, and to God.

He saw, where pale diseases wont to brave
The force of art, and crowd th' untimely grave,
With long-wrought life the nations learn to glow,
And blooming health adorn the locks of snow. 160
A countless train the healing science aid,
Its power establish, and its blessings spread;
In every shape, that varying matter gives,
That rests or ripens, vegetates or lives,
By chemic power the springs of health they trace, 165
And add new beauties to the joyous race.

While thus the realms their mutual glories lend,
Their well-taught sires the cares of state attend;
Blest with each human art, and skill'd to find
Each wild device that prompts the wayward mind; 170
What soft restraints th' untemper'd breast requires,
To taste new joys and cherish new desires,
Expand the selfish to the social flame,
And fire the soul to deeds of nobler fame.

 They

They see, in all the boasted paths of praise,   175
What partial views heroic ardour raise;
What mighty states on others' ruins stood,
And built, secure, their haughty seats in blood;
How public virtue's ever-borrow'd name
With proud applause hath grac'd the deeds of shame;   180
Bade Rome's imperial standard wave sublime,
And wild ambition havock every clime;
From chief to chief the kindling spirit ran,
The heirs of fame and enemies of man.

    Where Grecian states in even balance hung,   185
And warm'd with jealous fires the sage's tongue,
Th' exclusive ardour cherish'd in the breast
Love to one land, and hatred to the rest.
And where the flames of civil discord rage,
And kindred arms destructive combat wage,   190
The gloss of virtue rises, still the same,
To build a Cæsar's as a Pompey's name

    No more the noble patriotic mind,
To narrow views and local laws contin'd,
'Gainst neighb'ring lands directs the public rage,   195
Plods for a realm or counsels for an age;
But lifts a larger thought, and reaches far,
Beyond the power, beyond the wish of war;

                              For

For realms and ages forms the general aim,
Makes patriot views and moral views the same;   200
Sees with prophetic eye, in peace combin'd,
The strength and happiness of human kind.
    Now had the Hero, with delighted eye,
Rov'd o'er the climes that lengthen'd round the sky.
When the blest Guide his heav'nly power display'd,   205
The earth all trembles and the visions fade:
Thro' other scenes descending ages roll,
And still new wonders open on his soul.
Again his view the range of nature bounds,
Confines the concave, and the world surrounds;   210
When the wide nations all arise more near,
And a mix'd tumult murmurs in his ear.
At first, like heavy thunders, borne afar,
Or the dire conflict of a moving war,
Or waves resounding on the craggy shore,   215
Hoarse roll'd the loud-ton'd, undulating roar.
At length the sounds, like human voices, rise,
And different nations' undistinguish'd cries
Flow from all climes around in wild career;
And grate harsh discord in the aching ear.   220
Now more distinct the wide concussion grown,
Rolls forth, at times, an accent like his own;

                                                    While

While thousand tongues from different regions pour,

And drown all words in one convulsing roar.

By turns the sounds assimilating rise,   225

And smoother voices gain upon the skies ;

Mingling and soft'ning still, in every gale,

O'er the harsh tones harmonious strains prevail.

At last a simple, universal sound

Fills every clime and sooths the world around ;   230

From echoing shores the swelling strain replies,

And moves melodious o'er the warbling skies.

   Such wild commotions as he heard and view'd,

In fix'd astonishment the Hero stood,

And thus besought the Guide :—Celestial friend,   235

What good to man can these dread scenes intend ?

What dire distress attends that boding sound,

That breathes hoarse thunder o'er the trembling ground ?

War sure has ceas'd ; or have my erring eyes

Misread the glorious visions of the skies ?   240

Tell then, my Seer, if future earthquakes sleep,

Clos'd in the conscious caverns of the deep,

Waiting the day of vengeance, when to roll,

And rock the rending pillars of the pole ?

Or tell if aught more dreadful to my race,   245

In these dark signs thy heav'nly wisdom trace ?

And why the wild confusion melts again,
In the smooth glidings of a tuneful strain?

The voice of Heav'n replied :—Thy fears give o'er;
The rage of war shall sweep the plains no more;   250
No dire distress these signal sounds foredoom,
But give the pledge of peaceful years to come;
The tongues of nations, here, harmonious blend,
Till one pure language thro' the earth extend.

Thou know'st, when impious Babel dar'd arise,   255
To brave th' uplifted arches of the skies,
Tumultuous discord seiz'd the trembling bands,
Oppos'd their labours, and unnerv'd their hands,
Dispers'd the bickering tribes, and drove them far,
To roam the waste and fire their souls for war;   260
Bade kings arise, and from their seats be hurl'd,
And pride and conquest wander o'er the world.

In this the marks of heav'nly wisdom shine,
And speak the counsel, as the hand, divine.
In that far age, when o'er the world's broad waste   265
Untravers'd wiles their gloomy shadows cast,
If men, while pride and power the breast inflam'd,
By speech allied, one natal region claim'd,
No timorous tribe a different clime would gain,
Or lift the sail, or dare the billowy main.   270

Fix'd

Fix'd in a central spot, their lust of power
Would rage insatiate, and the race devour ;
A howling waste th' unpeopled world remain,
And oceans roll, and climes extend in vain.

    Far other counsels, in th' Eternal Mind,   275
Lead on th' unconscious steps of human kind;
O'er-rule the ills their daring crimes produce,
By ways unseen, to serve the happiest use.
For this, the early tribes were taught to range,
For this, their language and their laws to change ;   280
Tempt the wide wave, and ply the yielding soil,
To crown with fruits the hardy hand of toil,
Divide their forces, wheel the conquering car,
Deal mutual death, and civilize by war.

    And now th' effects, thro' every land, extend,   285
These dread events have found their fated end ;
Unnumber'd tribes have dar'd the savage wood,
And streams unnumber'd swell'd with human blood,
Increasing nations, with the years of time,
Spread their wide walks to each delighted clime,   290
To mutual wants their barter'd tributes paid,
Their counsels soften'd, and their wars allay'd.

    At this blest period, when thy peaceful race
Shall speak one language and one cause embrace,

                                    Science

Science and arts a speedier course shall find,   295
And open earlier on the infant mind.
No foreign terms shall crowd, with barb'rous rules,
The dull, unmeaning pageantry of schools;
Nor dark authorities, nor names unknown,
Fill the learn'd head with ign'rance not its own;   300
But truth's fair eye, with beams unclouded, shine,
And simplest rules her moral lights confine;
One living language, one unborrow'd dress,
Her boldest flights with manly force express;
Triumphant virtue, in the garb of truth,   305
Win a pure passage to the heart of youth,
Pervade all climes, where suns or oceans roll,
And warm the world with one great moral soul.
As early Phosphor, on his golden throne,
Fair type of truth and promise of the sun,   310
Smiles up the orient, in his rosy ray,
Illumes the front of heav'n, and leads the day;
Thus soaring Science, daughter of the skies,
First o'er the nations bids her beauties rise,
Prepares the glorious way, to pour abroad   315
The beams of Heav'n's own morn, the splendors of a God.
Then blest Religion leads the raptur'd mind
Thro' brighter fields and pleasures more refin'd:

Teaches

Teaches the roving eye, at one broad view,
To glance o'er time and look exiftence thro',   320
See worlds, and worlds, to Being's formlefs end,
With all their hofts on one dread Power depend,
Seraphs and funs and fyftems round him rife,
Live in his life and kindle from his eyes,
His boundlefs love, his all-pervading foul   325
Illume, fublime, and harmonize the whole;
Teaches the pride of man to fix its bound,
In one fmall point of this amazing round;
To fhrink and reft, where Heav'n has fix'd its fate,
A line its fpace, a moment for its date;   330
Inftructs the heart a nobler joy to tafte,
And fhare its feelings with another's breaft,
Extend its warmeft wifh for all mankind,
And catch the image of the Maker's mind;
While mutual love commands all ftrife to ceafe,   335
And earth join joyous in the fongs of peace.

   Thus heard the Chief, impatient to behold
Th' expected years, in all their charms, unfold;
The foul ftood fpeaking thro' his gazing eyes,
And thus his voice:—Oh, bid the vifions rife!   340
Command, celeftial Guide, from each far pole,
The blifsful morn to open on my foul,

And

And lift thofe fcenes, that ages fold in night,
Living and glorious, to my longing fight ;
Let heav'n, unfolding, ope th' eternal throne,   345
And all the concave flame in one clear fun ;
On clouds of fire, with Angels at his fide,
The Prince of peace, the King of Salem, ride, ,
With fimiles of love to greet the raptur'd earth,
Call flumb'ring ages to a fecond birth ;   350
With all his white-rob'd millions fill the train,
And here commence th' interminable reign !

Such views, the Power replies, would drown thy fight,
And feal thy vifions in eternal night ;
Nor Heav'n permits, nor Angels can difplay   355
The unborn glories of that blifsful day.
Enough for thee, that thy delighted mind
Should trace the deeds and bleffings of thy kind ;
That time's defcending vale fhould ope fo far,
Beyond the reach of wretchednefs and war,   360
Till all the paths in Heav'n's extended plan
Fair in thy view fhould lead the fteps of man,
And form, at laft, on earth's benighted ball,
Union of parts and happinefs of all.
To thy glad view thefe rolling fcenes have fhown   365
What boundlefs bleffings thy vaft labours crown ;

That,

That, with the joys of unborn ages bleft,
Thy foul, exulting, may retire to reft,
And find, in regions of unclouded day,
What heav'n's bright walks and endlefs years difplay.   370
    Behold, once more, around the earth and fky,
The laft glad vifions wait thy raptur'd eye.
The great Obferver look'd ; the land and fea,
In folemn grandeur, ftretch'd beneath him, lay ;
Here fwell the mountains, there the oceans roll,   375
And beams of beauty kindle round the pole.
O'er all the range, where coafts and climes extend,
In glorious pomp the works of peace afcend.
Rob'd in the bloom of fpring's eternal year,
And ripe with fruits, the fame glad fields appear ;   380
On each long ftrand unnumber'd cities run,
Expand their walls, and fparkle to the fun ;
The ftreams, all freighted from the bounteous plain,
Swell with the load and labour to the main ;
Where wid'ning waves command a bolder gale,   385
And prop the pinions of a broader fail :
Sway'd with the floating weight the ocean toils,
And joyous nature's laft perfection fmiles.
    Now, fair beneath his view, the vifion'd age
Leads the bold actors on a broader ftage ;   390
                                        When,

When, cloth'd majeſtic in the robes of ſtate,
Mov'd by one voice, in general council meet
The fathers of all empires : 'twas the place,
Near the firſt footſteps of the human race,
Where wretched men, firſt wandering from their God 395
Began their feuds and led their tribes abroad.
In this mid region, this delightful clime,
Rear'd by whole realms, to brave the wrecks of time,
A ſpacious ſtructure roſe, ſublimely great,
The laſt reſort, th' unchanging ſcene of ſtate.   400
    On rocks of adamant the walls aſcend,
Tall columns heave, and Parian arches bend ;
High o'er the golden roofs, the riſing ſpires,
Far in the concave meet the ſolar fires ;
Four blazing fronts, with gates unfolding high,   405
Look, with immortal ſplendor, round the ſky :
Hither the delegated fires aſcend,
And all the cares of every clime attend.
As the fair firſt-born meſſengers of Heaven,
To whom the care of ſtars and ſuns is given,   410
When the laſt circuit of their winding ſpheres
Hath finiſh'd time and mark'd their ſum of years,
From all the bounds of ſpace (their labours done)
Shall wing their triumphs to th' eternal throne ;

S

Each,

Each, from his far, dim sky, illumes the road,   415
And sails and centres tow'rd the mount of God ;
There, in mid heav'n, their honour'd seats to spread,
And ope th' untarnish'd volumes of the dead :
So, from all climes of earth, the gathering throng,
In ships and chariots, shape their course along,   420
Reach with unwonted speed the place assign'd
To hear and give the counsels of mankind.

Now the dread concourse, where the arches bend,
Pour thro' by thousands, and their seats ascend.
Far as the centred eye can range around,   425
Or the deep trumpet's solemn voice resound,
Long rows of reverend sires, sublime, extend,
And cares of worlds on every brow suspend.
High in the front, for manlier virtues known,
A sire elect, in peerless grandeur, shone ;   430
And rising op'd the universal cause,
To give each realm its limit and its laws ;
Bid the last breath of dire contention cease,
And bind all regions in the leagues of peace,
Bid one great empire, with extensive sway,   435
Spread with the sun, and bound the walks of day,
One central system, one all-ruling soul,
Live thro' the parts, and regulate the whole.

Here,

Here, said the Angel with a blissful smile,
Behold the fruits of thy unwearied toil.   440
To yon far regions of descending day,
Thy swelling pinions led th' untrodden way,
And taught mankind advent'rous deeds to dare;
To trace new seas and peaceful empires rear ;
Hence, by fraternal hands, their sails unfurl'd,   445
Have wav'd, at last, in union o'er the world.

Then let thy stedfast soul no more complain
Of dangers brav'd and griefs endur'd in vain,
Of courts insidious, envy's poison'd stings,
The loss of empire, and the frown of kings ;   450
While these bright views thy troubled thoughts compose,
To spurn the vengeance of insulting foes ;
And all the joys descending ages gain,
Repay thy labours and remove thy pain.

THE END.

THE
CONSPIRACY
OF
KINGS;

A POEM:

ADDRESSED

TO THE INHABITANTS OF EUROPE,

FROM ANOTHER QUARTER OF THE WORLD.

" But they, in footh, muſt *reaſon*. Curſes light
" On the proud talent! 'twill at laſt undo us.
" When men are gorged with each abſurdity
" Their ſubtil wits can frame, or we adopt,
" For very novelty they'll fly to ſenſe,
" And we muſt fall before the idol, Faſhion. "

MYSTERIOUS MOTHER, Act IV.

PREFACE.

THE following little Poem was publiſhed in London, in February 1792. It happened that two of the principal conſpirators, the emperor Leopold, and the king of Sweden, died in a few weeks after. The oppoſite effects, produced by the death of theſe two perſons, are very remarkable. From a view of the general character of the king of Sweden, and of the particular tranſactions of the laſt year of his life, there can be no doubt but he was determined to go any lengths with the powers which were then confederating againſt the liberty of France ; and it is a conſolation to human nature, that the vio-

lent

lent death of one sceptred mad-man has saved the people of Sweden from those horrid scenes of slaughter which now involve most of the neighbouring nations.

The character of Leopold, in some of its leading traits, was directly the reverse of that of Gustavus. The latter was prodigal of wealth, and excessively eager for what is called military fame, without the capacity or the means of acquiring it; the *former* was affectedly pacific, moderate in most of his vices, and remarkable for nothing but his avarice. He had sense enough to see that nothing was to be gained by a war with France; his avarice, had he lived, would have been a sufficient guarantee against that event; and his death may be considered as the immediate cause of the war.

The

The treaty of Pilnitz was doubtlefs fabricated in the court of Paris. The emperor agreed to it, for the purpofe of duping the king of Pruffia into meafures which might fecure the obedience of the people of Brabant, whom he had pacified the year before by a cruel deception. His defign was likewife to deceive the emigrant princes, who were then deceiving him; and to exhibit fuch a menacing appearance, as, according to his calculation, would induce the French people to fet down quietly under a limited monarchy; well knowing that, if they did this, their government would foon degenerate into a defpotifm, which would continue to give countenance to the general principle that had fo long enflaved the nations of Europe.

That he never intended, or had relinquifhed

quished the intention, of executing the conditions of the treaty of Pilnitz by going to war with France, is evident from the following considerations: the French constitution was ratified, and the revolution supposed to be finished, in September 1791. A war, to overturn that constitution, certainly ought not to have been deferred beyond the ensuing spring; and as it would require an army of two or three hundred thousand men, the winter must have been occupied in making the preparations. Leopold died suddenly, about the first of March. At that time no preparations had been made for offensive hostilities. The number of troops sent from Austria into the Low Countries, during the autumn and winter, was not more than was stipulated to be maintained there, and were scarcely sufficient to enforce the despotism to which he had destined

that

that unhappy people. Before the death of Leopold, the French emigrants at Coblentz began to defpair. The hopes, they had built on the treaty of Pilnitz had nearly vanifhed; the princes had an army of forty thoufand gentlemen to maintain; Louis was carrying on too great a fyftem of corruption at home, to be able to fupply them with money from his *civil lift*; they had exhaufted their credit in all the mercantile towns in Europe; and Leopold, confidering them in the character of beggars, began to treat them as troublefome guefts; for none of the objects of their demands could be flattering to his favourite paffion. At laft, to their great fatisfaction, the emperor died; and his fyftem with regard to France was either never underftood by his own minifters, or it was laid afide, in compliance with the predominant

paffion

paffions of his fon; which happened to be for war, expence, and unqualified defpotifm.

This young man began his career by a folemn declaration to all the powers of Europe, that he fhould follow precifely the fyftem of his father, with refpect to the affairs of France. This declaration might be underftood to mean the open and avowed fyftem, prefcribed by the treaty of Pilnitz, or the fecret and unexplained fyftem, which was to avoid the war. It was univerfally underftood, as it was doubtlefs meant, in favour of the avowed fyftem; whofe object, announced in the treaty, was " *to fupport the rights of crowns.*"

From this moment, a fpirit of hoftility was provoked by the Court of Vienna,

and

and encouraged by the French ambaſſador
there, who, like their other ambaſſadors,
was betraying the nation, to ſerve the
king ; till, on the 20th of April, war
was declared by the National Aſſembly. In
this war the deſpots of Europe will try their
ſtrength, and will probably ſoon be exhauſted.

Paris, 12 *July* 1793.

THE

CONSPIRACY

OF

KINGS.

ETERNAL Truth, thy trump undaunted lend,
People and priests and courts and kings, attend ;
While, borne on western gales from that far shore
Where Justice reigns, and tyrants tread no more,
Th' untainted voice, that no diffuasion awes,   5
That fears no frown, and feeks no blind applaufe,
Shall tell the blifs that Freedom fheds abroad,
The rights of Nature and the gift of God.

    Think not, ye knaves, whom meannefs ftyles the Great,
Drones of the Church and harpies of the State,—   10
Ye, whofe curft fires, for blood and plunder fam'd,
Sultans or kings or czars or emp'rors nam'd,
Taught the deluded world their claims to own,
And raife the crefted reptiles to a throne,—

Ye,

Ye, who pretend to your dark hoſt was given   15
The lamp of life, the myſtic keys of heaven ;
Whoſe impious arts with magic ſpells began
When ſhades of ign'rance veil'd the race of man ;
Who change, from age to age, the ſly deceit,
As Science beams, and Virtue learns the cheat ;   20
Tyrants of double powers, the ſoul that blind,
To rob, to ſcourge, and brutalize mankind,—
Think not I come to croak with omen'd yell
The dire damnations of your future hell,
To bend a bigot or reform a knave,   25
By op'ning all the ſcenes beyond the grave.
I know your cruſted ſouls : while one defies
In ſceptic ſcorn the vengeance of the ſkies,
The other boaſts,—" I ken thee, Power divine,
" But fear thee not ; th' avenging bolt is mine. "   30
    No ! 'tis the preſent world that prompts the ſong,
The world we ſee, the world that feels the wrong,
The world of men, whoſe arguments ye know,
Of men, long curb'd to ſervitude and woe,
Men, rous'd from ſloth, by indignation ſtung,   35
Their ſtrong hands loos'd, and found their fearleſs tongue ;
Whoſe voice of thunder, whoſe deſcending ſteel,
Shall ſpeak to ſouls, and teach dull nerves to feel.

Think

Think not (ah no ! the weak delufion fhun,
Burke leads you wrong, the world is not his own),   40
Indulge not once the thought, the vap'ry dream,
The fool's repaſt, the mad-man's thread-bare theme,
That nations, rifing in the light of truth,
Strong with new life and pure regenerate youth,
Will fhrink from toils fo fplendidly begun,   45
Their blifs abandon and their glory fhun,
Betray the truſt by Heav'n's own hand confign'd,
The great concentred ſtake, the intereſt of mankind.

    Ye fpeak of kings combin'd, fome league that draws
Europe's whole force, to fave your finking caufe ;   50
Of fancy'd hoſts by myriads that advance
To crufh the untry'd power of new-born France.
Mifguided men ! thefe idle tales defpife ;
Let one bright ray of reafon ſtrike your eyes ;
Show me your kings, the fceptred horde parade,——   55
See their pomp vanifh ! fee your vifions fade !
Indignant MAN refumes the fhaft he gave,
Difarms the tyrant and unbinds the flave,
Difplays the unclad ſkeletons of kings *,
Spectres of power, and ferpents without ſtings.   60

    * Offa vides regum vacuis exhauſta medullis.
                              JUVENAL, Sat. 8.
               T   And

And shall mankind,—shall France, whose giant might
Rent the dark veil, and dragg'd them forth to light,
Heed now their threats in dying anguish tost ?
And She who fell'd the monster, fear the ghost ?
Bid young Alcides, in his grasp who takes,   65
And gripes with naked hand the twisting snakes,
Their force exhausted, bid him prostrate fall,
And dread their shadows trembling on the wall.

   But grant to kings and courts their ancient play,
Recall their splendor and revive their sway ;   70
Can all your cant and all your cries persuade
One power to join you in your wild crusade ?
In vain ye search to earth's remotest end ;
No court can aid you, and no king defend.

   Not the mad knave who Sweden's sceptre stole,   75
Nor She, whose thunder shakes the northern pole ;
Nor Frederic's widow'd sword, that scorns to tell
On whose weak brow his crown reluctant fell.
Not the tri-sceptred prince, of Austrian mould,
The ape of wisdom and the slave of gold,   80
Theresa's son, who, with a feeble grace,
Just mimics all the vices of his race ;
For him no charm can foreign strife afford,
Too mean to spend his wealth, too wise to trust his sword.

                                                     Glance

Glance o'er the Pyrenees,—but you'll difdain   85

To break the dream that fooths the Monk of Spain.

He counts his beads, and fpends his holy zeal

To raife once more th' inquifitorial wheel,

Prepares the faggot and the flame renews,

To roaft the French, as once the Moors and Jews;   90

While abler hands the bufy tafk divide,

His Queen to dandle and his State to guide.

Ye afk great Pitt to join your defp'rate work,——

See how his annual aid confounds the Turk!

Like a war-elephant his bulk he fhows,   95

And treads down friends, when frighten'd by his foes.

Where then, forfaken villains, will ye turn?

Of France the outcaft and of earth the fcorn;

What new-made charm can diffipate your fears?

Can Burke's mad foam, or Calonne's houfe of Peers * !   100

Can Artois' fword, that erft near Calpe's wall,

Where Crillon fought and Elliott was to fall,

---

* M. de Calonne, at an immenfe labour, and by the aid
of his friends in England, has framed a Conftitution for France,
after the Englifh model; the chief ornament of which is that
" Corinthian capital of polifhed fociety," a Houfe of Peers. It is
faid that, after debates and altercations which lafted fix months,
he has perfuaded the emigrant princes to agree to it. It only
remains now for him and them to try on this new livery upon
the French nation.

Burn'd with the fire of fame, but harmless burn'd,

For sheath'd the sword remain'd, and in its sheath return'd † !

   Oh Burke, degenerate slave ! with grief and shame 105

The Muse indignant must repeat thy name.

Strange man, declare,—since, at creation's birth,

From crumbling Chaos sprang this heav'n and earth,

Since wrecks and outcast relics still remain,

Whirl'd ceaseless round confusion's dreary reign,   110

† Among the disadvantages attending the lives of Princes, must be reckoned the singular difficulties with which they have to struggle in acquiring a military reputation. A Duke of Cumberland, in order to become an Alexander, had to ride all the way to Culloden, and back again to London. Louis the Fourteenth was obliged to submit to the fatigue of being carried on board of a splendid barge, and rowed across the Rhine, about the same time that the French army crossed it ; and all this for the simple privilege of being placed above the Macedonian in the temple of Fame, and of causing this atchievement to be celebrated, as more glorious than the passing of the Granicus : as may be seen on that modest monument in the *Place Vendôme* in Paris.

The Count d'Artois has purchased, at a still dearer rate, the fame of being styled " *le digne rejeton du grand Henri,*" and of being destined to command all the armies of Europe in re-establishing the Monarchy of France. This champion of Christendom set out at the age of twenty-five, and travelled by land with a princely equipage, from Paris to Gibraltar ; where he arrived just in time to see, at a convenient distance, Elliott's famous bonfire of the floating batteries. He then returned, covered with glory, by the way of Madrid ; and arrived at Versailles, amidst the caresses of the court and the applauses of all Europe. The accomplishment of this arduous enterprise has deservedly placed him, in point of military fame, at the head of all the present branches of the illustrious house of Bourbon.

Declare,

Declare, from all these fragments, whence you stole
That genius wild, that monstrous mass of soul ;
Where spreads the widest waste of all extremes,
Full darkness frowns, and heav'n's own splendor beams ;
Truth, Error, Falsehood, Rhetoric's raging tide,   115
And Pomp and Meanness, Prejudice and Pride,
Strain to an endless clang thy voice of fire,
Thy thoughts bewilder and thy audience tire.

 Like Phœbus' son, we see thee wing thy way,
Snatch the loose reins, and mount the car of day,   120
To earth now plunging plough thy wasting course,
The great Sublime of weakness and of force.
But while the world's keen eye, with generous glance,
Thy faults could pardon and thy worth enhance,
When foes were hush'd, when Justice dar'd commend,   125
And e'en fond Freedom claim'd thee as a friend,
Why, in a gulph of baseness, sink forlorn,
And change pure praise for infamy and scorn ?

 And didst thou hope, by thy infuriate quill
To rouse mankind the blood of realms to spill ?   130
Then to restore, on death-devoted plains,
Their scourge to tyrants, and to man his chains ?
To swell their souls with thy own bigot rage,
And blot the glories of so bright an age ?

T 3

First

First stretch thy arm, and, with less impious might,   135
Wipe out the stars, and quench the solar light :
" *For heav'n and earth,*" the voice of God ordains,
" *Shall pass and perish, but my word remains,*"
Th' eternal WORD, which gave, in spite of thee,
REASON to man, that bids the man be free.   140

    Thou could'st not hope : 'twas Heav'n's returning grace,
In kind compassion to our injur'd race,
Which stripp'd that soul, ere it should flee from hence,
Of the last garb of decency or sense,
Left thee its own foul horrors to display,   145
In all the blackness of its native day,
To sink at last, from earth's glad surface hurl'd,
The sordid sov'reign of the letter'd world.

    In some sad hour, ere death's dim terrors spread,
Ere seas of dark oblivion whelm thy head,   150
Reflect, lost man,—If those, thy kindred knaves,
O'er the broad Rhine whose flag rebellious waves,
Once draw the sword ; its burning point shall bring
To thy quick nerves a never-ending sting ;
The blood they shed thy weight of woe shall swell,   155
And their grim ghosts for ever with thee dwell.*

* See note at the end.

Learn

Learn hence, ye tyrants, ere ye learn too late,
Of all your craft th' inevitable fate.
The hour is come, the world's unclosing eyes
Discern with rapture where its wisdom lies;   160
From western heav'ns th' inverted Orient springs,
The morn of man, the dreadful night of kings.
Dim, like the day-struck owl, ye grope in light,
No arm for combat, no resource in flight ;
If on your guards your lingering hopes repose,   165
Your guards are men, and men you've made your foes ;
If to your rocky ramparts ye repair,
* De Launay's fate can tell your fortune there.
No turn, no shift, no courtly arts avail,
Each mask is broken, all illusions fail ;   170
Driv'n to your last retreat of shame and fear,
One counsel waits you, one relief is near :
By worth internal, rise to self-wrought fame,
Your equal rank, your human kindred claim ;
'Tis reason's choice, 'tis Wisdom's final plan,   175
To drop the monarch and assume the man.

* De Launay was the last governor of the Bastile. His
well-known exit, serving as a warning to others, saved the lives
of many commanders of fortresses in different parts of France
during the first stages of the revolution. It may probably
have the same salutary effect in other countries, whenever the
agents of despotism in those countries find the people are determined to be free.

Hail

Hail MAN, exalted title ! first and best,
On God's own image by his hand imprest,
To which at last the reas'ning race is driven,
And seeks anew what first it gain'd from Heaven.   180
O MAN, my brother, how the cordial flame
Of all endearments kindles at the name !
In every clime, thy visage greets my eyes,
In every tongue thy kindred accents rise ;
The thought expanding swells my heart with glee,   185
It finds a friend, and loves itself in thee.
    Say then, fraternal family divine, ›
Whom mutual wants and mutual aids combine,
Say from what source the dire delusion rose,
That souls like ours were ever made for foes ;   190
Why earth's maternal bosom, where we tread,
To rear our mansions and receive our bread,
Should blush so often for the race she bore,
So long be drench'd with floods of filial gore ;
Why to small realms for ever rest confin'd   195
Our great affections, meant for all mankind.
Though climes divide us ; shall the stream or sea,
That forms a barrier 'twixt my friend and me,
Inspire the wish his peaceful state to mar,
And meet his falchion in the ranks of war ?   200

Not

Not seas, nor climes, nor wild ambition's fire
In nations' minds could e'er the wish inspire ;
Where equal rights each sober voice should guide,
No blood would stain them, and no war divide.
'Tis dark deception, 'tis the glare of state,   205
Man sunk in titles, lost in Small and Great ;
'Tis Rank, Distinction, all the hell that springs
From those prolific monsters, Courts and Kings.
These are the vampires nurs'd on nature's spoils ;
For these with pangs the starving peasant toils,   210
For these the earth's broad surface teems with grain,
Theirs the dread labours of the devious main ;
And when the wasted world but dares refuse
The gifts oppressive and extorted dues,
They bid wild slaughter spread the gory plains,   215
The life-blood gushing from a thousand veins,
Erect their thrones amid the sanguine flood,
And dip their purple in the nation's blood.

    The gazing crowd, of glittering State afraid,
Adore the Power their coward meanness made ;   220
In war's short intervals, while regal shows
Still blind their reason and insult their woes.
What strange events for proud Processions call !
See kingdoms crowding to a Birth-night Ball !

See the long pomp in gorgeous glare display'd,   225
The tinfel'd guards, the fquadron'd horfe parade ;
See heralds gay, with emblems on their vell,
In tiffu'd robes, tall, beauteous pages dreft ;
Amid fuperior ranks of fplendid flaves,
Lords, dukes and princes, titulary knaves,   230
Confus'dly fhine their croffes, gems and flars,
Sceptres and globes and crowns and fpoils of wars.
On gilded orbs fee thundering chariots roll'd,
Steeds, fnorting fire, and champing bits of gold,
Prance to the trumpet's voice ; while each affumes   235
A loftier gait, and lifts his neck of plumes.
High on a moving throne, and near the van,
The tyrant rides, the chofen fcourge of man ;
Clarions and flutes and drums his way prepare,
And fhouting millions rend the troubled air ;   240
Millions, whofe ceafelefs toils the pomp fuftain,
Whofe hour of ftupid joy repays an age of pain.

   Of thefe no more.   From Orders, Slaves and Kings,
To thee, O MAN, my heart rebounding fprings,
Behold th' afcending blifs that waits your call,   245
Heav'n's own bequeft, the heritage of all.
Awake to wifdom, feize the proffer'd prize ;
From fhade to light, from grief to glory rife.

Freedom

Freedom at laft, with Reafon in her train,
Extends o'er earth her everlafting reign ;   250
See Gallia's fons, fo late the tyrant's fport,
Machines in war and fycophants at court,
Start into men, expand their well-taught mind,
Lords of themfelves and leaders of mankind.
On equal rights their bafe of empire lies,   255
On walls of wifdom fee the ftructure rife ;
Wide o'er the gazing world it towers fublime,
A modell'd form for each furrounding clime.
To ufeful toils they bend their nobleft aim,
Make patriot views and moral views the fame,   260
Renounce the wifh of war, bid conqueft ceafe,
Invite all men to happinefs and peace,
To faith and juftice rear the youthful race,
With ftrength exalt them and with fcience grace,
Till Truth's bleft banners, o'er the regions hurl'd,   265
Shake tyrants from their thrones, and cheer the waking world.

   In northern climes, where feudal fhades of late
Chill'd every heart and palfied every State,
Behold, illumin'd by th' inftructive age,
That great phenomenon, a Sceptred Sage.   270
There Staniflaus unfolds his prudent plan,
Tears the ftrong bandage from the eyes of man,

Points the progreſſive march, and ſhapes the way,
That leads a realm from darkneſs into day.

    And deign, for once, to turn a tranſient eye   275
To that wide world that ſkirts the weſtern ſky ;
Hail the mild morning, where the dawn began,
The full fruition of the hopes of man.
Where ſage experience ſeals the ſacred cauſe ;
And that rare union, liberty and laws,   280
Speaks to the reas'ning race : to freedom riſe
Like them be equal, and like them be wiſe.

THE END.

* Some of the author's friends in England, although they join with him in censuring the writings of Mr. Burke on the French Revolution, are of opinion that the picture here drawn of that writer is too highly coloured; or at least, that the censure is so severe as to lose the effect that it might otherwise produce. It is impossible to say what effect, and whether any, has or will be produced by this poem; but, out of respect to the opinion above stated, it may be proper to make some observations on the effect that has already followed from the writings of Mr. Burke. I speak not of what has taken place in England; where it is supposed that, contrary to his intentions and those of the government that set him at work, his malicious attack upon liberty has opened a discussion which cannot be closed until the whole system of despotism, which he meant to support, shall be overturned in that country. The present war with France is doubtless the last piece of delusion that a set of hereditary tyrants will ever be able to impose upon the people of England.

But this subject opens a field of contemplation far more serious and extensive on the continent of Europe; where, if Mr. Burke can view without horror the immensity of the mischiefs he has done, he will show himself worthy of much higher attributes of wickedness than have yet been ascribed to him. It is a painful task to traverse such a wide scene of slaughter and desolation as now involves the nations of Europe, and then to lay it all to the charge of a single individual; especially when we consider that individual as having, for a long time before, enjoyed the confidence of all good men, and having at last betrayed it from the worst and vilest motives; as he had established his previous reputation by speaking the language of liberty, and professing himself to be the friend of national felicity. But it is not from a transitory disgust at his detestible principles, it is from deliberate observation and mature conviction, that I state it as an historical fact, That the present war, with all its train of calamities, must be attributed almost exclusively to the pen of Mr. Burke.

There is a peculiar combination of circumstances which threw this power into his hands, and which ought to be duly considered, before we come to a decision on the subject. The people of England had enjoyed for several ages a much greater portion of liberty than any other people in Europe. This had raised them to a great degree of eminence in many respects. At the same time that it rendered them powerful as a nation, it made them sober, industrious and persevering, as individuals; it taught them to think and speak with a certain air of dignity, independence and precision, which was unknown in other countries. This circumstance could not fail to gain the admiration of foreigners, and to excite a perpetual emulation among themselves. England has therefore produced more than her proportion of the illustrious men of modern times, especially in politics and legislation, as these affairs came within the reach of a larger class of men in that country than in any other.

In a nation where there is an enormous civil list at the disposal of the crown, and a constitutional spirit of liberty kept alive in the people, we must necessarily expect to find two parties in the government. In such a case, as the king is sure to carry all the measures that he dares to propose, the party in favour of the people are called the *opposition*; and it being always a minority, it gives occasion for great exertion of talents, and is supposed to be the nurse of every public virtue. Such has been the composition of the English government ever since the last revolution. The opposition has been the school of great men; its principal disciples have been the apostles of liberty; and their exertions have made the British name respectable in every part of the world. Mr. Burke had been for many years at the head of this school; and from the brilliant talents he discovered in that conspicuous station, he rendered himself universally respected. His eloquence was of that flowery and figurative kind, which attracted great admiration in foreign countries; where it was viewed, for the most part, through the medium of a translation; so that he was considered, at least in every country out of England, as the ablest advocate of liberty that then existed in Europe. Even kings and tyrants, who hated the cause, could not withhold their veneration from the man.

Under these impressions, their attention was called to the great event of the French revolution. It was a subject which they did not understand, a business in which they had no intention to interfere; as it was evidently no concern of theirs. But viewed as a speculative point, it is as natural for kings as for other persons to wait till they learn what great men have said, before they form their opinion. Mr. Burke did not suffer them to remain long in suspense; but, to enlighten their understandings and teach them how to judge, he came forward with his " *Reflections on the Revolution in France*;" where, in his quality of the political schoolmaster of his age, in his quality of the professed enemy of tyrants, the friend of the people, the most enlightened leader of the most enlightened nation in Europe, he tells them that this Revolution is an abominable usurpation of a gang of beggarly tyrants; that its principle is atheism and anarchy; that its instruments are murders, rapes, and plunders; that its object is to hunt down religion, overturn society, and deluge the world in blood. Then, in the whining cant of state-piety, and in the cowardly insolence of personal safety, he calls upon the principal sovereigns of Europe to unite in a general confederation, to march into France, to interfere in the affairs of an independent power, to make war with the principles which he himself had long laboured to support, to overturn the noblest monument of human wisdom, and blast the fairest hopes of public happiness that the world had ever seen.

Copies of his book were sent in great profusion by the courts of London and Paris to the other courts of Europe; it was read by all men of letters, and by all men of state, with an avidity inspired by the celebrity of the author and the magnitude of the subject; and it produced an effect which, in other circumstances, would have appeared almost miraculous; especially when we consider the intrinsic character of the work. M. de Calonne, about the same time, published a book of much more internal merit; a book in which falshood is clothed in a more decent covering; and in which there is more energy and argument, to excite the champions of despotism to begin the work of desolation. But Calonne wrote and appeared in his true character. It was known that he had been a robber in France, and was now an exile in England; and, while he herded with the English robbers at St. James's, he wrote to revenge himself upon the country whose justice he had escaped. His writings, therefore, had but little weight; perhaps as little as Mr. Burke's would have had, if his real object had been known.

But this illustrious hypocrite possessed every advantage for deception. He palmed himself upon the world as a volunteer in the general cause of philanthropy. Giving himself up to the frenzy of an unbridled imagination, he conceives himself writing tragedy, without being confined to the obvious laws of fiction; and taking advantage of the recency of the events, and of the ignorance of those who were to read his rhapsodies, he peoples France with assassins, for the sake of raising a hue-and-cry against its peaceable inhabitants; he paints ideal murders, that they may be avenged by the reality of a wide extended slaughter; he transforms the mildest and most generous people in Europe into a nation of monsters and atheists, " heaping mountains upon mountains, and waging war with heaven," that he may interest the consciences of one part of his readers, and cloak the hypocrisy of another, to induce them both to renounce the character of men, while they avenge the cause of God.

Such was the first picture of the French Revolution presented at once to the eyes of all the men who held the reins of government in the several states of Europe; and such was the authority of the author by whom it was presented, that we are not to be astonished at the effect. The emigrant princes, and the agents of the court of the Thuilleries, who were then besieging the anti-chambers of ministers in every country, found a new source of impudence in this extraordinary work. They found their own invented fictions confirmed in their fullest latitude, and a rich variety of superadded falshood, of which the most shameless sycophant of Louis or of Condé would have blushed to have been the author. With this book in their hands, it was easy to gain the ear of men already predisposed to listen to any project which might rivet the chains of their fellow creatures.

These arguments, detailed by proper agents, induced some of the principal sovereigns of Europe to agree to the treaty of Pilnitz; then the death of Leopold, as I have stated in the preface, unhappily removed the great obstacle to the execution of that treaty, and the war of Mr. Burke was let loose, with all the horrors he intended to excite. And what is the language proper to be used in describing the character of a man, who, in his situation, at his time of life, and for a pension of only fifteen hundred pounds a year, could sit down deliberately in his closet and call upon the powers of earth and hell to inflict such a weight of misery on the human race? When we see Alexander depopulating kingdoms and reducing great cities to ashes, we transport ourselves to the age in which he lived, when human slaughter was human glory; and we make some allowance for the ravings of ambition. If we contemplate the frightful cruelties of Cortez & Pizarro, we view their characters as a composition of avarice and fanaticism; we see them insatiable of wealth, and mad with the idea of extending the knowledge of their religion. But here is a man who calls himself a philosopher, not remarkable for his avarice, the delight and ornament of a numerous society of valuable friends, respected by all enlightened men as a friend of peace and a preacher of humanity, living in an age when military madness has lost its charms, and men begin to unite in searching the means of avoiding the horrors of war; this man, wearied with the happiness that surrounds him, and disgusted at the glory that awaits him, renounces all his friends, belies the doctrines of his former life, bewails that the military savageness of the fourteenth century is past away, and, to gratify his barbarous wishes to call it back, conjures up a war, in which at least two millions of his fellow creatures must be sacrificed to his unaccountable passion. Such is the condition of human nature, that the greatest crimes have usually gone unpunished. It appears to me, that history does not furnish a greater one than this of Mr. Burke; and yet all the consolation that we can draw from the detection, is to leave the man to his own reflections, and expose his conduct to the execration of posterity.